Original Color

NAN A. TALESE

Doubleday
New York   London   Toronto
Sydney   Auckland

# Original Color

## Hugh Kennedy

PUBLISHED BY NAN A. TALESE
an imprint of Doubleday
a division of Bantam Doubleday Dell Publishing Group, Inc.
1540 Broadway, New York, New York 10036

DOUBLEDAY is a trademark of Doubleday, a division of
Bantam Doubleday Dell Publishing Group, Inc.

Book design by Maria Carella

Library of Congress Cataloging-in-Publication Data
Kennedy, Hugh.
Original color / Hugh Kennedy.—1st ed.
p.    cm.
I. Title.
PS3561.E4264075      1996
813'.54—dc20          96-2052
CIP
ISBN 0-385-47736-8

October 1996
First Edition
1  3  5  7  9  10  8  6  4  2

This book is for Sue.

# Contents

Part 2

A man whose desire is to be something separate
from himself, to be a member of Parliament, or
a successful grocer, or a prominent solicitor,
or a judge, or something equally tedious,
invariably succeeds in being what he wants to be.
That is his punishment. Those who want a mask
have to wear it.

—OSCAR WILDE, *De Profundis*


Be nice to everyone and you'll sell art.

—UNKNOWN DEALER

# Part
# 1

## 1. Evidence

It all begins with a photograph. The scene is New Year's Eve at the auction house Sotheby's New York. The short, white-haired woman you see collapsing to her knees and out of the picture is Helen Wheeler, the industrial heiress and art collector. You can just make out the pendant on her gown, an old Venetian relic filled with bone dust from the remains of Christopher Columbus. I'm in the center, the fresh-faced young thing with the receding black hair and gold-rimmed spectacles, shielding a glass of champagne. Obviously, the focus of attention is that heavyset blond man on the left, winding up to smash me in the chest with a twenty-pound book of antique botanical prints. Until a few seconds before the photograph was taken, that man, Nelson Albright, was my boss.

Nelson is grinning so broadly in the photo that his eyes are almost shut; as if he, too, is tensing against a blow. Arrested in time for an instant, he gives you the impression of a man who knows precisely which role to play, a man who will transform this moment of chaos into pure entertainment. As I have learned, it is this gift of control, even in the face of the most anarchic evidence to the contrary, that makes for a successful career in the art business.

I still wake up some nights in a nervous sweat, jerked from a dream where I am hunched over the steering wheel of a white Ford van on the Mass. Turnpike, screaming toward Manhattan with a load of Louis Philippe torchères and framed hummingbird lithographs in back. I'm late for an appointment with Helen Wheeler, but whenever I try to pass the Mercedes in front of me it changes lanes and forces me to sit behind it. When the driver turns around it's always Nelson, and I wake with a shout. As I reach out in the darkness I often think of my photograph and wonder if I should throw it away. Somehow I never do. After all this time, it's the only piece of evidence I have left.

## 2. An Honest Face

Nineteen months before this photograph was taken, I was entering Nelson Albright's New York gallery for the first time. Over the course of my senior year at Princeton, which was just about to end, art dealing had come to represent my ideal job: it combined the best of an historian's knowledge with the financial returns, schmooze potential, and satisfaction of building important collections. The only problem was, you needed an advanced degree or a family friend in the business to do more than research at the major galleries, and I didn't think I could swing a lifestyle beyond hand-to-mouth on a $14,000 researcher's salary in Manhattan. This is where Nelson Albright came in. My part-time student job was assisting the curator of an antique print and map collection. Nelson was a Princeton alumnus who knew my boss, and Nelson had galleries all over the country that sold some of the same prints and maps I had grown to love at Princeton.

The morning of my interview, I stepped out of a cab at the corner of Park Avenue and Seventy-fifth Street into glorious May sunshine. Every brass doorknob seemed to sparkle, and every window box burst with pink and green. In the marble lobby of a pre-war building, a concierge mumbled formally and pointed me toward a door marked Albright Galleries. There a receptionist showed me into a suite of neoclassical rooms hung floor to ceiling with naive and surreal prints of tropical butterflies and snakes, hand-colored antique maps that depicted California as an island, and pristine mezzotint engravings of 1785's most significant horses. I'd seen a sampling of this material as a curator's assistant, but never framed in gold-leaf moldings with silk-wrapped mats. I glanced at a few description tags while I waited and saw commas in the prices where I expected decimal points. The phone on the receptionist's desk purred rather than rang, and a tiny black video camera swept back and forth in a corner of the wall like the hand of Elizabeth II offering benign greetings from her carriage. Although I'd felt confident on the train ride in, I now began to give in to acute self-consciousness, particularly when I recalled my friend Bridget's parting words at the station: "I hope for your sake you've been memorizing British sporting painters, Fred. Maybe the guy won't notice your blazer reeks of bong water."

After a few minutes, the receptionist led me through these central rooms and down a hall to a heavy white oak door. I knocked and stepped in to find a burly, blond-haired man in his mid-thirties writhing violently on an unmade bed. He was yelling, "Where is that horn, where is that horn?" in an earsplitting nasal voice while half a dozen auction catalogs bounced and slid over the sheets with him. The room around the man looked like an art gallery after a tornado—oil studies of fox hunts were scattered among color-plate books on a desk, a filthy pair of antique brass andirons lay a quarter inch from a pile of unmatted rose prints on the floor, and dozens of wooden mat drawers stacked in bays ten feet high were pulled fully open, the only closed drawer in the group looking as if it had been wrenched permanently shut in a fit of rage. I froze for fear of stepping on something priceless. It was as if I had walked into an early cinematic gag: if I stepped back through the door and opened it again, a steam locomotive might roar toward me, or a vast abyss open in place of the floor.

When I coughed to announce myself, the man looked up and demanded, "You know anything about eighteenth-century French-Canadian powder horns?"

"About who?" I said.

"Great," the man said. "Great!" And he returned to his writhing.

I'd never seen a grand mal seizure before, but I imagined, as the man's blond hair flew back and forth over his wide forehead, that it might look something like this. Then I saw that the man was not so much writhing as diving, scrambling on his back toward some object on the floor behind the bed. His big belly strained against the buttons on his pink business shirt, then with a great surge he bounced into a sitting position, grasping a glossy brochure in one hand and a telephone receiver in the other. He took note of me again with penetrating, possibly maniacal blue eyes, and after farting without the slightest reserve or embarrassment, began to shout into his phone.

"Marty! It was the 1745 one. You tell her so. Now did you see that Catesby set that's coming up? Good. No—stay away from the furniture. I told you, Arader is buying furniture at this sale. Look, Marty, the Catesby's your play, all right?" The man ran a hand through his hair and grabbed a dribbling carton of orange juice at the foot of the bed. After two lusty gulps he said, "Bid on the stuff I sent you to London to bid on, okay? I don't need any more fucking furniture. Call me back! Right, 'bye." Slam.

He surged forward off the bed and offered me a strong, hot hand. "Nelson Albright. You are?"

"Fred Layton," I said.

"And?" Nelson demanded. "You're Fred Layton and what?"

"Oh." I quickly reconfigured my sense of importance now that I was off the Princeton campus. "I came to talk to you about a job. I work with Parker Spitz at the Firestone Library."

"Damn!" Nelson said, as if I'd come in too late with important news. "Have a seat and I'll be right with you, okay?" He pointed to an ornate giltwood chair with two clear plastic containers of half-eaten sushi on its blue silk seat. Then he plucked up his phone again and punched into a waiting line. Six of the extensions on the phone's console were blinking green, undoubtedly for him.

"Hello? Hey, Whitney. What are we on, lot 62? Okay, I'll go to thirty-two five on that Catlin. What else is going on? Right, I'll do that. Right, 'bye." He punched into another line.

"Hello, Jay?" Apparently receiving no response, Nelson rolled through the rest of the lines. "Jay. Jay! JAY!" His voice expanded into a wallpaper-peeling yell. "Marjorie, I need Jay Archer on the line at 011-44-1-714-3848 immediately! So, Parker sent you up from the Firestone?"

I stared at Nelson for several seconds before realizing that he was talking to me again.

"He did," I got out. "Parker speaks very highly of you."

The slim blond receptionist who'd let me in now rushed through the white door into the room.

"Jay will be calling in a second—urgent," she read from a legal pad. "Whitney can't keep the Catlin under your price, on line 24. And Mrs. D'Amico is on 25. She likes the Brookshaw melons but thinks they're too expensive. I have two browsers out here, Nelson, or I'd help."

"Shit," Nelson said richly. A new call appeared on the phone console and he snatched it up on an eighth of a ring.

"Nelson Albright. Yes, Jay. Yes, he just sold his collection, and if he just sold he must want to buy. I will not argue on that point. I expect total results. Right, 'bye.

"Fred," Nelson ordered, as the receptionist fled the room, "pick up line 25 and tell Jenny D'Amico I'll knock fifteen percent off her melons. There's a phone under your chair."

"I beg your pardon?" I said.

"I said go!" he boomed at me. "You want to be an art dealer, pick up the phone!" He grabbed one of the Sotheby's catalogs and started yammering to the Whitney woman again. I got myself out of the giltwood chair so quickly I had to catch it before it fell over.

"Hello," I said into the phone, "Mrs. D'Amico?"

"Yes," a woman's smooth voice answered. "Who is this?"

"Fred Layton here," I said. "Nelson's on an overseas line at the moment. He wanted me to tell you he can take fifteen percent off your melons."

"I'd like it even more if we could come down to ten thousand," Mrs. D'Amico said. "Could you ask him for me?"

I covered the receiver with my hand and waved to get Nelson's attention. He was tearing through two catalogs in search of a description, cheering himself on like a veteran tennis star.

"Nelson, how about ten thousand dollars?" I asked, so politely I could barely hear it myself. Then I shouted: "Ten thousand! Can you go to ten thousand on Mrs. D'Amico's melons?"

"Ten thousand?" Nelson gripped his stomach as if he'd been brutally kicked. "How can Jenny D'Amico get over that hurdle every morning, waking up and knowing she's so unbe*liev*ably cheap? What was my price on those melons in the catalog?"

"I don't have the slightest idea," I laughed. "I just got here."

"Well, go find out!" he snapped. "I don't see a Dumpster tied to your ass."

"Look, Mr. Albright," I said, *"I'm* not selling these prints. This woman is not my client. I don't work for you!"

Without the slightest warning, Nelson froze. He dropped his phone and the auction catalog, which splashed on the mattress and was still. "Oh," he said slowly, and so sarcastically that I blushed, "I thought you *did* want to work for me. I thought that's why you called me and set up an appointment to talk with me and came into my office today. I guess I was wrong, Mr. Layton. I guess you set it all up as some sort of joke. Goodbye." He punched into his next call, having vaporized me from his consideration.

I was instantly overcome with guilt and self-loathing, and to redeem myself I said: "I'll close this deal if you want, just tell me what to do!"

"All right!" Nelson retorted. "She Fed Exes me the check today she can have the melons for ten. Christ!"

I smiled (why was I smiling?), removed my hand from the receiver, and said, "Ten thousand via Federal Express will do nicely, Mrs. D'Amico."

"Fabulous!" she exclaimed. "I'll get you a check right away. Now, I don't believe I've spoken to you before, Fred. Are you new?"

"I am," I said, and ducked out of my seat as a catalog in which Nelson had just lost a major lot came sailing across the room. It landed behind me with an enormous crash in a pile of gold-leaf frame corners. "I'm actually finishing up a short internship. I'll have Nelson call you later, all right?"

"Yes, thank you. This has been a wonderful experience, Fred, and *you've* been a part of it."

"I have. Bye-bye." I hung up, gripped the giltwood chair, and sat down again. Nelson finished up with bids in two more auctions, popping between one line and another while chugging the rest of his orange juice. The Catlin lot fell to him, the Catesby to another bidder. He hung up and fell back on the bed.

"How'd we do?" he said to the ceiling.

"Mrs. D'Amico's locked in at ten," I said. "You owe her a call."

Nelson rolled up to a seated position and looked at me closely. Then he dug around in his pocket. He handed over a business card with a few bills folded behind it.

"There's your first commission," he said. "If you can keep doing sales like that, there'll be a lot more."

"Thank you," I said, and pocketed the card. "Do you have time to interview me now?"

"Interview you?" Nelson sneered. "You want to work for me, you're hired. You dress well, you have an honest face: what else should I know? Where you from with that accent, Chapel Hill?"

"Charlotte, actually. Are you a native New Yorker?"

"No, Boston, Mass," he said proudly. "My roots have been there since the seventeenth century. Your parents still down in Charlotte?"

"They died several years ago," I said. "They were . . . in a plane crash in Bali."

He winced. "Damn it, that's tough. Did they set you up?"

"Actually . . ." I began, then stopped myself. My parents had set me up, all right, but probably not in the way Nelson meant it.

"Hell, don't be embarrassed about that," Nelson interrupted. "That just means you're hungry. You're smart and you're hungry, so you'll work hard. These trust fund kids I hire are usually complete fuck-ups. I'll get you up to speed in three weeks. Just leave me your résumé and tell me when and where you want to start."

"How does Boston sound?" I asked. "I've got a good friend who's moving up there."

"I've got a gallery right on Newbury Street. It's my number two moneymaking operation after New York."

"Great," I said. "Is September okay? I've got something lined up in Princeton through August."

"September is primo." He nodded firmly. "I'll start you in sales at sixteen grand with a four percent commission, okay? And if you stick with me, Fred, if you really stick with me and you sell art and you're willing to make sacrifices, I'll make you a millionaire by the time you're thirty."

"Wow." The smile felt glued to my face—I was sure Nelson had mixed me up with one of his phone calls and meant to say he might let me hold his bidding paddle in six months. But his voice was all conviction, and he was definitely talking to me. "You've got a deal, Mr. Albright," I said.

"It's Nelson! And give me a ring the last week of August so I'll know when to expect you."

"Fine." I stood. "Thank you, Nelson. I'll send my best to Parker for you."

But Nelson had already redirected his energies to search the wrinkled sheets for another auction catalog. I was going to remind him about the one he'd flung across the room, but decided to get out while I still could.

Out on the street, my head was buzzing with energy. I'd taken a leap in midair and Nelson Albright had appeared with a financially secure trapeze to check my fall. And I'd be dealing art, which beat the stuffing out of my friends' lower-rung investment banking jobs any way you looked at it. I decided to treat myself to another cab and checked my pockets to make sure I could afford it. I pulled out Nelson's business card and then remembered the "commission" he'd handed over with it. I fished through my pockets again and pulled out five fresh bills folded in a tight rectangle. They were all hundreds.

# 3. The Spider and the Sale

he next time I saw Nelson Albright was my first day of work in September. We had a nine o'clock appointment, and at 9:01 sharp I arrived at his corporate headquarters. These were housed in a converted eighteenth-century tavern in a posh suburb called Weston, half an hour northwest from Boston by train. On the way out the train passed a bleak string of abandoned mills near a town called Waltham, and I sighed with relief that I'd landed my job.

As I strode up to Nelson's office door, this one black walnut rather than white oak, he exploded out of it in a very unwashed pair of maroon wide-wale corduroys, his big belly lifting a polo shirt clear of his crotch. He bellowed, "Where's that new kid?" Given my timing, I was able to answer his query by raising my hand and thrusting it into his. In truth, the car I'd borrowed to drive to Boston had broken down in a dicey part of the city called Roxbury the night before, and I'd thrown eighty of my last hundred dollars for a hotel room and a train ticket to make the appointment, and I hadn't even checked in with the friend who was subletting me her South End apartment, but what did all that matter if I could be exactly on time for Nelson Albright?

"Morning, Nelson," I said heartily.

"Excellent!" Nelson boomed. "Number one, you're standing exactly where you should be. Number two, you're right on time and ready to work. Number three, where is the Morita invoice, Bish? Were you in toxic shock when I asked you for it?"

At a desk to my left an overweight woman in a raspberry jogging suit raised long-suffering eyes from her computer. "Number one, it's on your desk, where you asked for it," she said. "Number two, Marty's still waiting for you to call him back."

"Come with me, Fred," Nelson said. "We are going to *find* that invoice."

I followed Nelson into an expansive office filled with matted prints and antique furniture. A long line of windows at the opposite end of the room gave onto a columned veranda. Nelson pointed to a Chippendale chair and I took a seat in it. I was trying to think of people my new boss reminded me of, or looked like, but drew a complete blank. Half white-bread Bostonian, a quarter Italian, the rest Apache? The rest pure energy—perhaps that was what made him so hard to describe physically. Nelson stood well under six feet and had a wrestler's build, but gave you the impression of being quite tall. His ruddy face, save his aquiline nose, was too flat, his forehead too wide, to consider him handsome, yet there was something hugely attractive, even magnetic, about him. He wore the same expression that set the tone of my interview—that of a person with eleven hundred ideas who could spit out only three, a man with a handle on everything and a fix on nothing. He dropped into a weathered brown leather armchair behind a mahogany desk of presidential length and immediately began making calls, as if speaking to only one person at a time constituted an egregious waste of time.

"Tell him I'm not interested in his offer under any circumstances," he barked. "Yes, my offer stands. Okay, Marty, great. What was my offer, anyway? Look, he's not going to spend a penny until December, he's promised me that. What? Sure he wants to play, but he's like Picasso at eighty—the shot just isn't there. Follow up aggressively, though. Right, 'bye."

Nelson hung up, wrote three lines in a slanting cursive hand on a yellow legal pad, then looked up at me.

"Fred," he said, as if my name had at last come up for sentencing, "let's skip the pandering and brown-nosing stuff, okay? You'll find in my company none of that gets you anywhere. Only one thing makes you popular with me." He surged over a Lucite rug protector in his castered chair and grabbed a fistful of three-carbon invoices. "Sales. That's it. My director in New York makes $180,000 a year because he sells consistently, every day, and since he's selling my stock he's selling the finest antiquarian prints and maps in the world. If he doesn't make a sale he goes home at the end of the day feeling demoralized. No, stained—that's a better word.

"Now, you may be wondering what 'the finest antiquarian prints and maps' means. Well, I'm hiring you so you won't have to wonder! The finest means original color, Fred, original color. Not colored last week in a studio in London by some bimbo decorator, but colored at the time of printing in 1578, in 1692, in 1814. We are the world's leader in original color prints and maps, and you are going to study every print and map in my stock until you know the difference between original color and modern color. Have I made that clear?"

I swallowed. "You have."

"You want to make money, don't you, Fred?"

I sat back a little. "One-eighty sounds fine to me."

"Good! I like that kind of thinking!"

The intercom squawked. "Nelson, Kurt Schoch on 80."

"Kurt," Nelson said as he swept up the receiver. "That was a wonderful presentation, absolutely wonderful. Fantastic. Loved it start to . . . pardon? No, I didn't say any—Kurt! Wait a second, babe, I only meant that the whole market is hard to predict. It reflected on you in no way. . . . Oh my God no! She didn't. That's a lie. If she wants to piss away a ten-year relationship, that's her problem. Look, Kurt, I've got a dozen people in my office right now and I can't—" Nelson pinched the bridge of his nose between his thumb and forefinger. "No, fine. I'll talk to you about it Saturday night. The Country Club, seven o'clock. Kurt, I love you, okay? Right, 'bye."

Slam.

"Goddamn fuzzhead." Nelson made two fists and rubbed his eyes. "These purebred Wasps never buy anything from you. They just intermarry till they get what they want and their brains turn to silt. Remember that, Bernard."

I smiled. "It's Fred."

"Fred, sorry. I have Parkinson's disease. Alzheimer's! Anyway, sales. Think of it this way. You're the spider, and you spin an alluring web and hope that the right fly is going to come along and get caught. Sometimes it works and you get a quick meal, other times you've got to keep spinning for months, even years. You've got to spin your balls off: 'Let me come out to your house and show you this great map! I've got the cleanest, brightest copy of this print with the widest margins you've ever seen! It's going to push your collection from a C– to an A+. Yes, I can be on a plane in an hour!'

"So your mantra is that it's going to reflect well on *their* superb taste if they buy the map from you. You're doing *them* the favor by setting this map aside for them. You're giving *their* lives some structure while you relieve them of the burden of carrying so much money around. Eventually, then, your reputation builds:

you're interested in growing substantial collections for people, not just doing one-shot sales. And in the end you're going to get your meal, you're going to find the fifty- or hundred-million-dollar client who trusts your expertise. So *that's* your play. You make the million-dollar sale and you take home a forty-thousand-dollar commission the same afternoon. A lot of my people have done that. Just follow the procedure: you present the material, you get the check, you make the sale, and you write out a complete invoice with all the information about the material. Now, Fred . . ." A deep laugh began to build in Nelson's chest, as if it were obvious I'd been bonking babes all summer rather than studying art history. "The only thing is, how are you on the material?"

"The material," I said, feeling rather dizzy. My eye landed on a large eighteenth-century engraving of a baby elephant corpse, a human fetus in a bottle, and cross sections of a bat and two iguanas. Price: $950. How far off I would be forced to spin my balls in order to get this piece into a collection remained to be seen. A cosmetics company boardroom, perhaps? I slipped a notebook from my breast pocket and scribbled: "Fetus print: Estée Lauder? Lancôme?"

"Well?" he pressed.

"I have been reading up on Audubon," I said, "and Redouté."

"Fine, Fred," Nelson said, "that's fine for day one, but you've got to know *every* major natural history and sporting artist between 1700 and 1900 or you're going to be in deep trouble. Some customer will come along and ask you about Thornton when you're thinking about Weinmann and you'll go down swinging unless you can answer every question. And when you go down swinging I lose money to buy more top stock, and when I can't buy top stock I become very unhappy. And when I become very unhappy you, Fred, will become even more very unhappy."

I stared at my boss's flushed face for several seconds.

"I don't want to become very unhappy, Nelson."

"*Good.*" He got up and walked the length of his desk, four strides. "I'm going to send you down to my gallery on Newbury Street. Whitney Buck is the director's name there, and she's willing to have a look at you about a position. There's someone at that shop I'm getting ready to fire."

"Oh. I thought I already had—"

"Hey, don't worry!" Nelson sat and leaned back in his chair with a heavy squeaking of casters. "If she doesn't want you, you can always work out here for me. There's a lot to do. You can make my phone calls, all my old reference books have to be moved to the attic of my other house, my wife Kak has a million painting jobs on her list. You've still got a paycheck coming to you at the end of every month."

"Every month?"

"Once a month." Nelson nodded crisply. "Here—" He handed me a folder. "I want you to study some of this material before you meet with Whitney. Just don't walk all over her, okay? She got married six weeks ago and still doesn't know her ass from the side of a barn."

"Great." I stood up with the folder. "I guess I'll see you later, then."

"Fantastic." Nelson reached for his phone. "Give me a call when you're through and I'll give you your next assignment, okay? I want you to be my eyes and ears downtown. And I want a full report."

"Thank you, Nelson."

"Thank *you*, Fred."

A full report. Veni vidi vici. I walked back to my place behind the closed office door, and from there out into the warm sun of a boxwood-bordered path that wended its way to the world beyond. Still, I wondered.

Paychecks once a month: was that legal?

# 4. Total Beauty Presentation

I boarded the commuter train at Weston Station and went speeding back to downtown Boston. Cars on the turnpike floated past the windows as I stared out at the morning and thought back to what was probably the last carefree summer of my life.

After graduation, only a few people in my clique decided to stay on in Princeton. Then my friend Bridget capped our half-assed relationship by hooking up with a Salomon Brothers trader called Happy, who was in town for his tenth reunion. She disappeared with him into a BMW sunset the second week of June. Not to be outdone, I ended up having a fling with a divorced real estate broker from New York, a very sweet and confused man in town for his fifteenth reunion, but decided to let him disappear on his own. Within a few days of this event I picked up an apartment share with a couple of Ivy League-loathing Comparative Lit majors named Henry and Smooch, and thereafter spent all my time with them. Every night we talked ourselves blue in the face about

Giacometti's middle period or the errant immensity of meaningless eternity or whatever topic hit us as we did bong hits on the back porch of our dilapidated carriage house and listened to "Kind of Blue" for the sixty millionth time. We cooked, swam, read, toked, and lived from paltry university paycheck to paycheck, occasionally scraping up enough for a weekend in New York. Now that Princeton had washed its hands of us, the rich kids around town began to look like a different species again.

And here I was now, zeroing in on that world from an entirely different vantage point—the art the rich kids' parents bought. I smiled at the irony of it, then resigned myself to the folder Nelson had given me to study. It held just four sheets of paper. The first one read:

> *Personal calls are out of control. I've been checking. Since bonuses are at my discretion, you lose your commission for the month if I find a personal call you have made without reporting it to me first. With 100 employees in five galleries spending $40 a month on personal calls, this matter has been abused and there must be an immediate stop. My absolute #1 goal for this year is to have six employees make $150,000 a year, and personal calls are not part of this goal. As always, please help me look for new and better ways to make more money. Good luck.*

The second piece of paper, a fourth- or fifth-generation Xerox, read like this:

> *I am now insisting that all my employees beautify themselves up. Whitney is making $3 million a year and I can't afford not to have my employees not beautify themselves up anymore! I want*

*you to think about how you can take your present appearance and transform it into a total beauty presentation, utilizing your tits, your ass, your feet and legs, and your face and hair. You do not have to have been born beautiful to do this. Every woman has some sort of tits, but not every woman has enough sense to show them to the customer. In fact, I am making it a condition of continued employment with me that you* must *show your tits to your ten biggest customers. Also wear jewelry. If you're a man, I want you to wear a nice suit that shows off your best qualities and hides your stomach. Consider cuff links also. This does* not *mean you are supposed to pull down your pants at antique shows and show everybody your dick, but it* does *mean that if one of your ten biggest customers wants to have sex with you, you better have a damn good reason why not or plan to answer to me! My business depends on people who get down, kiss ass, and beautify themselves up. Good luck.*

The third sheet was a copy of a letter with some annotations scribbled along the bottom. It read:

*Dear Mr. Albright:*

*Please be advised that I have made the decision not to make any more payments on the artwork you voluntarily delivered to me this spring. Furthermore I would appreciate it if you would return the $40,000 already paid to you and pick up the artwork at your earliest convenience so as to avoid any further action on my part.*

> *Sincerely,*
> *Alison Malvern*

To which a hand I already recognized as Nelson's had added:

NO CAN DO!! STALL HER UNTIL I MAKE PAYROLL!!!

The last sheet seemed to be the final page of a contract of employment for someone named Doug Morrow, and stated three demands:

> *16. I do not work for nor take orders from Bish; however, I will make efforts to see she is comfortable, has necessary supplies to do her job, and that there are no major problems for her to deal with. Bish is to give no orders to any member of my staff. Her requests go through me.*
>
> *17. Employees advised to not run and tell Nelson every little thing I'm making other people do. That is not their job, it is my job and as to how I delegate it. It only serves to upset the system and slow progress down.*
>
> *18. Every employee of company to know my position and my authority, not to fear it, but to respect it. We are all pulling in the same directions for the same reasons.*

I looked up. We were back in Boston again. I addressed my reflection in a window of the train.

"Jesus H. Christ—what am I getting into?"

## 5. Very, Very Old

As I suspected, Whitney Buck did know her ass from the side of a barn. Certainly one intuits some intelligence while watching an icily pretty woman separate a corporate browser from $4,200 in exchange for an 1824 aquatint of three tigers tearing the life out of a wildebeest. Whitney was in the midst of this feat as I approached Geena, the receptionist, over the half acre of white marble between the front door of Nelson's Boston shop and its deathly quiet interior. Behind me was Newbury Street, a gentrified residential and commercial strip that began at the edge of the Public Garden with the elegant Ritz Hotel and ran for eight blocks to Mass Ave, becoming more inane and pretentious as you proceeded down it. I didn't realize then how fitting it was that Nelson's shop sat exactly in the middle of the fourth block. Geena had a languid, carefree manner, a gorgeous button nose, and shoulder-length blond hair. I'd seen her type a lot in college: no discernible flaws, but not much to get excited about, either.

"May I poke around until Whitney's ready to see me?" I asked.

Geena glanced back through the French doors into the main gallery. "We just have to wait until he writes the check. If we interrupt before Whitney gets the check she'll have a serious bird."

While I waited, I picked a colored print of a Pompeiian floor plan out of the rack that stood to the left of Geena's desk. The print was priced like a running argument: $3,200 on the top mat, $2,650 on the lower mat, and $2,950 on the back. I replaced it toward the middle of the pile and approached a matted sporting print on the nearest wall. Two beaglers were doing a stiff-limbed somersault over a broken fence, their chaotic horses just beneath them. One was saying to the other, "I've got a notion this is what they call a Bog." $3,600. Perfect for the butler's pantry at the shore house. I tried to imagine myself pitching this piece to a potential customer, but it wasn't working.

"Anything of interest I can show you today?" a voice behind me inquired.

I turned to a tall, pale, patrician man seven or eight years my senior. He had close-cropped black hair combed forward, shifty black eyes, and a narrow, jackal-like face that seemed on the verge of smelling something unpleasant. It was obvious his only interest was in showing me the door.

"Just looking, thanks."

"Please." He swept his arm around to indicate that the bog print and its mate, *A Few of the Sort Who Have Done the Thing,* were both available for viewing. I waited a moment for the man to slip away into the unseen space from whence he'd come, but he appeared to play a man-on-man rather than a zone defense.

"Can you tell me"—I pointed at the pair of prints—"if these are genuine antiques?"

The man smiled and suddenly became handsome, more a foxy look than a jackal's. "They're very, very old," he said.

"Yes," I said, and smiled back. "I see they're dated below the title."

"Whitney will see you now," Geena said.

I straightened my tie. "That must mean she has the check."

"Shake her hand really hard," Geena advised. "She likes that."


Whitney sat at a Louis XV *bureau plat,* armed with a battalion of reference books, a console telephone, and monogrammed In/Out boxes. She was thirtyish and attractive in a restrained way, with porcelain skin and short pale brown hair expensively cut in a bob. A hard hitter, and quite a study in contrasts with the laid-back receptionist, though I was soon to discover that anyone who lasted more than two weeks at Albright Galleries probably could thrive on the floor of the New York Stock Exchange. Although I'd sworn off women after Bridget, I had to admit there was something frankly sensual about Whitney's thin lips, sharp nose, and the curve of her calf in its sheer hose. I saw her in an imagined flashback, drunk with half the Smith College field hockey team at a Ronald Reagan post-election party, or seducing a white-haired CEO after three sets of tennis. I was willing to bet she'd once owned purse covers in every color of the rainbow before tossing them into the fire on the eve of a threshold birthday. She stared at me so as to suggest she was just as able to spin her balls off as the next guy.

"Good morning, Fred." She rose and offered her hand, looking me over as if I resembled an amusing toy that had just exited from a box of Cracker Jacks. "How'd it go with Nelson?"

"Not bad," I said. "He told me he wants me to be his eyes and ears for a while."

"Oh, *God.*"

"He also mentioned moving a lot of his reference books. So I guess I might be serving as his arms and lower back, too."

Whitney exhaled laughter while scanning my résumé, the tip of her tongue pressed firmly against the back of her front teeth. "Nelson's got a whim of iron, that's for sure."

I nodded. "Does that mean you'll protect me?"

She smiled, flattered perhaps, and handed back my résumé. "I think I could fit you in. Any questions?"

"No." I stepped back. Short interviews appeared to be the new trend. "Actually, I was just reading a memo, and I wondered—does this company really have a hundred employees?"

Whitney strode to her heavy glass office door and opened it for me. "Let's just say that depends on who you count."

# 6. Denny the Frogman

I felt a little more settled as I walked out of Nelson's Boston gallery, bordered on one side by an aggressively swish florist and on the other by a high-tech stereo shop. I realized that I had landed on my feet in a strange city, and that Whitney's eyes had accepted me at face value.

These reflections on place and face led me to thoughts of my family. My family did not interest me then as much as other people's families, but at that moment it was impossible not to peer back into the past for parental support and advice. Unfortunately, I couldn't come up with much of either. All I could think of was the lie I'd told Nelson, that my parents had died in a plane crash in Bali. What they'd died of was several hundred head-on collisions with their peeling wood veneer bar in Charlotte, and with each other.

My mother was an angry, proud hausfrau from a once prominent Atlanta family who expressed her sense of frustration with her own achievements by finding fault with everyone else's. She was the kind of woman who would jerk the circular earring display out of your hands while you were browsing through it in Saks, then call you rude and coarse if you opened your mouth to complain. Born into different circumstances, I always thought she would have made an excellent princess. My father, black sheep of the Laytons, was a stoic Egyptian history professor who swung through a wide, blank, uninformed present pursuing the goal of writing *the* book on daily life during the Nineteenth Dynasty. Like many modern academics, he clawed his way into a tenure track job only to find himself feeling buried alive by a stagnant salary, administrative nonsense, and students whose interest was aroused only if the points he made during lectures were prefaced by the words, "You'll be tested on this."

Together, Dani and Jack Layton raised their son Fred on a strict diet of drunken wisecracks and slams. Looking back, I'm surprised they didn't sue each other for Repetitive Motion Syndrome, they were so busy pushing each other's buttons. When Dad left on the liver train without any life insurance, which he called "a crock of shit invented by J. P. Morgan," my mother's demise followed within months. No one around to throw plates at, I guess. By that time I was sixteen and living with a nearby aunt and uncle under court order.

My Uncle Bill and Aunt Agnes let me sow a few wild oats after I moved in, but Bill put his foot down the morning he found me passed out in my underwear. That wouldn't have been so bad, except that I was also hanging halfway out of my bedroom window. All I could remember was being ejected from a truckers' bar with some friends after setting up the jukebox so it would play the same Lionel Richie song for the next hour. Thereafter, two hours each weekday night were spent studying, while Saturday nights were spent with Aunt Agnes at meetings of the Charismatics Society of Pineville. While a pair of nuns shouted the rosary at breakneck speed and Agnes fell into a pleasant snooze with her arms above her head, I would watch strait-laced octogenarian women from the parish be overtaken by faith and "go down." To the floor, that is, in ecstasy. It was easy to dismiss religion as twaddle in a home where muttering a mild profanity was grounds for my aunt to turn to her husband and say, "Bill, you pray for Fred tonight," but witnessing that such intense joy remained available to those ancient women turned my attitude and grade point average around.

Bill and Agnes tried to teach me above all that being poor is no shame, which stood me in good stead when I was filching half cups of laundry detergent from my freshman roommate at Princeton. By senior year I'd made enough slaving away at the Firestone Library to at least look the part of a dressed-down, well-to-do preppy. At Princeton it was look the part or find your place in the shadows.

Now, with Nelson, it appeared I could earn enough to make both ends meet for a change. In fact I could easily make ends meet on $16,000 in Boston, including the rent on the tiny apartment I'd be subletting. If Nelson was correct, I only needed to memorize the right reference books, assume a faux hauteur, and the commissions would roll on in. Seven or eight years at the silk-covered grindstone and I'd be a millionaire. My mother used to sit at the kitchen table laying out the plans for her life at forty-five—what harm would a few years as the Liberace of decorative arts rhetoric do me if I could pay off my student loans and put some money aside before I had deep wrinkles in my forehead?

I made it all the way down the street to a palatial Italian shoe store on this train of thought before Geena ran up behind me to say that Nelson wanted me on the phone that second.

"Hi, Nelson?"

"Why the *fuck* didn't you call with a progress report?" he barked.

I mustered calm into every fiber of my body. "I'm sorry, I just—"

"Look, Fred, I'm in a bind and I need you to make a delivery."

I watched my hands scramble wildly for a writing instrument. "Sure."

"The deal's just about set, and it's worth sixty grand to me if you can see it through."

"Isn't this the sort of thing Whitney should be handling?" I said.

"You've been there half an hour and you're already giving away my leads?" Nelson said incredulously. "Jesus, maybe I was wrong about you."

"No," I said emphatically, *"tell* me."

"This is Marty's deal, but he just left for an appointment and I can't wait for him to get back. You know where the Catlin portfolio is? The 1845 one?"

"The?" I wasn't even sure who Marty was.

"Just ask Whitney to get it for you. Wrap it up in brown paper and get into a cab. His name is Denny D'Amico. You sold his wife Jenny the Brookshaw melons. Denny used to be a frogman for the Mafia. He's worth ten million dollars and has a million in cash in the bank. If he says he can't pay he's blowing smoke up your ass. You're there to make his collection an A+. Questions?"

"One thing: what's a frogman?"

"The guy who swims from ship to shore with the cocaine on his back. He runs a clothing store now. The price is $60,000, we discussed it. I'll give you the address. And, Fred—"

"Yes?"

"If he tries to get you to move some cocaine for him, just say no, okay? He's Marty's client, and I don't want Marty getting his tits in a tangle, so just be polite and say no. That's an order."

———

Marty's ex-frogman client ran a Versace knockoff boutique called Illusions on a North End square of funeral parlors and coffee bars. A dusty festival banner strung over the street said, "The Immaculate Conception, now thru August 1st." A Japanese woman in black buzzed me into Illusions, threw me some attitude, then let me browse over seventy-dollar ties while I waited for the man himself to appear. I felt a sort of power over seventy-dollar ties I never had before, and even frowned at a couple.

When Denny D'Amico walked out, I decided that as far as Boston was concerned, he singlehandedly filled the quota of drop-dead handsome men each city in America is allotted by the hands of fate and genetics. He was six foot four and broad-shouldered, black-haired and olive-skinned, and had a tiny scar centered just above his penetrating green eyes. He had one of those faces on which everything had gone right, and moved in his light chocolate double-breasted suit as if each moment spent inhabiting his body was pure pleasure. His diction was a bit forced, but there's the Mafia for you.

"Hi, Mr. D'Amico, I'm Fred Layton."

"Denny, I insist," he said. "It is a pleasure to meet you, Fred. Come right this way." Denny approached a wall of floor-to-ceiling mirrors, the central one with a recessed metal ring in it at waist level. He struggled momentarily to twist this ring, stole a quick look at himself in the glass, then pulled open the mirrored door to his suite of offices.

# 7. Where I Get It Back

enny and I sat on either side of a black marble coffee table in a track-lit office with uncomfortably low ceilings. Three bronze sculptures of perfectly built nude women with patinas like polished fenders shared the room with us. If these statues formed the centerpiece of Denny's art collection, bringing him up to antique prints would be more an act of common decency than a sales challenge. Denny unwrapped the brown paper package I'd brought from the gallery to reveal a burgundy morocco leather binder, about 28 by 18 inches. He nodded solemnly.

"Should we be wearing gloves?"

"Pardon?"

"For fingerprints."

I paused. Did Nelson Albright own a pair of protective gloves? "You know, I'm sure we're fine as long as you just touch the edges."

He unknotted the limp red ribbon at the edge of the portfolio's top cover and folded it back to reveal a splendidly preserved set of hand-colored lithographs. In a Western American landscape of absurdly rounded hills and grassy valleys, Osages and Iroquois and Sioux jumped buffalo, shot arrows into the blue yonder, ran around under white wolf skins, and played an ancient version of lacrosse, where for safety's sake only six hundred players were allowed on the field at one time. Denny might have been looking at Rembrandt sketches. When we got to the print called *Wi-Jun-Jon*, a before/after image of an Assiniboine chief who became an alcoholic dandy while visiting Washington, Denny stared at it without moving for nearly three minutes. I imagined that art salesmen were supposed to contribute critical readings of the work at such junctures, so I spoke up in a confident voice.

"Sold his soul for a nice suit."

Denny's eyes slid to the right. "What was that?"

My heart stopped. "I mean, that would be a knockout framed."

Denny grunted and moved to the next print. "How long have you been working for Nelson?"

"For Nelson?" I noticed that we'd come to a portrait of a buffalo urinating on a wolf corpse, and stayed my hand from reaching out to flip it over. "Uh, two hours, at least. I just moved here."

"A veteran, huh? I know what that's like." He leaned back. "And how do you like Boston?"

"It's fine," I said. I decided not to tell him that the most memorable sight thus far hadn't been the glittering gold leaf dome of the State House, but watching a transvestite walk up Arlington Street in a red wraparound dress, falsies like croquet balls on his chest, hands thrown up above his head in pleasure as a breeze snaked down the filthy sidewalk.

"Boston's not so bad," Denny said. "You ought to get someone to show you around a little. . . . Hey now, what about this?" He pointed to a particularly chalky cumulus cloud in the urinating-buffalo print. "Is this color original? Nelson said I should always look out for original color."

"Sure. If Nelson's representing it as original, it must be." I stared at the fine web-weave of Denny's sleeve. I had memorized another fact or two about the Catlin series in the taxi, I just couldn't cough them up. "So, you collect bronzes too?"

"Yeah, you like this stuff?" Denny smiled at last. He reached up to caress a sculpture's brassy forearm and a Rolex with diamonds in it like rock salt appeared on his thick wrist.

"It's . . . classic," I said. "Do you buy here?"

"No, I buy in Italy!" Denny exclaimed. "That's where you get the really good bronzes, in Milan."

I nodded. "You like Brancusi?"

"Who?"

"No one important," I said. "But it's great that you're breaking out into prints. Breadth is the mark of a mature collector."

As Nelson had predicted, Denny's chest swelled measurably in size. "Yeah, it's a good move, I think. And Nelson said they're a great investment. That's my main concern."

"Absolutely topnotch," I said. "This portfolio will grow in value north of ten percent a year."

Denny rose. He towered over me in his splendid suit. "You're getting into the right business, Fred, I'll tell you that. I have to put my stock on sale after a few months; your stuff you just mark up as it gets older."

"Right." I smiled, which killed his.

He reached behind a black leather chair in a corner of the room and brought out a wrinkled Purity Supreme grocery bag. "You can count this back at your gallery. By the way, will you be coming out for Nelson's party tonight? My wife would like to meet you."

I took the bag and instantly dropped it on my foot. It was heavy with (oh, Lord) $60,000 in small bills. This was a hundred and twenty times more money than I'd ever held in my life.

"The party?" I stammered. "Sure, wouldn't miss it."

———

Out at the street corner, Denny flagged a cab for me. As one pulled up he put a hand on my arm and a hand on the bag of money. He turned me slightly so that I faced an alley that ran behind his store. His manicured tough-guy face glowered.

"Okay," he said.

I attempted to swallow. "Okay?"

He gave a clipped, military nod. "Yeah. This is where I get it back."

My face must have gone white at this point, because Denny instantly grinned and slapped me on the shoulder. "That's just a joke, kid. See you at the party, all right?"

I was still nodding dumbly as the cabby pulled away.

## 8. Quick Study

Due to road repairs in downtown Boston, half of them scheduled by the Department of Public Works to affect east-west traffic, the other half scheduled by the state of Massachusetts to affect north-south traffic, it took nearly half an hour to get back to Newbury Street. Nelson had called eleven times in my absence.

"Welcome, you're our most-wanted man," Whitney said. She held the front door for me. "You also smell like an old man's wallet."

I lifted up the wrinkled grocery bag. "It's this stuff. I've got to count it out."

Whitney looked into the bag and then back at me, her eyes

wide. "Fred, if you bring in this kind of money every day you can be as late as you want!"

"Actually, it's not—"

"Aha!" Now the tall, black-haired man who had tried to assist me earlier stormed up and relieved me of the bag.

"How dare that maniac send some college kid out to one of my top clients!" he said to Whitney. Then to me: "Look, new person. I can get you fired before your feet touch the ground in this place. If I ever see you sharing the same *air* with one of my clients again, you're history." He slammed the French doors shut behind him and disappeared into the main gallery.

I turned to Whitney. "Who shat in his corn flakes this morning?"

"Shh," she said, with a hint of a smile. "That's Marty Ifft, in case you haven't met. He can get a little emotional. And I don't think he's predisposed to like you since you sold that pair of Brookshaw melons to Jenny D'Amico. He's highly averse to having his clients stolen."

"Stolen?" I said incredulously. "That was a call I took during my job interview! I didn't steal anything."

"You can try telling Marty, if you like," Whitney said. "That or give back his five-hundred-dollar commission."

I frowned. "All I can do at this point is wish him luck counting Denny's pile."

"I might board a plane for Costa Rica, the way things are going around here. Can you buzz me out, Geena? I'm going over to the frame shop."

I held the door for her. "Where is that?"

"It's right around the corner on Exeter," Whitney said. "I've got to make sure everybody's still awake."

"You're the woman for the job," I said.

"Nelson on the line for you, Fred," Geena announced, and held out the receiver.

"The focus of everyone's attention," Whitney said. She clicked into the vestibule and then out of sight. It seemed so safe outside, I wanted to follow her.

"Yes, Nelson," I said into the phone. "Marty's got the money."

"You're incredible," Nelson said. His mouth was packed with food. "I'll see to it that Whitney offers you a permanent position by the end of the week. Fred, I need to ask you another favor, okay? We're having a very important party out at my house tonight, with some big, big hitters, the kind of people I've been telling you about, and there are going to be lots of sales opportunities."

"I'm sure I can make it," I said grandly.

"Good. Now my executive assistant, Doug Morrow, is on his way into Boston with the white van, Fred, the white Ford van, and I would be forever in your debt if you would simply take that van, drive it to the New York gallery, drop off the pieces in it for their stock, get three British marine watercolors from Marjorie Warren, my New York receptionist, and . . . just a second"—Nelson screamed something over his shoulder to a person named NoNo— "and bring them back to my house by nine o'clock for the party. Whitney will be going up with you to see some clients too, okay, so if she looks out of it I want you to put a little salt on her tail. I would happily do this myself, but my wife's parents are in town from Dallas, and the poor woman hasn't seen them in two years."

"New York and back by nine?" I felt dread rising in my chest. "I guess that's doable, but I've got to pick up my friend's car from the garage and—"

"Whitney will be there to give you all the directions," Nelson reassured me. "Would you do this for me, Fred? I won't forget it."

I sighed. I supposed I would be paying my dues for a while. "Sure, Nelson. I can't control the traffic, but I'll do my best."

"*Thank* you, Fred. Call me with a report when you get there." He hung up and I looked at Geena, who was smirking as she doodled on an issue of *Town and Country*.

"Where do I get change for tolls?"

"The petty cash box is upstairs," Geena said, "but I think Marty just raided it for lunch. It's always empty anyway."

Whitney appeared at the door again, and Geena buzzed her in.

"I hear we're going to New York," she said. "We ought to sneak a few decent pieces of stock away from that crowd while we're at it. Nelson certainly isn't going to donate it for the asking."

"Sure thing," I said. "As long as none of it is for Marty."

Whitney laughed. "You're a quick study, Fred, what can I tell you?"

## 9. No Radio, No Audubons

You could practically taste the fetid Manhattan air when Whitney and I arrived in the van. The potholes were probably visible from space, and I nearly got trapped in one of them when six people cut me off getting onto West Ninety-sixth Street. We lurched to a stop at a red light with a thin stream of smoke wisping out from under the van's hood, and an old man in a red bandanna and a filthy johnny shirt instantly appeared at the windshield. With the indifferent expression of a carwash employee, he sprayed a dollar bill on the glass in Windex and began to wipe. Whitney might have just stepped off a punt in Henley, she was so appalled.

"Who asked for this?" she exclaimed. "And, God, look at that rag!" She leaned back in her seat. "Nothing makes me more disgusted than a dirty rag."

"Let's just be calm," I said, and rolled down the window. "Excuse me! We don't want any." At once a gnarled hand covered with purplish splotches shot into the tiny open space. It grabbed my rep tie, pulled down twice, then opened, palm up, as the other hand circled uselessly over the glass.

"*Give* it something," Whitney implored, "the light's about to change."

"I would, but I'm out of small bills," I said.

"Come on, Fred, I've got to meet the Asquiths in fifteen minutes."

"Yes, but all I have is a twenty," I said, "and I mean that quite literally." Still, Whitney didn't make a move. My head reeled in the highly distilled stink from the man's diseased arm. Would I really have to ask her to unlock her three-hundred-dollar leather purse? Had she not noticed that I'd paid the tolls all the way down the Merritt Parkway?

"Oh, here." At last Whitney thrust a piece of paper at me. I put it into the man's hand and he receded for a split second to view his catch. Then the light bloomed green, a squall of horns erupted behind me, and a furious pounding of fists ran over the van's outer body. I walked on the accelerator.

"What did you give me?" I said.

"A traffic ticket." Whitney began to laugh as we turned toward Central Park West. "Maybe he can take it over to the parking authority and have this piece of junk booted."

I honestly thought I was hearing things. "You just gave me a parking ticket?"

She shuddered. "All those homeless people ought to be rounded up and put on an island somewhere, God forgive me."

I didn't have time to point out that we already were on an island, because when we pulled up for another red light at Ninety-second Street the horns around me began to blow again. I rolled down the driver's side window, now much cleaner than the windshield, and a huge drag queen like a black Divine who was crossing the street pointed to the van's back doors.

"You got company, baby."

"Fred," Whitney yelled, and hit my right arm, "it's getting in! Didn't you lock up?"

I pulled my head back into the van and saw that the man in the johnny shirt had opened one of the doors. He must have held onto the back bumper and door handles as I pulled away.

"Hey, get out of there!" I hollered. The man made some incomprehensible noises and heaved himself up into the van.

Whitney had stuffed her purse under the seat and was adjusting the rear-view mirror. "Put it in reverse and knock him against the truck behind us!"

I glared at her. "Jesus Christ, Whitney, that is not something you lose a couple of points on your license for. Hang on." I climbed out of my seat and scrambled over the tires and the Asquiths' newly framed Audubons toward the back of the van, digging for my wallet in my blazer pocket. By the time I got to the doors, the man had already claimed one of the quilted shipping blankets and was moving in on Audubon's *Carolina Parakeet.* Fully matted and framed, the print dwarfed him in size.

"Here." I thrust my twenty-dollar bill in his face. "Leave the blanket and the print alone."

The man stared directly into my eyes. His were the color of light caramel, with flecks of pale olive. He looked almost demure until a line of spittle began to droop from one corner of his mouth.

"The light's about to change!" Whitney shouted.

"I'm sorry," I said, trying to sound reasonable to the man, "but these are for a *client.*"

He took the bill from me in slow disbelief and crawled back out of the van without another word. His legs looked like prosthetic limbs—no muscle tone or contour to speak of. I pulled the door shut, locked it firmly, and ran up to the steering wheel. This kind of glitch definitely didn't qualify as part of my art dealer fantasy.

Whitney hadn't budged from her seat. In fact, she was laughing when I sat down.

"Too much," she said. "Did he take the *Parakeet,* or did you have to give him the *Wild Turkey?*"

I flipped off a taxi and ran the next red. Unless I drank off my Diet Coke that instant it was going to end up on Whitney's knit suit. "No, all right? He said he's already got a *Wild Turkey.*"

# 10. Poised to Take Advantage

Nelson's personal residence, Château Delapompe, was a turn-of-the-century robber baron mansion constructed from ruddy brick and slate shingles. It was cut in the Gothic suburban style and sat on a three-acre lot in the West Newton Hill section of Newton. At first, Delapompe reminded me of depictions of the entire Jamestown settlement, circa 1640. Later it would invite comparisons with the House of Usher and Wuthering Heights. A designer I came to know called it one of the best examples of a my-cock-is-bigger-than-your-cock house in suburban Boston.

Since I had to make a drop at the downtown gallery and drive Whitney to her house, it was going on nine-thirty when I arrived at the château. After parking Nelson's van I grabbed the portfolio of British watercolors I'd brought from New York and jogged through a drenching rain into the shelter of the carport. There I met Nelson's shady-looking executive assistant, Doug Morrow, who was parking cars.

"Fred!" Doug said in a Maryland twang, and slapped my back. "The Sixty Thousand Dollar Man! Thanks a lot for helping me park the cars, dude. Everybody's already here."

"Park the cars?" I looked at him closely. "I drove that lousy van all the way out here for Nelson and he only wants me to park cars?"

"You can start with this asswipe," Doug said, and indicated an approaching pair of headlights. "Oh yeah, hang on a second, man." He produced a folded white envelope from his back pocket and handed it to me. "This was waiting for you in the box where we keep all the car keys. Maybe it's your commission on the Catlin."

"Somehow I doubt it, but thanks." I glanced at the envelope but didn't open it. "What's this party for, anyway?"

Doug shrugged. "Nothing, just a party. They throw a lot of them to sell shit. Nelson's always desperate for cash. As you can see from the shack he lives in."

"I do see."

"All right, man, we'll talk to you later." Doug walked off, lighting up a cigarette despite the rain, and I turned toward the approaching sedan. As it pulled up under the carport, I leaned the watercolor portfolio against my leg and tore open the envelope. Inside was a Xerox copy of a scene from a small-format Audubon *Quadrupeds* print. A large rodent at the left rearing up on its hind legs was labeled "Nelson," while a much smaller rodent crawling into the composition on the right was labeled "Rich Potential Customer." In the middle, the smallest but most vicious-looking rat stared straight ahead and bared its teeth. The original name— Marty, I guessed—was whited out, and in its place someone had typed "Fred." Someone had also drawn a large red X through the Fred rat. The caption under the scene read, "Poised to take advantage."

I smiled, though I could feel the fur on the back of my neck rising. "Thanks, Marty," I said. "I won't forget it."

"Yo, Fred!" a deep voice called. "Where should I put this?" A few feet away, Denny D'Amico was sidling out of a gold BMW 750il. I leaned forward, looking, if Denny's tinted windows were accurate, like a small drowned rodent.

"Put it anywhere you like." I tried to smooth down my hair. "What are you drinking?"

"Anything wet." He paused as he climbed back in. "I was going to take off the suit, but I could tell you liked it."

"Where's your wife?"

"Jenny couldn't get a sitter. Looks like you'll have to keep me entertained." He smiled and winked.

"Cool." I took a weak-kneed step toward the porch door and nearly tripped over my portfolio. "I'll do my best."

## 11. God Bless America

Nelson's wife, Kak Albright, met us at the door of Château Delapompe, just as I became aware that Denny smelled strongly of Scotch. Kak was a short blond Texan with huge blue eyes, a tiny sharp nose, and a slim, Junior League bandwidth of expressions. She gushed with the sort of social warmth learned entirely by rote. Her mode of greeting at parties shifted subtly according to intimacy with the guest: For old friends or customers who had spent in excess of $50,000, it was, "How ARRR yew?" For new friends and clients who had spent less than $50,000, it was something closer to "How-arr YEWW?" For new male employees under thirty-five, it was a silent once-over that calculated how many van trips between Boston and New York the employee could bear before complete mental breakdown. I didn't realize until I watched Kak's eyes sweep disparagingly down my damp, exhausted body that employees of Albright Galleries might be called upon for any task at any hour of the day, night, or weekend. I inched closer to Denny D'Amico as Nelson dashed forward from a Gothic Revival arch near the entry door and relieved me of the British watercolors. He was still in those filthy corduroys, though he had switched from tennis shoes to wingtips. He spoke close to my ear.

"D'Amico's the plague for you, okay? He's Marty's deal."

"Marty made that clear," I said crisply.

"I just met my new buddy Fred outside," Denny began in a loud voice.

"Terrific!" Nelson exclaimed. "Glad to hear it. Why not get Denny a drink, Fred, and then find Marty? We've got some incredible things to show him for his collection."

"Sure, Nelson," I said. We moved off toward the other guests. "How are those Catlins treating you, Denny?"

"Good," Denny said enigmatically. "My wife thinks they're cute."

"In that case we'll send you some reference books."

Down in the crowd of guests, Marty Ifft happened to look up from a gin and tonic and see us. Based on the homicidal look he gave me, I pointed him out to Denny from the top of the steps and made for the gallery bar on my own.

Château Delapompe was bisected by a long passage that began as a hall at the carport door. From the hall, this passage dropped three steps and widened into a central gallery that divided the main fireplace and dining room on the left from Nelson's library office and a bay of Gothic windows on the right. Then the passage narrowed again to end in the living room and back patios at the far end of the house. Midway down the gallery, a dozen bottles and snacks were arranged on a Tudor table that sat under the Gothic windows. Thirty or so people radiated out from this table, chatting and dipping into Navajo bowls. The difference between these clients and me, even between most of the other employees and me, was glaring: they were here to display and describe as much about themselves and their possessions as possible; I was here to egg on such display and avoid reference to my negligible past.

I got halfway into preparing a drink before realizing that Nelson might not want me to partake, but under the waiting glare of a thirsty, pin-striped man whose eyes convinced me I was no more than a napkin under his shoe, I poured a double. Denny, the client of the hour, made another approach at four o'clock sharp. Marty followed him and elbowed me aside.

"Denny!" he said. "You've got to see these British watercolors I just brought up from New York."

"The new watercolors are an *ex*cellent idea," Nelson said as he rushed up. "First, Denny, let me take you into my confidence on something. Two *major* fashion people called me this afternoon to ask about collecting antique prints. One of them was asking about *Catlin* portfolios, and I had to tell her she was too late! You are way ahead of the curve, man."

"Gentlemen, gentlemen," Denny said with a gracious flourish, "no one has said a word about framing some of these puppies. Might I expect a discount?"

"A framing discount?" Nelson exclaimed. "Denny, for a $60,000 sale we'll sponsor a coup d'état in the Third World country of your choice!"

Denny laughed, after a mysterious delay. "And what kind of commission is Fred looking at for all his hard work?"

I spoke up before Marty had the opportunity to lean forward and scratch my eyes out. "Mr. D'Amico, it wasn't my sale. You know that."

"He'll be getting commissions soon enough," Nelson said.

"He's a Princeton man, like me. He'll be taking over Newbury Street in a year, if he plays his cards right."

At this prediction, Whitney Buck swooped down on us from the dining room like a gyrfalcon. "Nelson, may I speak with you for a sec?"

"You look lovely tonight," Denny said.

"Denny!" Whitney said, and laughed as if gargling with mouthwash. "I didn't even see you. Nelson, Kurt Schoch is interested in having a look at the new watercolors, if you . . ." She batted her eyelashes.

Nelson adjusted his belt. "Of course, of course. See what I mean, Den?"

Denny grinned. "Can't hold back a—"

Marty stepped forward. "Denny, I—"

Whitney pulled Nelson aside. "Nelson, I—"

I was alone again, and went back to finishing my drink. I'd just garnished it with lemon when a voice began to whisper in my ear.

"Fred," the voice said, "could you come here?" I was sure I was imagining things until I turned with my double vodka and saw Kak Albright, who was trying not to be seen talking with me. "Fred, would you do me a *fabulous* favor and get a bag of ice from the kitchen? Y'all just go straight into the dining room and the door's on the left."

My heart thumped in wild fear of displeasing her. Whitney had made it clear in the van on the way to New York who oversaw firing decisions in the company. "Sure, Mrs. Albright."

"That's grayte." She sighed. "And you call me Kak from now on."

I excused my way through the guests into the dining room, accidentally nudging what appeared to be a structurally significant lemon in a decorative fruit pyramid that sat atop a Regency table. I was about to push through the dining room's swinging door to the kitchen when I heard Whitney's voice, wound tight with emotion.

"I didn't even give official permission for him to be downtown!" she hissed. "And he'll get commissions over my dead body!"

"Whitney," Nelson's voice pleaded, "he worked with Parker Spitz at the Firestone. He's *good stuff.*"

"I don't care if he worked with Lee Iaccoca at Chrysler, it's my gallery and I make the goddamned rules."

"Right, you make the rules until you have another breakdown and then we don't see you for three weeks."

"Don't you *dare* bring that up!"

I stopped in my tracks. Several minutes passed as I was roasted in the kitchen and felt my ears burning to a crisp, charred consistency. Then I heard Kak's voice rise up from the gallery. "Ex*act*ly. I mean, what are we doing walking through life, carrying all this extra baggage? Sorry, Jack? You're right, I *did* send someone. That new guy must be retarded!"

I tried again to push through the door, but this time a loud crash stayed my hand.

"What the hell are you doing?" Nelson yelled.

"I'm throwing this," Whitney yelled back. Another crash followed. "What do you want me to do?"

"Do whatever makes me the most money!"

I turned around to find Kak at my heels. She looked like she was about to pull out a switch and give me a Texas-style whomping.

"For pete's sake, Fred, is your sense of direction that bad?"

"Nelson and Whitney are having a private discussion in there," I whispered.

Kak frowned at me, a frown of interrupted privilege that could have frozen boiling water. "Since when is anything private around here?" she said, and pushed through into the kitchen.

Whitney was in tears, her tear-stained face like a little girl's as she pulled tissues from a converted duck decoy. Nelson was holding a brass egg whisk at the marble-topped counter and trying not to laugh. The kitchen maid, a tall black woman in her sixties, was sitting at a phone nook in the corner with her arthritic hands over her ears. The remains of two dinner plates covered the floor. Although Nelson's kitchen was six times the size of my senior-year room at Princeton, it was in such a luxe setting that I began to beg to keep my $16,000 salary.

"Look, I don't have to go on commission right away," I announced. "Anything you say is fine, Whitney."

"I'm sorry, Fred," Nelson began, as Whitney rushed past me. He extended his hands as if to present me with the egg whisk in substitution. "Commission after six months, how about that? But my millionaire promise still sticks, okay? Millionaire in ten years. And you're definitely starting downtown in sales. Tomorrow, bright and early."

"That's *fine*," I said. "I didn't mean to cause so many problems."

"You ought to talk to Marty," Kak said, dragging a five-pound bag of ice from the freezer with a grunt. "He's thrilled with the whole arrangement."

"Here," I said, "let me take that, Mrs. Albright."

"It's Kak," Kak said. "I told you."

"Did you park any of those cars, by the way?" Nelson said. "Jack Klake can't find his keys."

"Well, Fred's off to a flying start," Kak said, glaring at her husband. "God bless America, honey, where do you find these people?"

They arranged smiles on their faces and filed out of the kitchen into the party again. I looked back at the maid in confusion, but she refused to remove her hands from her ears.

## 12. Looking for the Peach

At work the next morning I had a call from Ruth Feinberg, my good friend from Princeton who'd spent the summer in Israel trying to escape the clutches of a decidedly pre-feminist kibbutz where her father had enrolled her. Ruth had moved to Boston in late August to help an historical society in Wayland mount an exhibit of silver horseracing trophies. It was her car that had bitten the dust on me when I drove into Boston two days before.

"Ruth," I said, "I haven't had a second to call you."

"Fred?" She exhaled a long, ragged line of breath, quite near tears. "Does Nelson need any new people?"

"Why?" I said. "What happened?"

"Dad did not pay $70,000 in tuition so I could Xerox articles from *Country Life*, that's what happened. That's for starters."

"You poor *thing*." I stared off into the gallery. "I'm just trying to think. How are your house-painting skills?"

"Funny." She sniffed. "Things must be pretty good for you,

though. The woman who answered had to see if you were *available*."

"Right, buttocks raised and awaiting the whip. It's not so bad, actually. Nelson says I can become a millionaire in ten . . . no, wait a minute. In ten years I'll be thirty-two." Numbers floated vaguely in my head. "He said a millionaire by the time I was thirty, didn't he? When did he say ten years?"

Ruth laughed obligingly. "Let's have breakfast tomorrow, okay? Drive out in the car and we'll chat."

"Excellent idea," I said. "Why don't you sit for a second, and I'll tell you about the car."


Nelson knew who Ruth Feinberg was, or at least he knew her father, the part-time antiquarian print dealer. Actually, Dr. Feinberg had had a rather bitter argument with Nelson after a Sotheby's auction in the early eighties, and in general thought him a price-gouging scum. I clearly remembered the spring break picnic at the Feinberg compound in Sandy Hook, Connecticut, where Ruth and I were interrupted from marveling over the lavishness of an Albright Galleries catalog by the good doctor, who grabbed one of his own hand-stapled price lists and rose with wrath from his chair.

"I'd rather sell my daughter into a harem than have her work for Nelson Albright!" he announced. "Your grandfather would have blushed at the things he called me, that swindler, that *schwein!*"

Nelson never forgot an argument either, and during Ruth's interview he pulled out a coffee table magazine that had recently published a puff piece about his success. One reader's letter of response to the article interested Nelson very much, and he thought it might interest Ruth, too:

*Dear Features Editor,*

*I enjoyed the paean to Nelson Albright in your last issue. If your writer requires assistance in prying his puckered lips from Mr. Albright's buttocks, I am happy to suggest several plastic surgeons who would be up to the task.*

*Yours sincerely,*
*Dr. J. Feinberg*
*Sandy Hook, CT.*

Ruth had blushed and then laughed, and Nelson hired her on the spot for $20,000, as if she had become, in Dr. Feinberg's prophecy, the prize daughter of a military enemy he was procuring for his harem.

Ruth was the first woman I met at Princeton, a freckled, brown-eyed, big-boned, and slightly baffled Jewish bohemian. I'd seen her run from a dining-hall table in embarrassment after saying something harmless, and later the same day zoom down Nassau Street on the back of a friend's motorcycle shouting, "Princeton sucks!" which always made the freshmen skittish. The real Ruth was somewhere between these extremes, I guessed, and still a few years from full bloom. In any case, she knew worlds more natural history and antiquarian print lore than I did, and Nelson seemed to realize she was a find. Yet something about her hardiness, or her zealous scholarly passion for the stock, or her weight, stopped him short from placing her in a gallery sales position. She was instead retained as a researcher and Nelson's second "executive assistant" at the Weston headquarters. Within a week she had moved from the bed and breakfast in Wayland where she'd been staying into a spare bedroom at Château Delapompe.

At first, Ruth's thanks to me knew no bounds, and in pecuniary terms this produced a hundred-dollar cash loan that saw me through the remainder of September on a diet of tomato soup, sliced bread, apples, and ears of sweet corn I haggled for at the outdoor produce stalls in the Haymarket. With Ruth's help, I was able to hold my first dinner party on a Friday evening at my little one-room apartment on Chandler Street. My entire guest list, Ruth, showed up wearing a long madras skirt and bearing a jug of wine. Fifi, a six-foot freestanding cardboard maid I'd received from my friend Bridget for graduation, stood just outside the door with a small calling card on which I'd inscribed the menu:

| | |
|---|---|
| *Appetizer:* | *Soup of tomato* |
| *Entree:* | *Maize on the stalk, butter* |
| | *Waters* |
| *Dessert:* | *Tea cake in heavenly thin slices* |
| | *Coffee* |
| *Postprandial:* | *Waters* |
| | *Pommes Fred Layton* |

"Fred," Ruth gushed as she entered my closet-sized kitchen and kissed me, "this is so awful, I'm eating up your larder. I hope you finally got reimbursed for driving to New York."

"All but the twenty bucks I gave to the homeless guy. Whitney said I had to have a receipt for it."

"Witch."

Given the state of my apartment, which previous tenants had painted in lurid greens, oranges, and blacks, we dined in the small courtyard beyond my kitchen door.

"I've been meaning to ask you," Ruth said as she poured her third glass of wine and sampled it. "What went wrong with you and Bridget? You were such a great couple."

I looked off and shrugged. "Who knows? All I said was, 'Let's try that thing where you come while giving me head.'"

She poked my chest. *"Fred."*

"What can I tell you, sweetie? Bridget caught me in the bathroom with Mark."

"Andrea's Mark? What did you say?"

"I said he was helping me floss."

"What did she say?"

" 'Bisexuality is for earthworms.' "

"That's awful!"

"Don't worry," I said, "I deserved it. That and more. I spent far too long hiding behind her."

A long pause, while a line of fire engines roared down Tremont Street.

"Fred, sexuality is like a peach. Do you see this peach?"

I leaned across the table. "Ruth, you have no peach."

"Exactly."

"I feel so relieved."

## 13. The National Organization for Women

Back on Newbury Street, Geena the receptionist took a three-month leave of absence to follow the Grateful Dead (she was The Daughter of a Client, after all, and could not be fired), so I was obliged to sit at the front desk manning the phones and pushing a small concealed white button to buzz people into the gallery. Whitney busied herself preparing for a sales trip to a gum doctor in Miami who had floated the purchase of 600 thirty-dollar-a-night motels entirely on credit, while Marty came and went with large deli sandwiches wrapped in white butcher paper, complained constantly about our frame shop, and seemed to outsell everyone in Nelson's New York, Greenwich, Chicago, and Los Angeles galleries between cigarette breaks.

On an average day, Nelson would telephone for sales updates between eight and twenty-one times. Whenever he decided to visit the Boston shop in person, we would have ample advance notice, since calls and messages preceded and followed his movements as dust and intrigue did the Sun King's carriage. Bish in Weston tracked him more like a hurricane. "Nelson left New York an hour early," she would warn us, and Whitney and Marty would look at each other in their designer clothing with pale, drawn faces.

It soon became clear to me that Nelson was the essence of fearlessness and insecurity combined in one flesh. To work for him was to fill in his silences and fill up his day, the same way that a pedestrian or bicycle courier or limousine seems to wedge into every free inch of space during a Manhattan rush hour. My boss *had* to ensure that his life ran at breakneck pace, all the time. If interesting leads didn't exist when I spoke to him, I simply made them up. If all I could report after two days of work was selling an 1865 chromolithograph of a tulip to a librarian from Natick for ninety dollars, I expressed my certainty that the librarian would be back with her decorator in a week. If a lunch-hour browser confessed to thinking about owning a collection of eighteenth-century maps—if he knew what the eighteenth century *was*—he got my card, a catalogue, and three follow-up letters inviting him to stop by again.

In such a state we all arrived at the morning of October 19, 1987. The day felt out of kilter from the moment I got up, though my bright orange bathroom made such subtleties hard to detect. I even had a headache, which was rare for me.

The scene as I turned onto the fifth block of Newbury Street was vaguely post-assassination: Ruth and her fellow executive assistant Doug Morrow were standing frozen in time beside a black Volvo station wagon, while Nelson was dashing back and forth between the curb and our storefront to no apparent end, his thick blond hair still damp from the shower. Now he pulled open the back hatch of the Volvo and began rifling through a pile of freshly matted prints, as if his wife might be discovered committing adultery with Denny D'Amico at the bottom.

"Pump it up," he was saying as I approached, then: "Ruth! I want everyone out here, *now.*"

"Doug," Ruth said irrefutably, "Nelson wants everyone out here, *now.*"

Doug ran to the vestibule and stuck his head in. "Everyone, Nelson wants everyone out here, *now!*"

Silence. We waited. Presently Whitney walked through the

green gallery door, brushing off her tweed skirt with anxious sophistication.

"Now," Nelson snarled at her, "don't you know what *now* means, Whitney?"

"I believe I was on the phone with an important client," Whitney said. "Marty still is, so don't interrupt him." She peeked under the station wagon's hatch and drew in her breath. "Wow! That is ter*rif*ic."

Nelson, caught between sputtering rage and Whitney's infectious enthusiasm, went with the latter, though this, like all his emotional choices, had about it an air of pure contingency.

"*Awesome*ly beautiful super minto," he said, and drew out for our small circle a pristine aquatint of four American city views from 1817.

"I've dated this girl once or twice before," he continued, "but I've never slept with her till now. Here, Whitney; have those fuzzheads around the corner frame it in the two-inch gold leaf I like. We'll pop it at eighteen thousand. Offer it to Swifty Williams. If he doesn't take it, offer it to his ex-wife at twenty-two five."

Whitney held the aquatint by either edge of its mat and mouthed "Twenty-two five?" to me as she passed. The rest of us circled the Volvo's hatch like Eritrean farmers queued up for wheat flour.

"Ruth," I whispered, as Nelson filled Doug's arms with prints, "I need to talk to you, *now*."

She shook her head. "Don't push your luck, dude. Bobby Hammerstein just canceled the big Miami trip. Plus Nelson found out you let that homeless guy into the van."

"Who told him about that?"

She smiled. "Who do you think? If you start doing well and outselling Marty, Nelson will stop giving him leads and good stock for his clients." Ruth took off her glasses and polished them on her sweater. "We had a major meeting this morning. You should see the way Nelson runs things out in Weston. If you're a man you can come and go as you please; if you're a woman you've got to get Nelson's permission. Women can't leave."

"Would you rather be Xeroxing racing trophy articles?"

She looked at me as if this were beside the point. "God, did he ever wig when he found out the Miami trip was off. Bish put him on the intercom and I could hear him upstairs in the bathroom."

"Nelson!" Whitney called. She clicked up to the edge of the vestibule. "Your broker's on the line: the Dow is down thirty points in the last hour."

Nelson's dismayed face popped up from the hatch. "Jesus *Christ.* We are meeting as of now. Whitney, pick out what you need for stock. Everyone else into Whitney's office. That includes Marty."

Whitney ran out to the street. Nelson pushed past Doug and brought his angrily knit forehead and plunging nose right up to my face.

*"Now."*

We watched him ball-and-heel his way into the gallery. Ruth giggled and gave me a little shove forward.

"Jeez, Fred; don't you know what *now* means?"

"I believe it stands for the National Organization for Women," I said.

Whitney picked up an imposing pile of prints and stiff-shouldered her way past us. "Not in this goddamned organization it doesn't."

## 14. Designing Lunatics

To open the meeting, the six of us gathered in Whitney's office and watched Nelson take calls. I was very interested to see how many of us would still have jobs when we closed.

"Hello," Nelson said. "Speaking, and you are? Yes, but could you please speak faster, please? Could you send me those questions in writing, because you're speaking incredibly slowly. In fact I can't understand why you're speaking so slowly, I feel like you're insulting me. Okay, shoot. No, that's not true: next question. No, they were in terrible condition. They were in terrible condition. They were chipped, dirty, stained, and had gouges taken out of the corners because someone had torn off all the blind stamps. That's all I have time for. That's your headache. I've got fifteen people in my office and I . . . yes, send them in writing. Right, 'bye. You moronic bitch."

Whitney rolled her eyes with finishing school finality and I sat down in the space she cleared on the couch.

"First order of business," Nelson said, as he dug a finger around in his ear. "We are at this moment plunging into a nationwide depression."

"Jesus," Marty laughed into his coffee, "shouldn't we at least start with a roll call?"

———

An hour later the morning's mail was borne in, but without the eloquence of checks about it. As the stock market continued to plummet, many clients called to return prints they'd recently bought. Nelson, his hands balled into fists, asked about their trips to the Cayman Islands and St. John, praised their consummate skills as collectors, and in the end headed off a selling spree. No one announced a meeting agenda, unless the agenda was to watch our boss's tight mouth grow tighter. The combination of intense pressure and enforced stasis exhausted me. Marty, in the absence of a cigarette, chewed his finger.

"No, Tony," Nelson was saying, as he browsed through an antiques show contract and we approached lunch, "just thinking of the stomach juices I'll need to make that trade gives me ulcers. The walls are too thin. Tell you . . . tell you what, though; I'll *give you* the Mouzon map of Georgia plus my 1875 Krebs birdseye of Pittsburgh for only twelve grand. . . . What? You want me to bid for you? Which auction? You bet, I'll be there anyway. I'll intimidate anyone who goes near that lot. Christie's, right? Not a problem. Of course I'll do it for free. . . . Oh, Gloria wants it. Why don't you buy her an engagement ring instead of a print? Tony, she knows what you're like and she still loves you. What you need is a tolerant woman who's a giver, and Gloria's a *gooood* woman, Tony, a *gooood* woman. Close the sale, man, close the sale!"

Slam.

"As I was saying," he addressed us, taking up the thread of a sentence whose opening I no longer remembered, "I've got a contract here for a new antiques show in Baltimore. Six days, lots of media coverage, big preview, Young Collectors Night, reduced booth rent if we go in by the end of this week. Someone could do it with one vanload of stock, or two."

"Whoever heard of an East Coast antiques show before Philadelphia?" Marty said. "I wouldn't touch it."

"I agree," Whitney said. "We do more business at the Boston show than with Baltimore people all year. Count me out."

"I just might do that," Nelson said, his voice resolving into a whine. "In fact, I'm seriously considering sending Fred here, and Ruth, to do this show, so they'll get some experience selling to a lot of traffic."

"That's a great idea," Doug said. He was cleaning his fingernails with a small hunting knife.

"Perhaps you'd like to man the front door for walk-in traffic while Fred's away," Marty sneered at him.

"Oh, please," Whitney said, "not even in jest."

"There isn't going to be any more walk-in traffic after today," Nelson said darkly. "Have you not landed on that extremely subtle conclusion yet? You should have closed this gallery to everything but appointments two months ago. I'm tired of the two-hundred-dollar birdshit sales you're doing here."

"Two hundred bucks four times a day adds up to a lot of birdshit," Marty countered.

Nelson stared at him blankly as the phone began to ring. He didn't seem to recognize anyone. "Hello, Nelson Albright. What! Oh, my God. Sell, Jason, sell! Sell everything I've got!" Slam.

"Now we're into it," he said. "I mean we are *into* it. This is crash, and unless we start to extend ourselves in every direction there's going to be trouble. I insist that we do this show. In fact,

I'm going to commit Fred and Ruth to this show as of now. I'll ask that you do ten thousand each as a minimum, okay, and if you can't sell that much then I'd have to say you aren't hungry enough for the business and in this bust economy I'd have to consider dropping you."

"Ten thousand each in Baltimore?" Whitney said. "Why can't New York do it?"

"New York does *one* show a year," Nelson droned, as if the topic were discussed frequently, "and Greenwich doesn't have the stock or the manpower."

"But ten thousand each?" Whitney repeated. "The mind reels."

"Ten grand is tit, and I know you can do it," Nelson went on, looking at me. "You're both intelligent and fresh and hard workers. And shows can be great fun."

"Oh, a ball," Marty said. He and Whitney shared a knowing laugh that chilled my blood.

"In fact, Whitney, you can give them a hand with the preview," Nelson said, his voice resolving into cold rage. "It's in Baltimore next Friday."

"But I've got to—" Whitney began.

"In *fact*," Nelson went on, "I'd say that the next person who opens their fucking mouth in this room is history. That's what I think I'm trying to say."

Dead silence. An agonizing minute ticked by. Presently Doug walked over to the Victorian tole tray in front of the couch and scribbled a note on a Post-it pad. He passed the pad to Nelson and stepped back. Nelson read the note, mumbled something that sounded very much like "Korea Palace," and stood up.

"I have an appointment in ten minutes. Marty, I need two hundred dollars from petty cash, please."

Whitney strangled a laugh and Nelson pounced on her.

"Yes, Whitney, two hundred dollars. It happens to be for a new squash racquet. Maybe you'd all be performing a little better around here if you joined a club and worked up a sweat once in a while. Mr. Ifft?"

Marty jumped to his feet and exited the office via the green swinging door to the left of Whitney's *bureau plat*. We heard him moving up the back stairs to the second floor, then the footfalls faded away. Nelson began to pace from the couch to Whitney's desk and back again. For a man with such a big belly, he moved with surprising agility.

"Fred," he said quickly, "there's a Christie's sale in London in ten days I want you to monitor."

I sat up. "In London?"

"I want you to make sure they fax me the realized prices. There's a Catlin portfolio in that sale identical to Denny D'Amico's, and if it sells for more than sixty grand you've got a loyal client for life."

"*Marty's* got a loyal client for life," Whitney said, her voice rising. "Can we please not open that can of worms again?"

"All right, fine," Nelson snapped. "But I want those prices on my desk at Château Delapompe the second they're available."

"I'll let him know, sir," Whitney said sarcastically.

Nelson's restless eyes fell on three just-unwrapped Brookshaw cherry prints with triple marbleized mats. The marbled paper was flat gold with a blue fleur-de-lis pattern on top. He stopped pacing and regarded the prints like Godzilla about to obliterate a small city.

"If *this* is the kind of framing we're doing for stock . . ." he began.

"Those prints are for Jenny Dilforth's client and we have the check," Whitney said. "Do calm yourself."

"Hmm." A smile played over his lips. "Ms. Dilforth is working with an aesthetic sense that constitutes either jailable lunacy or unbelievably bad taste. Standard discount?"

"She got twenty-five percent."

His eyes bugged out. "Twenty-*five?* Are you trying to soak me, Whitney? Do you realize it takes $30,000 a day for us to stay afloat?"

"You took the bath on it," Whitney said firmly. "You cut the deal on *that* telephone."

"All right, all right," he said placatingly. Then, unable to resist: "Did you mark the framing up three times, or did you just throw that in gratis?"

"Three point five, as usual," Whitney said. "Asshole."

Marty broke the spell of Nelson's silent delight by pushing through the green swinging door again. "There's only $180 in petty cash, chief."

"I'll be burned in hell," Nelson said. He stuffed the money into his pocket and called back over his shoulder as he rushed out, "Everyone sell, okay? You can give thirty percent off if you have to. We're in a depression. Ruth, meet me at The Country Club in an hour."

Doug flicked back the stray locks of his poodle perm, gave our body language a final once-over for signs of insubordination, folded his hunting knife, and followed Nelson out of the office as close to the manner of his walk and set of expression as he could. Whitney made a sickened face and stood up.

"Remember to use a condom with your new squash racquet."

"I'm amazed at how Korea Palace is branching out," Marty added. "Hot oil massages, escort services, and now a full line of racquet sport supplies."

Ruth, who had been reading *Fine Bird Books* all morning, seemingly oblivious to everything that had transpired, now uncrossed her legs and stretched them. "I wonder what Tang Li leaves out when he hasn't got the whole two hundred?"

None of us could answer.

## 15. No Boat Data on File

On the morning of my planned departure for the Baltimore Antiques Show, Whitney paid me a little visit at the front desk. Since the first Delapompe party we hadn't spoken much.

"I want you to look this over and become familiar with it," she said crisply. She handed me a list of Maryland and Delaware clients who belonged to her and Marty and were one hundred percent off limits.

"By the way," she warned, "this Baltimore show is managed by Jetty Smith. Your booth is going to have to be eye-catching."

I nodded confidently. "You bet."

"I'll also want to see daily reports of what you do and whose names go into the daybook," she added.

"Consider it done."

"In fact, Marty and I have decided that daily reports in general might be a good idea. You're going to have to start producing much bigger sales to get my clearance for commissions at the end of six months."

"I understand."

"And I don't want you to start packing up stock until we close today. Marty and I have a lunch date with a decorator. I don't want any clutter around."

"Not a problem."

"I'm expecting an important check from Jack Klake, too." Whitney leaned over the phone and wrote "Whitney expecting check" in the front desk daybook. "I'll send you over to the bank to deposit it when it arrives."

"I'm there."

She smiled sourly. "And let's cut the sarcasm, okay?" Whitney and her bobbed hair and her pearls swung around the French doors and slammed into the main gallery. The phone purred and I picked up.

"Albright Galleries."

"All packed?" Ruth began.

"I understand," I said.

Our body-builder Federal Express man knocked on the door and I buzzed him in. "Hey, George," I said. "Your shoulders are looking a little fat today."

"Up yours." He grinned and handed me a pen.

"Ruth," I said, "let me put you on hold."

"No, Fred—"

"Whitney," I said into the intercom, "there's a Fed Ex letter here for you."

"That'll be the check," her muffled voice answered. "Open it and tell me what you've got."

I flashed a parting smile at George, pulled the envelope's ripcord, and read from the small white card inside.

*"Dear Mrs. Whitney Hallirake Buck,*

*"We are unable to complete your recent application for entry into the 1988* Social Register *without the following missing information: No Boat Data on File."*

Marty's high whinny came through the intercom, then Whitney said, "Is that your idea of a joke? It's easier than you think for me to cut off your antique show commissions."

"I understand," I said, and punched into Ruth's blinking line. "You were saying, my sweet?"

"You *never* put me on hold!" Nelson screamed. "What the *fuck* do you think you're doing?"

I stared at the phone console in terror. "Nelson, I didn't. You were Ruth a second ago."

"You think Ruth sits around using my private line all day? Jesus Christ!"

"I'm—"

"Look, this is important," he went on. "I'm driving down to Dover this afternoon and I must have the Fay views of New York. I've checked all the other galleries. They are un*speak*ably rare."

"I'll find them right away," I said.

"The *nano*second you do I want you to call me, okay?"

"Yes." I hung up. "Unspeakably rare."

But there I was stuck. When Nelson already called everything in the gallery incredibly rare, what did unspeakably rare look like?

By the end of the first hour of searching the gallery, I still hadn't found the Fay views. En route, however, I had passed over dozens of bays of mat drawers containing just about everything else we sold: Civil War lithographs; American and English vignettes; architectural engravings; *Vanity Fair* caricatures; Audubon birds and quadrupeds; six lower-range German poultry series; various butterflies, cats, cowboys, shells, Indians, snakes, and insects; and images of possibly every flower and decorative fruit cultivated in Europe between 1610 and 1880. "These I've got to memorize," I said, then I turned my search to the map drawers.

After ten minutes among the maps, Whitney stopped by to watch. Maps were her thing, so her attitude softened noticeably when she saw me hard at work.

"Hang on a minute, Fred, I'll give you a little lesson," she said. She floated to a drawer, removed two copies of a 1648 Blaeu of the Americas, and pulled back their clear Mylar top mats so I could examine them more closely.

"All right, the $64,000 question," she said. "Which map has original color?"

I looked from one example to the other. The map on the left was painted with muted greens, browns, and blues that appeared to have aged over a long period. I rubbed the edge of the heavy rag paper and tipped it up to look at its underside—here were the deep greenish-brown stains of oxidized pigment I'd read about in Nelson's catalogs. These stains were shaped in mirror image to the land masses on the front and showed none of the thick blotting that gave away the existence of new watercolor daubed over old paper. The map on the right had a different palette altogether: turquoise, pink, green, bluish green, and orange, with the fanciful American natives who lounged in decorative niches at the borders highlighted in gold leaf. I didn't bother to flip it over.

"The one on the left has original color."

Whitney looked at me doubtfully. "I'm afraid not."

"Damn!" I slapped my forehead. "Now I remember: the one on the right has gold leaf, so it's a deluxe copy. They were colored for the special subscribers when the atlases were printed, right? It's just been better preserved."

"Fred, Fred," Whitney soothed. "Don't work so hard. You haven't looked at the most obvious point."

I stared down at the cartouches, the vignettes, the wonderfully inaccurate land forms. "I give up."

"Price, for heaven's sake, price!" She directed me past each map to Nelson's angry pencil scrawl in the lower right-hand corner of the mats. "This one's $3,800, the one on the right is $7,500. Obviously, the one on the right has the original color."

"Oh, right," I said. The point of the whole lesson seemed to drop a notch. "I should have guessed."

"Fred, line 65 for you," Marty called over the intercom.

"I guess the rest will have to wait," Whitney said. "Or you can ask Marty if he has a minute."

"Why risk my life?" I punched into the blinking line. "This is Fred Layton."

"Fred, this is Marjorie Warren in New York. Have you all seen the Fay views?"

"You don't mean that old portfolio I just gave to the recycling guy?"

"Fred, please," Marjorie said quietly. "It's too early in the morning."

## 16. Mild Foxing with Eight-Ply Radial Tread

ow obnoxious," I said. "Would you look at this thing?" Ruth completed an inventive lane change into a small space between two eighteen-wheelers on the treacherous, rain-flooded surface of I-95, glanced over at Whitney's list of off-limits clients, and frowned crossly. This was one of the first acknowledgments of my existence she had offered since pulling away from Newbury Street over seven hours before.

"Fred," she began, "if you drag that list out in the booth I swear I'm leaving."

"I don't know that I have much choice," I said calmly.

"You certainly didn't choose to pack any stock all day yesterday."

"I'm afraid you'll have to see Whitney Buck on that point."

"Sure, and because she's a prima donna we lose a whole day to set up!" Ruth stared ahead and chewed her lower lip. She wasn't blaming me, I suspected, just the way things ran in the Albright organization. After a spine-shattering packing session at the gallery the night before—packing I was supposed to have completed by the time Ruth arrived with the van, and instead spent looking for the Fay views, which Nelson eventually found in the back of Kak's Range Rover under a pile of Bergdorf Goodman bags—we'd put off our departure until early the next morning. As a result, we were now tempting the antiques show Fates: the Baltimore preview began in less than five hours and we were still in Delaware. An ever present, Nelson-shaped cloud of tension seemed to hover above us. "What's going on?" the cloud rumbled. "I expect total results!"

We drove on for a moment and Ruth sighed, quietly resigning herself to the situation. I was actually feeling charged up at the idea of selling without Whitney and Marty monitoring me, but I didn't dare share the feeling until I knew I wouldn't ignite one of Ruth's semi-legendary tantrums. I watched a sign pass and checked my watch.

"Can I ask you something? How can we still be eighty-six miles from Baltimore if it's only an hour and a half from Philadelphia?"

"They keep moving it." Ruth punched the horn and frightened one of the eighteen-wheelers out of our path. We drove over what looked like a roll of toilet paper but apparently was cast in concrete. The Federal lift-top desk in the back of the van groaned miserably.

"We've also got to repack a little," Ruth said through gritted teeth. "Everything's a mess."

I looked over my shoulder at the thicket of mahogany legs, bubble-wrapped frames, print drawers, and tools. The load was stuffed as high as the ceiling all the way back to the double doors. In fact, we were so full up that I was leaning forward slightly as I sat. I noted that we were also gliding to the right and clutched the door handle. "Sweetie, aren't we sort of hydroplaning?"

"Fred," she cried, "what do you expect me to do?"

"Let me drive for a while. You can sit over here and take a nap."

"A nap," Ruth said derisively. "I dreamt of Nelson screaming at me last night, what good is sleep going to do?"

"We'll get set up in time. Come on, let me pitch in."

"All *right.*" She pulled over to the breakdown lane and decelerated. Somewhere between fifteen and five miles per hour, several ragboard-backed, Mylar-wrapped double-elephant-folio Audubons shot free of the crazy pile behind us and slammed into the back of my neck. Had my hand not been there already, soothing some knotted muscles, my head might have landed in the ashtray.

"Fred!" Ruth shouted. "Are you okay?"

I pushed the flood of natural history out of the cab area and applied direct pressure to my bleeding knuckles. "You're right," I said, "we do need to repack."


Some kind soul had actually left a first-aid kit in the Albright toolbox, so I dressed my surface wounds in the driver's seat while Ruth pulled out several piles of matted prints and a set of chairs and replaced them in safer positions in the van. After a few minutes she jumped in on the passenger side, leaned over, and pecked my chin. She was soaked with cold rain even under her anorak.

"Yow! Thanks for cutting yourself, Fred—it really snapped me out of that funk."

"Any time. Are we ready?"

"You bet." Ruth sat back and started braiding her shoulder-length brown hair, a sign that her mood was improving.

I gunned the motor, checked my mirrors, and pulled away from the shoulder onto the highway. At about twenty-five miles per hour I glanced into my sideview mirror and noticed a momentary flurry of color and wet plastic at the upper edge of my sight. This spectacle was accompanied by a distant ripping sound like a parachute opening above us. Whatever Ruth saw in her sideview mirror was far more disturbing.

"Fred! Oh my God stop stop oh my God!"

In the first three seconds of deceleration I nearly sideswiped a minivan full of Navy personnel in white shirts and just missed skidding into a twisted filigree of guardrail. I managed to slow just enough so that Ruth didn't break her legs when she jumped out of her seat. By the time I got out of my own and ran back into the hiss and whip of passing highway traffic, the Audubon she'd accidentally left on the van's roof had already shed its Mylar trappings and burst into flight like a badly made paper plane. The jumbled aerodynamics of the busy highway, the wind, and the press of rain defeated this impulse, though, and it was to the sound of Ruth's horrified scream and the sight of her nearly suicidal leap that I watched the $9,500 *Louisiana Hawk* flatten out onto the asphalt, be mowed down under the tires of an eighteen-wheeler truck cab, and at last allow itself to be scooped up and brought to the side of the road. Ruth took one look at the black, webbed slash laid across the hawk's midsection and burst into terrified tears. If I hoped to snap her out of this funk, I knew I'd probably have to disembowel myself.

## 17. Fredgetable Dip

R uth's hysteria did wonders in eliminating barriers for the rest of that day. The traffic police on the McHenry Bridge who pulled us over for speeding, the surly men at the parking lot barrier outside the Baltimore Museum of Art, the guards at the museum loading dock who were unaccustomed to any action going forward without unrolling spools of institutional red tape—all ceased and desisted at the sight of Ruth wiping away tears.

I mentally planned out a booth as we parked, unloaded, trundled into and out of a museum elevator, and pushed our first handcart of stock past the Cohn Matisses and a pickup Motherwell show from the permanent collection. The museum's neoclassical spareness helped me to discover a certain mental calm on the far side of terror, even though most of the other forty-two dealers in the exhibit halls were down to putting finishing touches on their track lighting or luxuriously deciding which platinum rings to lay on the top shelves of their display cases. They surveyed us coldly as we passed. A couple of scared college kids Albright's got representing him now, their eyes seemed to say. Wonder if the big man himself will grace us with his presence?

So as not to keep my paranoid imagination in suspense, Jetty Smith, the show manager, intercepted us on the way to our booth and rolled through a long list of her fears and reservations. Jetty looked like Kate Smith in the later years and had the ultimate tough thing going. She wielded no little power in the rarefied forum of antiques show management, and inspired the proper degree of respect in Ruth and me almost immediately.

As we wedged the last few foothills of our small mountain of stock into the corner of our booth, a 13-by-20-foot space at the edge of an enclosed fountain court, it occurred to me that the show workmen hadn't put up our booth paper. All we had to work with were four bare wooden frame walls.

"I guess this is what Bish gets for being late with the rental check," Ruth said lifelessly.

"What *we* get," I said, "if you don't mind the correction."

We found and hefted up a roll of hunter-green booth paper and tilted it against one of the walls. It was over a foot too long.

"Did we bring a saw?" I said.

"I didn't see a saw," Ruth said, and giggled, and then started to cry again, clutching her stomach as if she hadn't eaten in several days. "Ninety-five hundred dollars . . . I don't even like hawks."

I hugged her big, surprisingly hard body close to mine. "Sweetie, there are such things as restorers. While you're crying you might want to ask around for a saw. Some of these bastards might take pity on us, seeing that the preview starts in five seconds."

Ruth dried her eyes and surveyed our closest neighbors. Most had strung velvet rope across the entrances to their completed booths to keep them virgin until the opening gala that evening. I crossed the thin carpeted walkway and took some comfort in the fact that the exhibitor directly across the corridor looked in as bad a state as we did. All she had accomplished was stapling up her sign—OKSANA OUTKA INTERIORS—and displaying a few cut-rate English sporting oils and *objets de secondhand virtu*. In the center of this booth, three pine packing crates with reinforced metal edges sprouted Corinthian column capitals, anatomical drawings, truncated marble feet, and handfuls of yellow packing filler like the plastic ersatz straw from Easter baskets. Several hammers with clear, sparkle-filled handles lay around this booth, but no saw.

"I'll start on the other side of this hall," Ruth said behind me. I nodded. "Good idea."

I had just knelt down to peel a packing blanket off our stock when I heard an efficient swish of hose and heels. I looked up to see a black-haired woman in a cream Chanel power suit. She was about forty and, as they say, very well put together.

"At last!" She extended a long, beautiful hand to me. "Perdita Bowles, nice to see you."

"Fred Layton, nice to see you."

She seemed to understand my lack of further response and pointed to her badge. "Mrs. Perdita Bowles. Show chairman."

"Oh." I stood up. Whitney had warned me to be wildly delighted by any and all chairpersons. "*Very* nice to see you," I said.

"I'm also assistant director of this museum," Perdita added, "though I really spend most of my time fundraising."

"It shows. I mean, how great."

"You're cutting it close, but I'm sure you've brought some fabulous things." She handed me a white envelope and looked for a long moment at our mountain of stock. "I hope to see you at the dealers' party after the preview tonight."

"Thank you, Mrs. Bowles, you probably will."

"Perdita. And thank you for coming. We've had a wonderful response. Have you got a theme for your booth?"

I looked searchingly at our mountain, then at our lights, which reminded me of a pile of Christmas tree bulbs before they were untangled from their cords.

"We're leaning toward 'Prints and Maps for Your Home' this year," I said.

"What about the corridors?"

I followed the sweep of Perdita's exquisite arm across four

fifteen-foot lengths of hallway that bracketed the courtyard entrance and defined the limits of our neighbor, Oksana Outka. Now
I understood why these walls had no border paper—we hadn't put
any up yet. At that instant I entered an entirely new zone: the
terror on the far side of the mental calm on the far side of terror.

"For those walls, lots of Redouté," I said brightly. "He's the
Raphael of flower painters, you know."

"I get the picture," Perdita said, "you need to set up. You've
certainly got some stiff competition across the way to motivate
you."

I stared at the jumbled pile of packing crates and unmatted
sketches again. "Wait—is that a theme?"

Perdita gazed admiringly at our neighbor's patrician squalor.
" 'Unpacking the Past.' It's the most inventive booth I've seen in
years. Oksana is always two or three seasons ahead of the rest of us,
I'm afraid. It took her two days to get that look. Just give me a
scream if anything comes up, all right, Fred? I've got some signage
to finish."

"We'll talk to you later." When Perdita had gone, I opened
the white envelope she'd handed me. It contained several pages of
fifth-generation Xeroxes on Baltimore nightlife as well as our
badges, beautifully calligraphed and imaginatively misspelled. As I
laid the envelope aside I was interrupted again.

"Did you bring any Baltimore prints?" a white-haired man
asked. He had a haggard, dour face and that inverted elderly gentleman shape—belly convex, crotch concave. He handed me a card
with his name on it. "You've got your work cut out for you, son."

"Yes." I smelled strong alcohol on his breath. "Are you a
dealer?"

"No. My wife, Martha, is on the committee. But she won't

come in until the preview. Some of the up-fronts in this show have been forcing her out, know what I mean?" He jabbed me quite painfully in the ribcage. "A few women, like my Martha, work hard all their lives and get no appreciation. Then some nigger in South Baltimore can have seven kids and live her whole life on welfare."

"Well," I said, suddenly thankful that Ruth hadn't yet returned with a saw, "I guess everyone wants to be in their own driver's seat."

"You're *goddamned* right," he said. "What's your name, son?"

"Fred Layton."

"Harold Pillsbury. You keep any Baltimore prints aside for me, Fred Layton. I'll go as high as $750. You get me?"

"Yes, sir." I seemed to remember packing a small Baltimore plan that Nelson had priced at $7,500—could we possibly meet in the middle?

"I've got a saw!" Ruth said, and ran into the booth. Her eyes were quite dry now. "We have it for the next hour."

"Where'd you get it?"

"A very cute porcelain dealer." She was grinning. "He said three words and I knew he was from West Hartford. I could only call him 'Uh.' I'd scoop him if I wasn't so upset."

Harold Pillsbury stepped back. "Mr. Layton, I'll leave you to your lady friend." He took three more steps down the corridor and watched us for a moment.

"Keep the far end straight," Ruth said, pointing to the roll of booth paper. "Who's he?"

I smiled at Mr. Pillsbury as he moved away and walked over a velvet rope into one of the neighboring booths. "I have a strange feeling he's indicative of something."

———

The next five hours blur in my memory. Among other tasks, Ruth and I learned how to staple up booth paper; how to attach Scalamandré border paper along the top fringe of booth walls; how to hang track lights; how to hang prints on curtain hooks and arrange furniture beneath them; and how to stuff packing materials and tire-tracked Audubons under tight museum stairwells, in direct violation of fire codes. With less than an hour remaining before show time, Ruth raced out to the van to find some framed stock for our last wall, which ran along the left side of the corridor next to Oksana Outka's booth. I sat cross-legged with a print rack to prop me up and looked wearily about. I was by this point so wrapped up in my thoughts that when a compact, handsome man with chestnut hair and very, very blue eyes passed by and offered a word of encouragement, I didn't bother to hold my tongue.

"Smile," he said, with an engaging grin and a Texan accent, as he hurried past.

"Make love to me," I answered back.

At the time it had seemed straightforward enough—someone proposes a condition, you state the action required to produce it.

Before I even had time to blush, though, the man was gone around the next corner. As I decided whether to follow him Ruth reemerged, triumphant and dripping with rain.

"I found a Furber!" she cried. "Let's blow this clambake."

So it was that our last wall for the show had but one print on it, a Robert Furber engraving called *October* with a bouquet of flowers at its center. Short of stapling up the Audubon *Hawk,* this was the only item we had left.

"It's a great touch," I said to Ruth in the van. "Very postmodern. Behold the single object."

"You've obviously never been to an antiques show," Ruth said, suddenly glum. "These people are still fighting modernism."

"I'm fighting collapse," I said, and screeched our tires on an illegal left. "I can't even make a fist. I am a Fredgetable, suitable for dipping."

"Oh, look at that skinhead about to cross!" Ruth exclaimed. "Aim for the puddle."

With my liberal soaking of the skinhead, Ruth's mood bounced back. I only hoped the skinhead wasn't planning on attending the preview.

## 18. George Washington from Sloane Square

Back at the museum, the custodians had cleared away the last five percent of clutter and set out bowls of roses on tables along the walkways. Here and there a caterer bustled past, looking for a committee member to be flustered to. Ruth and I strolled up the stairs and into the show on the strength of our misspelled badges. In the previous forty minutes Ruth had rinsed the red from her eyes at our hotel and put on a smart black dress. Black made her rugged hiker's calves look nearly svelte. The carafe of wine at the hotel bar had done wonders for both of us.

As we walked past the completed displays, I noted that our

booth was situated at the very end of the show's garden paths rather than at the beginning. This fact offered a few extra moments to surround the lone Furber bouquet with a trio of framed Audubon octavo birds we'd found wedged in the very back of the van. I was hammering in my first nail to do this when a woman who was at least six foot two emerged from behind one of the Oksana Outka crates. She appeared to be approaching fifty, though as Groucho Marx once noted, it was hard to say from which direction. She had a large smudge of badly dyed red hair like a peaked dollop of meringue, a high forehead, two enormous watery blue eyes, a tremendous hook of a nose, a smudge of lipstick, and a wandering smudge of a voice whose origin I couldn't pin down. She was all legs in her green knit suit, nearly lopsidedly so, and gave you the impression of a second-string London society matron looming up in a television camera's lens, denying a bit of her husband's parliamentary wrongdoing with rehearsed absent-mindedness. *"Right,"* she would begin, and then lose her place.

"Can't they get this done . . ." was all I heard, a rhetorical question directed at my hammering. Before my blood had a chance to congeal, however, she receded behind the crates again.

When I turned around, Nelson was rushing into the booth like a tanked alumnus after a college football game. Kak and Whitney were close behind. This sight congealed my blood quite effectively. Ruth froze with her hands folded below her waist as Kak threw down a small red Pakistani carpet and kicked at it until it had unrolled in the center of the booth.

"That's much better," she said to herself.

"Hey, honey," Nelson said, "did you see that boo-boo Herring in Michelson's booth? It's been stretched within an inch of its life." He paused. "Didn't we own that at one time?"

"It was awful," Kak agreed.

"Yo, Ruth," Nelson called, "how do you think you're going to sell anything with your hands over your cunt?"

"*Nel*son," Whitney scolded. Ruth's mouth opened slightly but no sound came out. She balled her hands into fists and placed them at her side, looking straight ahead.

Kak laughed and surveyed the booth. "Fred, y'all have done a nice job."

"Very nice," Nelson announced, as he threw his trench coat over the back of a print rack for some underling to deal with. "*Very* nice."

"I like the way you mixed in the hummingbirds with the Thornton passion flowers," Kak continued. "That's really cool."

"I keep telling you," Nelson said, as he flipped through a handful of prints he'd brought with him, "Fred has a lot of talent."

Whitney saw my face and spoke up. "We just flew down for the preview, Fred, then we'll get out of your way."

"Fred," Kak said from the back of the booth, "now why did you put this Redouté here, next to this big old Audubon? It's just choked to death."

"He'll learn," Nelson said. "Whitney can only teach him so much. You have to let him step on his dick a few times."

Whitney's pale face reddened. "*Nelson,*" she hissed. "For the last time: this is a family show."

"*Nel*son Albright," a voice chirped. We turned. It was the British smudge. She looked at my boss in a way that suggested she'd just put in contact lenses for the first time. She wobbled over the walkway and took Nelson's hands. Nelson perused her and her booth with some amusement.

"Ok*san*a, you look incredible."

"Ok*san*a," Kak inhaled, "how arrr YEW! What a fabulous booth you've got!"

Nelson's hands shot into our front print rack and pulled out a large Pompeiian wall design. "Oksana, you could definitely use a few of these for your shop."

"Oh yes?" Oksana said, instantly disinterested.

"My Boston director, Whitney Buck, can show them to you any time. Or our new star, Fred Layton. Fred just completed the Courtauld program and worked at Christie's in Philadelphia for three years. Fred, meet Oksana Outka. We used to run around in London together."

I extended my hand and received two tenths of a second of eye contact from the smudge. I pulled back the unshaken hand and showed it to Ruth as a charred, arthritic stump. She smiled and looked away.

"Now see, this image is only $2,950." Nelson flipped the Pompeiian wall design on its back. "I'm sorry, $3,200."

"Inflation in action," Oksana said, "rather like shopping in Argentina. I saw $2,650 on the other . . ."

Nelson lifted the top mat and frowned. "Fred," he said, without looking at me, "can we please be a little more accurate here?"

"Great idea," Whitney mumbled to me. "According to my calculations, he's got you entering college at the age of twelve."

"It looks like he hasn't seen Oksana in ages," I answered back.

"Are you kidding?" Whitney said. "They see each other fifteen times a year at shows. They get all excited like that because they can't stand each other. Nelson christened her George Washington one time and the name stuck. Everyone in the trade calls her that now, and Oksana's never forgiven him. Look at her in profile sometime."

"Washington," I said, now seeing the bizarre resemblance, "yes, that's dead on!" But this response was drowned out by a cry from the rafters, or the fountain court, as two white-haired, tanned men in identical blue chalk-stripe English suits and rep ties, one of them carrying a white net purse thinly disguised as a "bag," rushed up the walkway.

"Oksana!"

All at once, Oksana transformed herself from smudge to diamond. "Reuben! And Danny! Hallo!"

Reuben grinned and kissed her cheeks. "What have you got for us this year, Oksana?"

"That *booth*," Danny said, and rocketed toward a framed charcoal sketch of male buttocks, "is *just* . . ."

"Joe Mead!" Nelson called, not to be outdone. He walked into a booth catty-cornered from us and proceeded to drag out a bank president type with a steam-iron part in his hair. The man's wife meekly followed. "Have I got some terrific stuff to show you two!"

"Hey, *Peggy*," Kak drawled.

Joe and Peggy Mead were conveyed into our booth, whereupon Whitney observed that things had become a bit crowded, and we migrated toward the edge of the walkway. Ruth was still trying to find a suitable place to put her hands.

Peggy Mead now indicated a framed map. "What's this one, Nelson?"

"Peggy, what an eye you've got!" Nelson roared. "That's the best Dutch map of the Chesapeake ever made!"

I smiled and strolled up the walkway on my freshly polished

shoes. Actually, the map was an English plagiarism of a French edition of a Dutch nautical chart, and about seventy-five years out of date, though I supposed in 1725 one didn't worry as much about such inconsistencies. As I approached the arches that led to the reception hall I heard a swell of excited voices. There followed the fat pop of a champagne cork and a patter of applause like a flock of pigeons lifting off from a distant fairway. Behind me, Nelson pulled the framed Chesapeake Bay map off the wall, secured it on an easel, and launched into a cartographical shaggy-dog story that made my hair fairly stand on end. Peggy and Joe Mead stood a little closer to each other for protection. I tried my "Good evening" on a passing dealer and received a smile that remained a smile until the dealer saw Nelson's logo on my badge. When the dealer turned the corner I saw the man called Danny approaching from Oksana's booth with another charcoal sketch in his hands.

"Is that Nelson Albright over there?" he asked me.

"Yes, it is," I said grandly, "would you like me to introduce you?"

"Nelson Albright," Danny said, with raised eyebrows, "is a terrible man. Terrible." A wad of ersatz straw from one of Oksana's crates that had caught on his shoe followed him back across the walkway.

"What did that guy say?" Nelson said, suddenly behind me.

"He said we have a fabulous booth," I said. "I gave him a card and some catalogs."

"Good job," Nelson said. "Separate these people from their money. That's what you're here for."

# 19. Perfectly Good Wives

We were presently surrounded on all sides. Here were the Baltimoreans untouched by the vicissitudes of the general economy, chartered members of that five percent of America that finances and constructs and controls what the other ninety-five percent of us hazily know as reality. I grinned at my first customer, a very tall woman all in black.

"And how are you?"

"Indeed," she said. A few steps out of our booth and she was in Oksana's clutches.

"Hallo," Oksana began. "Lovely evening."

The woman started. "Quite!" Off she went.

"George!" a man shouted, as a passel of lawyers rounded the corner. "How's your horse?"

One woman gasped at a passing friend, as if she'd come naked: "That brooch!"

"Oh, Bea!" the friend shrieked. "It *is* you; how *are* you; good to *see* you!" She and Bea moved into gracious, air-kissing proximity, then whipped their heads away like strangers. A white-haired man caught up with the Bea woman and steered her toward the Albright booth.

"Thought I lost a perfectly good wife there," he said.

I smiled. "Yes, sir."

"How much are these Thornton passion flowers?" a wrinkled woman in a blue gown asked. A poodle popped its head out of her bag.

"Fifty-eight hundred," I said.

Her face dropped. "Oh, crumbs."

"Well, I'd like to purchase this," a portly, mustached man said as he walked up to me. "Seven hundred fifty is your price?"

I was handed a tinted lithograph of Jarvis Medical Hospital, Baltimore, 1865, and took a peek under its top mat. Seven fifty for this thing? "Yes, sir! Let me get you an invoice."

"Fine." The man held the print at his side as Perdita Bowles, show chairman, strolled up behind him. She had changed into a tulip-shaped crushed velvet dress with sheer arms that ended in a foot-long bow tie over her cleavage. I couldn't tell if it was a real bow tie or a pretied one.

"Hi, Fred," she said in her FM disk jockey voice. She curled her hand over the man's shoulder. "Are you thinking of doing that, honey? Remember Timmy's going to Vail for Halloween."

Mr. Bowles nodded sagely. I dug into our toolbox for an invoice and felt a vigorous tapping at my elbow. A ghoulish figure leaned close, a woman of about seventy with skin like deer hide stretched over an Inuit tanning rack.

"My husband would like a word, Mr. Layton."

"Wonderful. I'll be right with you," I said. I looked into the aisle and saw Mr. Pillsbury fuming beside Mr. Bowles.

"Hey, you!" Pillsbury said. "I thought I told you to save Baltimore prints for me."

I opened my mouth in surprise. "I beg your pardon? Didn't you say not to put anything on hold?"

"How could you hold or not hold something when I haven't even looked at it? That's dirty poker, Mr. Layton."

"Don't pay any attention to Harold Pillsbury," Perdita Bowles said discreetly, as she looked up at a wall of our botanicals. "He's out hunting for controversy, as usual."

"Cool down, Harold," Mr. Bowles was saying to him. "You've already got one of these. I saw it up at your house."

"The condition's not half as good as this copy," Mr. Pillsbury shot back. "Dirty poker, Mr. Layton. Dirty poker."

I paused with the invoice and looked at the satisfaction on Mr. Bowles's face. Obviously I had entered into some long-standing rivalry between the two.

"Are you going to sell me this print or not?" Mr. Bowles said at last. "If it was on hold, why was it in this rack?"

I felt Nelson's hand on my shoulder. "Do it, Fred, but see if you can get him up to a thousand with the framing. And don't sell to Pillsbury. He'd haggle over the price of a blow job with a five-dollar whore."

"Okay," I said.

"But don't get him angry, either."

"Maybe you should finesse this one."

"This is good training." Nelson reached out to receive a hug from Mrs. Bowles. "Hello, Perdita."

"Nelson," she purred, "I was hoping to see your pretty face."

"I haven't got a pretty face. Christ, though, you look a*maz*ing."

I wedged my way behind the two and handed over the invoice to Mr. Bowles.

The sight of someone writing a check drew a dozen more people into our booth, so I had to step out into the aisle to bag the print. Here I was nearly run down by a svelte octogenarian with a black patent leather bag hanging several inches up her forearm. She stopped in front of my face, and the two women following at her heels nearly collided.

"And look at who *that* is!" she exclaimed, her hyperthyroid eyes bulging. "Look at who *that* is!"

One of her friends pointed at a Redouté watercolor. "Now this lovely little thing," she said, "what's it painted on?"

"That's on vellum," Ruth said dramatically. "It's almost two hundred years old."

The woman turned to her friend and touched her cheek. "Vida, that's what we gotta get us, some of that vellum."

"*Mmm*-hmm," Vida said. "Trade this stuff in."

"This is a lovely rug," the octogenarian said.

"I thank you," I said.

"When I was in Istanbul," she continued, "they sat me down in one of those rug shops, gave me a cup of the best tea I ever put in my mouth."

"I must get over there someday," I said.

"You have an armed guard with you, you can go," the woman said fiercely.

I smiled. "I'll keep that in mind."

Now an exhausted man in a kelly gabardine jacket limped up to the ancient woman. "You have to stay with me," he complained. "All these people are comin' up and sayin' hello, and I can't remember who they are."

## 20. Leg of Columbus, Excellent Condition

With twenty minutes to go in the preview, the local television people arrived. This was fitting, as the last few hours had begun to feel like a series of meaningless quickie visuals—one overdone, searching face after another. A not unattractive reporter with a clipboard and a great deal of blond hair rushed over to Nelson as he was holding forth on maps. She waved for her minicam crew to follow. Nelson had been pitching like a man possessed for over two hours, but he hadn't sold anything.

"Mr. Albright," the reporter said, "any comments for us on the first night of this exciting new show?"

Nelson's face hardened into a dissatisfied pout. "The art market is about to implode," he said. "The economy can't bear these outrageous prices anymore, it's as simple as that. Has anyone sold a big-ticket item here tonight? I haven't heard."

The reporter showed her teeth unsurely and waved her crew into Oksana Outka's booth, where half of the merchandise had already disappeared. If Oksana had priced her packing straw that evening, I think she probably could have sold it. When the reporter and her crew were out of sight, Nelson pulled Kak close. "I've had enough of watching that British bag of shit snow me under," he said. "Let's go."

"Hon-ey," Kak said, "what?"

"And I hate pitching to these cave dweller society people," he added. "They're like the living dead."

Kak frowned. "Don't you want to stay around for the party?"

"With these junk dealers?"

"We'll do our best in your absence," I said.

"It's tough, Fred, it's *tough*." Nelson shuddered. "If you do ten thousand on this show you can stretch me out and drive a stake through my heart."

"In that case I'll shoot for twenty."

"Fly safely," Ruth said. Her hands were now hovering at chest level. She smiled as Nelson, Kak, and Whitney Buck—whose whole face had become an "I told you so" smirk directed at Nelson—made their exit. Then she cracked her knuckles and stuck out her tongue.

"Ruth," I said, "how could you let him insult you like that?"

She shrugged. "He doesn't mean it personally: that's one of the things you don't see in the Boston gallery. You wouldn't believe what comes out of his mouth in Weston."

"Still."

"I don't expect to be treated like I'm made of crystal. Besides, he pays me more than you. He should expect more." She took a few steps toward the walkway and left the topic behind her. "Looks like you made the only sale."

"And the Pillsburys are out in the parking lot filing down our brake shoes." I rubbed my face in my hands. "This Fred need a head."

Ruth pressed two drink tickets into my hand. "Here. Compliments of Perdita Bowles. I'll have a vodka tonic. This is probably the only break we'll have before the party."

"Just point me toward the bar and shove," I said. Ruth did so.

Ruth didn't shove me in the right direction, but that was all right, since I got to see the other dealers in action on the brilliantly lit main walkway of the show. There were notes of both gentility and hucksterism, dealers who did not deign to notice browsers and browsers who did not deign to notice dealers. Not a one measured up to Nelson. Back in our corner, my boss made pitches like some kind of checkbook-seeking missile; here the commercial air was so conservative you could cut it with a John and Peter Targee knife (New York, circa 1810, $2,500 subject to prior sale). Glancing from left to right down the crowded walkway and into its culs-de-sac, I saw life-size porcelain borzois, Massachusetts Federal high-post beds, comb-back continuous-arm Windsor chairs, paintings of colonial boys in green satin walking clothes discovered on drawer bottoms, and other bits of the elite American past I'd never imagined sitting in my room at Princeton writing frothy papers on neo-expressionist canvases with hay and deer antlers stuck to them.

Near the end of the main walkway, I spied a large, raised Plexiglas box that looked entirely out of context. Even so, a small crowd was buzzing around it. Most took one look at the crude gold cross mounted inside, smiled, and moved on. Others lingered over its unpolished blue and red stones in the way skeptics do when snake oil is being sold by the quart. As I approached the cross I noted that it had depth as well as height. It was about the size of a playing-card box and held a glass vial in its center. I wondered at the whitish-gray powder inside. World's first cocaine accessory?

"Within this pendant," I read, halfway down a smudged description card, "are preserved one and one half ounces of the ground femur of Christopho Colombo, the discoverer of the United States of America. THIS SAMPLE CONSTITUTES THE LARGEST EXAMPLE OF COLOMBO'S REMAINS STILL IN PRIVATE HANDS AND THE LARGEST AND MOST IMPORTANT EXAMPLE OF HIS BODY ON THE AMERICAN CONTINENT." I checked my frown under the disapproving eye of the nearby dealer. The price, at the end of the description, was on request.

"May I?" I asked the dealer. "The Columbus?"

He smiled at my badge through full braces. "Certainly. $975,000. The perfect item for a cannibal like Nelson."

I smiled back. "As a rule he just sucks out the marrow."

"*Won*derful," a woman on my right said in a South Carolinian drawl. She was short, with bright white hair though only in her mid-fifties, and had kind, inquisitive blue eyes behind updated English-teacher glasses with red Cadillac fins. I imagined her as an enlightened society matron who marched for civil rights and had a winter apartment in Rome. I instantly liked her pluck. She noticed my attention and smiled.

"This is a very special item, don't you think?"

"Absolutely," I said. "What an entrance you could make at the symphony."

"Yes, oh yes. Much better than a Dali watch or something." The woman raised her eyeglasses slightly. "Is this your display, Mr. . . . Layton?"

"Unfortunately not."

I was edging away to give her more room when she asked, "Would you replace the glass in the outer pendant there?"

"The glass? I certainly wouldn't," I said. "An object like that, you'd want to keep it . . . secure in its original idea, I suppose. That's probably sixteenth-century Venetian glass."

"Yes, I imagine you're right," the woman said. The animated, sophisticated way she spoke sent a pleasurable tingle over my scalp. "Thank you so much."

"Not at all," I said. If she was a professional shoplifter, she had me fooled.


When I wove back through the show with the drinks a few minutes later, the woman, the dealer, and the Columbus cross were gone. Dozens of grandfather clocks around the exhibition hall were just striking nine.

# 21. What We Do to Our World

red, where were you?" Ruth grabbed my arm as I reentered the booth. "Harry, the guy who loaned me the saw, wants us to go over to the preview party with him. He said he knows an amazing restorer who can clean up the Audubon!"

"Ruth," I said, "what I saw back there you would not believe. Nine hundred—"

"Just bring the hawk down to the van and we'll stash it in the hotel until Harry can see it," she cut in. "Have you got the keys?"

"What about your drink?"

She took her V&T and threw it back in four gulps, then handed me the plastic glass and punched my chest. "Wooh! Maybe I still have a job after all."

The bustle of the preview had fallen back, by degrees, to the scattered voices and near hush that preceded it. I took off my blazer and hung it on one of the print racks. Then I slipped behind the walls of our booth, stepping over octopodes of extension cords, and felt my way around in the dimness for the *Louisiana Hawk*. I reemerged with the image side facing into the booth and leaned it against our longest wall so I could fetch a couple of print bags. It was then I noticed a damp envelope taped to the print's ragboard backing. I sat on my haunches in a patch of overhead light and read the enclosed note:

*One-half of the proceeds from the sale of this* Louisiana Hawk *will go to the John James Audubon House Project of New York, as per agreement with the consignee, Mr. Nelson Albright of 25 East 75th Street, New York.*

It was dated in mid-1985 and signed by Nelson, the head of the Audubon House, and Mayor Edward Koch.

"Great," I said under my breath. "We don't even own the thing."

"Hello there, Mr. Layton," a woman said. I stood up so quickly that I startled her. It was the short society matron with the Cadillac-fin glasses.

"Nice to see you again," I said. "*Now* you're at my booth."

"I didn't even know you all were here down in this little corner," the woman said genially. She put her hands on her slim hips and gazed around. "And look at that, there's my friend Oksana right across the way. She sold me my very first print. But my goodness, you have some *love*ly things as well."

"Thanks," I said proudly. I smiled at the sly charm in her voice.

"I hope I'm not keeping you," she said. "I'm having something wrapped up and thought I'd look around. I never get halfway through one of these events on the first go."

"You're not keeping me at all," I said. "I hope you decided to stay with the original glass."

The woman paused for a moment, then seemed to remember the specifics of our encounter.

"Yes, I think I will. I'll have to let my curator look at it."

I concealed the Koch letter in my pocket and folded my arms.

"It would be wonderful, wouldn't it, if you could pour out that bit of bone and add water and get instant Columbus? I'd have so many questions to ask him."

"I would as well," the woman said, and dipped into a deeper drawl. "That *would* be an interesting afternoon."

"And if the old tale is true about the water he poured over the side of the *Santa Maria,* that every glass of water you pour today could contain two molecules from it . . ."

"Exactly," the woman said. "Magic's already built in, wouldn't you say?" She slipped off her eyeglasses and offered a brisk hand-shake.

"I'm Helen Wheeler."

"Mrs. Wheeler, it's a pleasure."

"Please call me Helen, Mr. Layton."

"Only if you call me Fred."

"I will, thank you." She took two more steps into the booth and squinted. "Now how much is that big old Audubon *Swan* on the wall? He is homely, isn't he?"

"I believe he's in first-year plumage in that print," I said. At the same moment I felt a light static tingle against one of my trouser legs and stepped back. The *Louisiana Hawk* had taken that opportunity to fall face up at our feet. The oily tire tread on it had only deepened in color now that some of the water had evaporated.

"Oh dear," I said mildly, as my heart began to hammer out in panic, "this one keeps asserting its independence."

"*What* . . ." Mrs. Wheeler inhaled and circled the canceled bird, shaking her head silently. "What in the world's happened to it?"

"It's . . . from an ornithological artist," I said, and felt something like a caffeine rush kick in, "a friend of the gallery who gives us her work on consignment."

Her wide blue eyes stared into mine. "How in the world does she expect you to sell it?"

"She actually made it look that way," I said.

"Is it some sort of statement?"

"Oh, yes," I said, my eyes averted from her. At that point, my only intention was to slip the print out of public view, then get her interested in something else. "It was environmentally intentional," I went on. "We have a couple of clients who buy these Audubons. Feinberg, the artist, used to live near a huge tract of marshland, but she's been evicted by a real estate interest."

"That's scandalous," Helen said, her face flushed with anger. "We had a conservancy problem once down in Sanibel, and I had to fight it tooth and nail against those developers. I've got my fingers crossed the next recession will cool their ardor."

"Let's hope."

She looked down at the hawk. "What we do to our world. . . . It's being canceled out, that's what she's saying. We build six-lane highways over our beautiful country."

"The metaphor is pretty clear," I said, and then, stupidly, went on. "Audubons are obvious art, like most of what we sell, but Feinberg likes their unambiguous qualities. They provide her with a perfect point of departure for her statements. They're simple but quite forceful."

"Brilliant," Helen declared. "How much is it?"

"It's . . ." I turned the print over as if I didn't know. "It's ninety-five hundred. And it comes with this letter of authenticity signed by Mayor Koch. Have a look."

She laughed and unfolded the note. "Mayor Koch from New York? Well, that does make it a conversation piece."

"And half the proceeds go to the Audubon House project in Manhattan. The family had a huge farm there in the 1850s, in present-day Harlem."

"Mmm, right in the heart of the wilderness." Helen scanned the letter and handed it back. "Fred, I'd like you to hold this piece for me until Young Collectors Night tomorrow. Could you do that?"

"Hold it for you?" I said slowly.

"I had only the one check with me, you see, and that's gone. I'm just in town for the weekend. But I promise to come back. I must try to say hello to Oksana in any case."

"There you are!" The Columbus bone dealer with the braces appeared at the end of the main aisle with a petite boutique shopping bag of the type aging suburban queens hang on bedroom doorknobs to impress their guests. If she had ordered him to run his tongue along the walkway carpeting to close the sale I probably could have captured it on film.

"I must get along, Fred, and I'm so sorry for keeping you," she said. She took one of my hands in both of hers and my blood jumped—at the energy of her grip or perhaps the agreement I saw in her eyes, that we were kindred spirits. How could I have just set myself up to screw her?

"I'll see you tomorrow, Helen," I said, and felt the other dealer react. "And I'll keep the piece for you."

"Good." She let herself be led away by the dealer, who threw a more appreciative glance back at me. One of the maintenance people flicked a master switch and the remaining lights in the booths went out.

Our beat-up Ford van was the last dealer vehicle in the lot. Ruth was revving the engine to the point at which engines explode.

She rolled down her window. "Damn it, Fred! Where's the Audubon?"

"Well," I said, "it's sort of on hold."

## 22. The House Praises the Hostess

The dealers' party was held at the renovated firehouse of Allegra Kunkle, one of Baltimore's major new art collectors. Kunkle was thirty and had just come into her inheritance. She'd had plans to donate art to the city, the story went, or even to buy pieces for the Baltimore Museum, but once she started renovations on the firehouse she decided to spend everything on herself. You reached the upper floors of Kunkle's house via an industrial elevator, but even inside you were still essentially outside—it was all brick and iron shell, with plate-glass floors and walls. Maids circulated with crudités on large pieces of copper like asteroid remains, while Red Bank oysters were accessed from a multi-ledged cliff of carved ice that sat in a brass tub. Downtown Baltimore glittered on the other side of the harbor. I ate several asparagus spears and drank vodka tonics while Ruth hooked up with Harry, the cute, bearded Audubon restorer, a few feet away.

The two dozen other people at the party were avoiding all

reference to their jobs, save the upcoming Young Collectors Night, and making much of the vodka, which was from the Netherlands and exceptionally rare. Behind me, Perdita Bowles was comparing notes on Bangkok with Oksana Outka's clients Reuben and Danny, who were, as it turned out, important local patrons of the arts. Our buzz-cut, emaciated hostess approached me while I was having a look at her suite of Bernd and Hilla Becher water tower photographs, which might have been titled *My Overcast Vacation in East Germany.* They were depressing to the point of exhilaration, and hung in a group over a behemoth of a Regency commode with lion's paw feet, the only object in the house more than sixty years old.

"Ms. Kunkle," I said, "I love your Bechers."

"Bless you," she said. "All these morons think I took them."

"They make a very witty reference to the house."

"I think houses should be passionate, don't you?" She placed her thin, baubled hand on my right bicep. "Buildings are repositories of energy. If you give them enough energy when you construct them, they repay you when you inhabit them. If you don't, they never let you fully dwell."

"You're quite right."

She shrugged. "Mostly I'm creative, but sometimes I get accuracy."

The black box of the elevator shuddered like a furnace firing to life and opened into the party. Ms. Kunkle moved me back slightly before going to admit the new guests. "Don't get too close to the commode or you'll tear your trousers on those drawer pieces. I only put the damn thing there to keep it out of the way."

I watched her skip to the other side of the space and get animated. As she did, a man in his mid-thirties who'd just gotten out of the elevator glanced at me, did a double take, and approached.

I froze. It was the chestnut-haired guy I'd asked to make love to me while setting up for the show. Valdemar Abbot of Dallas, according to his dealer's tag. Up close he was handsome as an astronaut, his hair cut short enough to reveal tiny red ears and a quarter-size patch of gold hair at the crown of his head. A sunburned ruddiness glowed on his large face.

"Fred," he said. "Nice to see you again." He offered a powerful hand at half normal speed. I shook it and unsuccessfully fought off a blush. He had impeccably manicured fingers to go with his manners.

"Mr. Valdemar Abbot," I said. "How are you?"

"Very well." He gave one nod and studied my tag. "Right, you work with Nelson. I hope your booth came together."

"Yes," I said, "but you should let me explain. That was sort of a slip of the tongue back there at the booth."

"I see," Valdemar said, adopting my serious tone in a way that made me sound like an idiot. "I found it pretty refreshing, to tell you the truth."

"I mean the way it came out," I stammered. "I was a little punch-drunk when you came by, so I guess 'Smile' wasn't what I wanted to hear, although—"

Valdemar raised his hand. "Let's just say you 'pushed back' a little, shall we?"

"That's right, I pushed back. That's fine." I nodded. I was a basket case. "Um, so. Are you having a good show?"

"Very good. Just sold an unfucked Lancaster table I bought out of an attic."

"I beg your pardon?"

"Unrestored," he said. "I guess you're new to the business. If a piece of wood is in original condition, you say it's unfucked."

"Ah."

"What a beautiful piece it was, too. You could see right along the top where the plane left grooves in the wood two hundred years ago."

"And you bought it out of an attic?" I said. "I didn't know you could still find great pieces that way."

"You still can, from time to time." He folded his arms. "It's just everything else that's changed in this business."

"How so?"

Valdemar searched his memory. "Well, sometimes I think back to '78 and how things were the year I got started. I remember one time in New York a bunch of dealers were pulled into the little crawl space they clear for you at the Armory show. We were unloading and a guy I know from Nashville opened the back of his truck and called us over. I think he had a New York pier table he'd bought out of an old lady's tag sale on the way up. Whatever it was, he brought it to the edge of his truck and we gathered round. He said, 'All right, anyone interested in this piece of wood before I drag it in?' We looked it over and talked about a price, and in a couple of minutes one of the dealers decided to take it off his hands. But then somebody else got interested, thought of a client who'd like it, you know, and she bought it from the first dealer for a hundred dollars more than the original price. Then somebody else stepped in and bought it for a hundred above what the second dealer paid. I think that table turned over six times before it hit the street. And six dealers made a hundred bucks, which can pay a bill or two. Today, though, forget it. A fellow buys a good Adam mirror or a Biedermeier chair and takes it straight to auction. No middleman. 'I want it all,' that's the attitude. That whole mentality has taken over."

"That's awful," I said.

Valdemar looked at me with slightly narrowed eyes. "It stinks, Fred; it stinks."

"If it stinks why do you keep on doing it?"

His expression softened. "Dealing? It's the one area of my life where I don't have to accept any compromises."

"You're a rarity," I said. "I think my boss wakes up in the morning looking for them."

"Ah, your boss," Valdemar said. "How did you do for Mr. Albright this evening?"

"Our corridor did all right," I said, "but we didn't. Oksana Outka must have done twenty or thirty grand. It made Nelson a little uncomfortable."

"Oksana, our founding father," Valdemar said knowingly. "I call her the antiques bed-hopper. Two years ago she was selling Italian plywood furniture. The year before that it was the silver she stole from her grandmother's house in England."

"I'll make a note to stay on your good side."

He smiled. "It's the mark of a faddish dealer, changing her display window all the time. But you can never tell in this business. In April down in Washington, Arader's New York people sold their entire *booth* to a woman at the preview. Two booths down I did $46,000 for the week. Oksana, sitting right between us, didn't open her book once."

"No kidding."

"Yup." His voice trailed off, then he said, "Listen, Fred, I'd be very grateful if you'd let me take you to dinner tonight. I've got a table at Gunning's Crab House in an hour."

I looked at Valdemar closely, trying to feel him out. As I did, a strange sort of pause held us, a trusting pause whose long duration we both allowed and welcomed. It was as if Valdemar saw the way I looked at him and let something unlock between us. My bones, as the Brits say, went floaty.

"Sure," I said, "that sounds wonderful."

"What sounds wonderful?" Valdemar said.

"Whatever you suggested."

He grinned. "Don't worry, you won't be disappointed." This task accomplished, he glanced around the room and signaled a waiter for a drink. I caught Ruth's eye and winked at her.

"So how does this commode look?" I said. "Fucked or un?"

Valdemar placed a hand on the Regency commode's marble top, then went down on one knee and began to examine it. "This piece is what you call prepubescent," he said. "It hasn't even been fondled. I wonder what in the world she paid." He stood up and let the blood drain from his head. "You ought to try doing this business on your own, Fred. You're unique at an event like this, that your personal ass isn't on the line."

"That doesn't mean I won't get a hernia breaking down my booth."

"This is also true. Allegra," Valdemar called, "your commode is fantastic. Is it an André Boulle?"

"Bless you, Valdemar," Allegra said as she passed, "all these morons think it's a John McLean."

# 23. Mr. President

hy are you sniffing up my neck, Valdemar?"

"It smells great."

"Ah."

"I have a friend back home, you know."

"Yes?"

"We're both safe, it's all right. It's just that he's relieving me at the booth tomorrow so I can fly to Atlanta, and he's very jealous."

"Don't worry. I learned how to be discreet in college."

"So . . . you're always safe, right?"

"Depressingly. Tell me about your friend."

"Remember all those hundred dollars the dealers make on the table before it hits the ground?"

"He spends them for you."

"When he walks into shoe stores they call him Mr. President."

"If I gave you a hundred dollars, could I have your back?"

"Fred, you have the kind of personality people go through years of therapy to get to."

"Val?"

"Hmm."

"When you're doing that to my neck?"

"Mmm?"

"Try using your tongue."

"Wow."

# 24. A Quick Look at the Dailies

I was a bit confused about why the dealers placed so much emphasis on Young Collectors Night until Ruth put a copy of the Young Collectors Survey into my hands the next morning. She got it quite late from Harry the restorer, judging by her blissfully exhausted face as she sat down at the booth with a croissant and hot chocolate. I was blissful, too, as blissful as a heartbroken man could be, having kissed Valdemar goodbye an hour before dawn so he could pack for the airport.

"Isn't it great when it's over," she said, "and you lie there and your whole body is just tingling?"

"You'd thank me for strangling you," I said. "I've never seen you look so happy. It's sure to be downhill for the rest of your life."

"Strangling would be *fab*ulous," Ruth said, leaning back in her chair. "I wouldn't have to break down the booth."

"I'd watch what you do break."

"No, it's cool. You certainly scored, though. Pretty hot guy there, Fred."

"Don't remind me. I'm head over heels for a married man. Still, he showed me some amazing uses for those crab mallets you get at Gunning's."

"Pig." She slapped my arm. "Oh, I almost forgot! Look at this." She unfolded a sheet of paper and handed it over. It was a survey of some sort, titled "L'Enfant's Lifestyles of the Rich and Anonymous." Under the title it read, "This year win up to $500!"

"You bet ten bucks on your description of the ugliest outfit you see at Young Collectors Night," Ruth said, "and the best description wins all the money."

The survey was built around eighteen "cattygories" into which a showgoer might fall:

| | |
|---|---|
| *Bangles* | *Found Objects* |
| *Beaucoup* | *Heat in the Kitchen* |
| *Cadillac Walk* | *Hem Hoist* |
| *Creative Engineering* | *Leading Horticulture* |
| *Cruel Shoes* | *Poor Things* |
| *Cycologne* | *Sparkle Plenty* |
| *Folds, Pleats, Gathers* | *Toys in the Attic* |
| *Forelock Foliage* | *Trophies* |
| *Foundation Faults* | *Value Engineering* |

"This is the sort of thing Albright people never see," Ruth added, as if I might be at fault. "We're *personae non gratae* at shows. You're not even supposed to be seen talking to us!"

"It's good to know all those sneers last night weren't meant personally. Who's 'L'Enfant'?"

"Some guy who used to work for Oksana Outka and then sued her."

"That figures."

Ruth smiled and stretched back in her seat. "Fred, if you sell that Audubon I'll carry your child."

"It may come to that."

I ducked as half of Ruth's croissant sailed past my head.

"Everyone's counting on you to sell it," she whispered.

"What!"

"Fred, these dealers have no secrets. They're like an incestuous family."

"Then tell me what happened with the restorer last night."

"Well . . ." Ruth raised a rakish eyebrow. "We certainly didn't need a crab mallet."


The late morning and afternoon that followed were far more indicative of what happens at an antiques show: the antiques age. You walk back and forth within the confines of your booth. You stare across the walkway at the other dealers, who become like wallpaper—you see them and you see them. The chairman brisks around in another stunning knit suit and you order an eleven-dollar cheese sandwich for lunch. A collector who has been pitched to you as intimidatingly brilliant drops by, and you discover that his knowledge ends abruptly at an idiot savant level of factual recall about this battle's death toll or that cabinetmaker's clientele. A noted decorator pores over your racks for an hour and concludes, just as you believe she is reaching for her checkbook, that what she needs must be half your price and in much better condition. You resist the urge to ask whether she has considered time travel, or why she didn't buy Currier & Ives prints as a young woman, when they first appeared. Your sandwich arrives. The cheese is spoiled.

Ruth spent a good part of the day with Harry, her restorer fling, leaving me to watch Oksana Outka pick at her bloodless French assistant about various booth discrepancies that were far beyond my limited powers of perception. Oksana made more than one foray into our booth to mumble and record some of our prices for future reference, but didn't say a word to me. I sat and dozed while the bread from my cheese sandwich digested, then I had a daymare about dozens of Whitney's clients coming into the booth and asking, "What is this? What is this?" about pieces I'd never seen. With the first tinkle of bar ice at four-thirty, eight dealers stampeded past me with their purses and wallets. Drinks after preview night were rarely allowed within the carpeted areas of shows, so the halls became bereft even of dealers.

At about five o'clock I shook out of my snooze completely and saw two elderly Californian carpet dealers surveying me from behind one of Oksana Outka's packing crates. They seemed to have grave news to impart.

"Mr. Layton," one of the carpet dealers said, glancing down at me through half-glasses and fingering his vest. "A friendly note of warning to you."

"Yes, sir," I said. I was expecting to hear that Valdemar Abbot's lover was gunning for my hide.

"If you do sell your Audubon *au pneu* to Mrs. Wheeler . . ."

I exhaled with relief. "Oh, you mean Helen."

" 'Helen.' Well . . ." The second dealer smiled and strolled away to look at our prints.

The vested dealer held his jaw as if retaining a mouthful of water in it. "Helen or Cressida or whatever you call her, you must identify that print as an antique on your invoice. If you sell it as a piece of modern art you'll be tossed out of the show and Nelson could permanently lose his license to deal. Not that I'd go into deep mourning, should that happen."

"I will dance at his retirement party," the second dealer mumbled.

"Yes, of course," I said. I felt sobered by the inanity of what I was about to attempt.

"In closing, have you a survey for tonight?"

"I do, yes. You're encouraging a dangerous habit here."

"They are the best kind."

Both men departed with illicit martinis in hand. I sat musing on what Oscar Wilde might do in my situation until Jetty Smith wheeled round a corner bearing a newspaper. She stopped and held it before me, looking almost happy.

"This is *USA Today*," she began.

I reached up. "That's so kind of you. I only got through the *Times* this morning."

"I want you to look at column four, paragraph *one*."

My eyes slid over to the story, BALTIMORE ANTIQUES SHOW MAY BE WAVE OF FUTURE.

"How great!" I said. "I should have congratulated you."

"Please read it all." Jetty Smith deposited the paper in my lap. "Once you have, you can pack up your booth and leave. You will vacate the premises within two hours, under my supervision."

I stared up at her and then back at the article. It began, " 'The art market is about to implode,' quipped Nelson Albright, renowned antiquarian prints dealer, at the opening of the first annual Baltimore Fall Antiques Show." I didn't read on.

"What possible effect can this have?" I said. "How is it Nelson's fault the Dow Jones dropped five hundred points in a day?"

"Two hours, kiddo," Jetty said. "And I'll only mention in passing what I heard from Oksana Outka, that you've been offering modern pieces at my show. I'm only going to mention it, because if I investigated further and discovered it was true, I could revoke your license on the spot. If it were in my power Nelson Albright would never do a show again. Anywhere."

Jetty's motor turned over and she strutted out of sight. As I watched her go, the whole concept of Heat in the Kitchen suddenly made perfect sense.

## 25. Bill of Goods

Our expulsion was greeted with quiet glee by most of the dealers, though as mere pawns of Nelson we were afforded some sympathy by a few others. Oksana Outka was granted the space we would vacate and began dragging pillars and buttocks sketches into our booth before I'd even taken down the lights. Until the last few minutes of the cleanup, Ruth was out painting the town with her friend Harry.

A booth is easier to deconstruct than construct, I discovered, but under the staring eyes of every person who passed, including a delighted Mr. Harold Pillsbury, who slithered underfoot while continuing to dress me down for selling his precious Jervis Hospital print, I had no choice but to will myself invisible. I thought out my legs, then my arms, back, chest, and head. Just as I had forgotten that I was there at all, Perdita Bowles stopped by to vent her outrage at Jetty Smith, and I got her to clear away Mr. Pillsbury before I impaled him on an easel. I could smell the rank cloud of sweat I was producing, from embarrassment and exertion and anger. At the height of this chaos, and just as I'd finished loading the first handcart with framed prints, Helen Wheeler walked into the booth, her prematurely white hair newly curled.

"Fred!" she exclaimed. "What's happened?"

"Helen," I said, "I can't explain now, but it's a matter of dignity between me and the manager of the show. We're breaking down the booth and leaving as soon as possible."

"Oh, no, you mustn't," she said. "That would be too horrible. Why don't you have Oksana Outka talk to the management? She has a lot of sway in these events."

"Oksana isn't here right now," I said, "but never mind, Helen. My boss is expecting us back."

"My goodness, aren't they making you put in the hours," she said, shaking her head. "I hope you'll still be able to sell me that Audubon."

"The Audubon," I said, so low it was nearly a whisper. "Are you sure you're still interested?" It suddenly occurred to me that if I didn't sell the print I was heading back to Philadelphia $9,250 under my sales quota. "Are you sure you're still interested?"

"I'm here to tell you my curator was excited to death by the idea. May I have another look at it?"

I wiped the sweat from my upper lip. My moral impulse staged a momentary showdown against its amoral and unethical siblings, then the unethical siblings ran over the moral impulse in an eighteen-wheeler, and the matter was decided. If she really wanted the thing, why should I stand in her way?

"Tell you what," I said. "I've got to run down in the elevator with these prints and start loading our van. I'll leave the print here with an exit pass, and if you like it well enough, you take it with you and I'll send along the invoice later."

She tapped my hand. "Why don't we do that? This is certainly the last time I'll visit this show."

"And I," I said. "Just leave your telephone number and the other relevant information, all right?" I dug out a sheet of paper from my breast pocket and handed it to her.

"Fine," she said firmly.

"Here it is." I drew out the print and unveiled it. My face winced. Her face lit up.

"Yes, there it is."

"Good luck, Helen. I'll be in touch," I said. I hurried up to the handcart and began pushing.

"Oh, Fred," Helen called. She opened one button of her splendid blue suede coat and flashed a highly polished Columbus cross at me. "What do you think?"

"Helen," I said, "if that doesn't break the ice at parties, you should get some new friends."


## 26. My Perfect One

e's on a high boil this morning," Whitney said ominously. She was dropping me out at Château Delapompe for a debriefing session on the Baltimore show. I'd been back in Boston for six hours, three of them unpacking the van and three of them trying to sleep.

"What's the problem?" I said between yawns.

"One of his prostitutes wants to work for him."

"One of his whats?"

"Tang Li is her name. Then last month's sales figures came in." Whitney sighed. "He said if our numbers don't improve he's going to apply for nonprofit status and force us to volunteer."

Whitney left me at the end of the Château Delapompe driveway and zoomed off to deliver some framing at a nearby client's house. The intense suburban quiet that followed her departure was broken by a distant crash and a child's scream as I approached the stone pile of the house. About fifteen seconds later a much perturbed Kak Albright emerged from the carport door. She wore a glossy green rain slicker and had her blond hair pulled into a tight ponytail. She gripped a can of processed cheese food in one hand as Nelson followed her out onto the walk. Nelson, looking more amused than angry, took a shortcut through a clump of boxwood to the macadam driveway.

"Kak," he pleaded, "she wants to reform her life! She's tired of servicing seven or eight men a day."

"You ought to put her in laid paper." Kak yanked the key to Nelson's Mercedes out of her slicker pocket. "Or those restrikes. She obviously can't drive to New York without training wheels."

"Honey, if I don't cut costs how am I going to keep paying your allowance every month, and the $700 for flowers, and then the payroll, if there's anything left over?"

Kak shoved the key into the Merc's door. "Aren't you forgetting your account at Korea Palace?"

Nelson smiled. "If you're going to see your father, tell him he still owes me for that restoration job."

At this, Kak's can of cheese food took to the air and caught Nelson square in the belly. He ran toward the Mercedes as his wife engaged the engine. The sedan roared to life, four windows rose in hydraulic symmetry, and Nelson sprayed about six ounces of fluorescent orange cheese over the windshield before Kak roared away, spitting gravel and—I noted as I scrambled out of her path—

laughing. Nelson began to laugh too. He waved as I approached like the owner of a country provisions store.

"Marriage is a great institution, Fred. How was the rest of the show?"

I shrugged. "Got laid."

"Good for you!" He beamed and flicked back his thick blond hair. "Come in and have a seat. I want you to wait by my fax machine until the Christie's prices on that Catlin set come in from London."

"Which Catlin is that?"

"The one that'll get a higher price than Denny D'Amico paid! Jesus, I thought Bish sent you a catalog."

"I just got back last night."

"Of course, that's right." Nelson nodded. "Don't worry about that bitch Jetty Smith. I take full responsibility. And congratulations on the Audubon sale to Helen Wheeler! She's one of those people I was telling you about, the hundred-million-dollar client who trusts your expertise."

"Oh, right," I said miserably. "My expertise."

"She's your meal, man! We are going to design a whole marketing campaign around that woman. Every time Helen Wheeler sneezes, we'll be right there beside her."

"To say, 'God bless you'?"

"No!" Nelson shouted. "To say 'Can I show you these prints?' Would you please pay attention?"


Choix Albright, Nelson and Kak's only child, led us into Nelson's private library office. At five, she was the spitting image of Kak, with silky blond hair and delicate features. According to Ruth, each morning Choix took many tranquilizers of great strength with her Flintstones chewables to prevent her from burning down the château. The phone on Nelson's desk rang and she ran ahead to answer it. Her fingers were orange with processed cheese food.

"Who is it *now?*"

"She learned that from her mother," Nelson said proudly.

"It's for you, Daddy," Choix shrieked. She dropped the receiver and backed herself up against the bay of windows. "It's for you!"

"Thank you," he crooned, "thank you, my perfect one!"

I refrained from retching and took a seat on a green-gray burnt leather couch. When she sensed that the call would be a long one, Choix skipped back to the desk in her pink taffeta dress and landed in Nelson's lap. I popped into the nearest bathroom and returned with an issue of *Maison et Jardin*. It was safe to say that the debriefing session would be a little late getting off the ground.

"They are super-primo, Joel," Nelson was saying. "Super-primo."

Choix frowned and looked up at her father. "Daddy."

"I would need fifty today and the other twenty on delivery. Right."

"Daddy! Daddy!" Choix whined.

Nelson glanced down at his daughter and tapped his finger on the mute button as he listened to Joel's response. "Yes, Choix, what is it, my angel girl?"

Choix smiled and looked straight ahead, as if reading from cue cards. "I love you, Daddy."

"Oh!" Nelson squeezed her tiny ribs. "Thank you! Thank you,

my perfect one! I—" He lifted his finger from the mute button and dropped his voice an octave. "Right, Joel, you could courier it to me, or I—no, that's fine."

Ignored again, Choix wrenched free of Nelson's grip and stormed into a tiny room that adjoined the office and appeared to house only leather-bound books. I heard a ghostly telephone ringing inside.

"And we'll—okay, to the Parsippany office. Great great great . . . fantastic. Okay, my man. Give my love to Kimberly. Whisper my name tonight when you . . . right, right! Kak? Yeah, I got her good this morning. And please call me next time you're in town. For real. We'll take Kimberly to Sturbridge for the day. She'll shit dolls when she sees this place. All right, thanks."

Nelson hung up, ran his hands over his groin and clapped once. "Yes! Hey, Fred. Where did Choix go?"

I bent forward from the leather cushions and watched Nelson's daughter staring intently at something in the office annex. "Looks like she's getting you a fax."

At that moment we heard the sound of tearing paper. Choix disappeared from view, then reappeared in the hallway, running out the door of what looked like a linen closet beside the entry bathroom.

"I hate you, Daddy, I hate you!"

"Fred!" Nelson exploded out of his chair. "She's got the Catlin prices from London. Don't sit there like a pudwad, get them from her!"

I threw aside my magazine and offered pursuit. Choix's patent leather oxfords clattered from the front hall to the kitchen and up the winding staircase to the servants' wing on the second floor.

I'd never seen a little girl move with such single-minded coordination. She ran through the upstairs hall shrieking with glee until she looked over her shoulder and saw that I wasn't Daddy. Rather than give up her fax, Choix stopped at a turn in the hall and faced me in front of a washer and dryer. When I got within three feet of her, she balled up the fax and tossed it in an overhand loop so that it landed behind the dryer. Pretty soon she'd be rotating her head three hundred and sixty degrees and projectile-vomiting pea soup.

"Little girls rot in hell for that," I said buoyantly.

"Fred!" Nelson bellowed up the stairs. "What's it say, what's it say, what's it say?"

"Shit." I tried pushing the washing machine aside, but since it was full of water it weighed a ton. The dryer seemed to be bolted in place. I hopped on top of it and started feeling behind it for the fax.

"Fred, Fred, I need that number! That fax is worth $5,000 to me!"

"Just a second!"

"Take it from her, for Christ's sake! I'll break her fucking neck!"

By pushing at the head of the washer with one arm and wrenching the other down into the few inches of space between the dryer and the wall, I found it possible to get within two inches of the ball of fax paper. It had caught on a black air hose and was precariously balanced there. I saw dust rhinos of such magnitude that I immediately began to sneeze.

"Fred, are you so incredibly inept that—"

"Aah!" I surged forward, seemed to dislocate and relocate my shoulder in the space of four sweaty, claustrophobic seconds, and pulled out the paper ball. It only occurred to me then that we could have just called Christie's London and had them fax the page again.

"Fred, Denny D'Amico's calling me back in three minutes!"

I unwrapped the page as Nelson's pumping legs came into view.

"Fifty-three thousand one hundred pounds," I gasped, "at 1.3512 to the American dollar."

"Nooo . . ." Nelson stopped in his tracks and did mental arithmetic. "That's over $70,000! We just made Denny ten thousand bucks! Fred, you're incredible!"

I eased myself down beside the washer as Nelson ran back to his office. Choix darted out of her hiding place and he swept her up into his arms as they hit the stairway again.

"Great news," I said to the empty hallway. "I can barely contain myself."

## 27. That's a Heart Doctor

Before I knew it Christmas was coming to Boston, and I could make plans to get the hell out of town. I'd spent an unhealthy amount of time at the gallery pursuing my fortune, sixty-five or seventy hours some weeks, and had just escaped with my life on the snowy morning when Nelson decided to drag-race an inconsiderate Porsche driver down the Mass. Turnpike following a sales presentation in Marlborough. Smooch, a summer roommate who had recently landed a job with the *Village Voice,* wanted me to come down to Manhattan and meet her new roommate, Clint, so as we drove away from the Porsche ordeal I asked Nelson for the weekend off. At that moment I knew how Bob Cratchit felt pleading with Scrooge to come in at noon on Christmas Day.

"Sure, you need a break," Nelson said loudly. "I can see you've been busting your nuts, rehanging the gallery and writing to Helen Wheeler every week. Why not take tomorrow for yourself and meet me at Sotheby's Saturday afternoon? I'm going down for a sale with Ruth. We can all ride back to my Christmas party together."

"Oh, terrific." I made a mental note to ask Whitney next time.

"Here." He reached over the seat and dropped his wallet into my lap. "Take two-fifty out for yourself. Some fuck-you money."

"Some what?"

"Fuck-you money. What's the point of working so hard if you can't carry around enough money to be able to say 'Fuck you' to whoever you want?"

I nodded, too cash poor to disagree with this reasoning, and extracted five fifties.

Smooch and I agreed to meet on the Lower East Side at a renovated Victorian building that was hosting a Soviet poster show. I shared a cab from Grand Central Station with two fur-coated women who were going to the same event, and soon wondered why I'd been so nervous about taking the subway.

"So I said, 'Gift packs for the Soviet Union,'" one of the

women said to her friend. "I've got so many pairs of old shoes I could send, which is ideal because they *really* need shoes. And they've got such a *fabulous* distribution system over there."

"They really do," the other woman agreed. "Gift packs would be fabulous."

Smooch spotted me at the building's coat check and ran down a long entrance hall with a shot of Stoli in each hand. Her short black hair now ended in a fringe over her dark eyes. She had a sensuous, never quite extinguished, almost aggravatingly contagious smile. I slid my arms under her shot glasses and we hugged.

"Fred!" she cried. "I've missed you so much!"

"How many of these little monsters have you had, darling?"

She handed me a glass. "I can't remember. The food spanks. They have, like, Perestroika nachos. Anyway, come on—you have to meet Clint of the icy blue eyes. God, I feel a ton better now that you're here."

I decided to throw back the shot. "How's life at the *Voice?*"

"Oh, please." Smooch relieved me of my overnight bag and hooked her arm through mine. "At every other paper in the world you copy-edit for grammar and flow. At the *Voice* you copy-edit for political correctness."

We entered an enormous room with Egyptian columns and two central chandeliers. Three dozen framed posters and two hundred people were on view, a cross section of patrons and peons, each trying to bear with the other. A lot of Princeton people were milling about too, which made me wonder why Smooch would consider coming. At her signal, a very skinny, self-possessed blond man in tinted glasses approached. He was twirling a lollipop in a clear mug of beer.

"Here's Clint," she said, pretending to draw my attention to a heavy metal/Bureaucracy/gagged man poster. "He just got out of jail for an AIDS sit-in at the Federal Plaza. Doesn't he look like Sting?"

I looked hard for this resemblance in Clint, then saw a much more familiar person behind him. This person bore a remarkable likeness to my ex, Bridget Peabody, probably because it was Bridget.

"Smooch," I whispered, "it's Bridget!"

"Fred," she said, "this is Clint."

"Hello, Fred," Clint said.

"Fred!" Bridget exclaimed. "What are you doing here?"

"You look gorgeous," I said.

"I beg your pardon?" Clint said.

I waved him away. "No, not you."

"Nice friend." Clint dropped his lollipop back into his beer and stepped up to the heavy metal poster.

"Harshness heard from," Smooch added. She gave me a disapproving look and followed him.

Bridget appeared to be making ends meet quite nicely on her measly 30K salary. In fact, she looked the picture of New York youthful affluence, as if she'd been consuming exorbitant foods at lavish events and then working them all off by the next evening—a sort of passive social bulimia that enabled her to slip into the eye-popping black sleeveless dress she wore as if it were jeans and a sweatshirt. She'd chopped off most of her long, formerly braided brown hair and frosted it blond. In doing so she had successfully moved one notch up the beauty ladder from pretty to very pretty. I considered telling her she might go in for braces, since she'd come this far. I wasn't quite sure what to do.

"Honey," I said, "the bank lets you dress like that?"

"I made the bank $400,000 today," she said.

"Terrific. Did they give you a rain hat?"

She kissed me, finally. "I've missed you, Fred."

"Like fish."

"Really. I was down in Princeton and saw about fifty of your friends. 'Oh, how *is* Fred? He taught me *so much.*' "

"Enough. Why were you down at Princeton?"

"I went down with my boyfriend."

"How nice for you both."

"Sorry, pal, you're not going to make me feel guilty." She took a step back and nodded her approval. "You look great. How's the job?"

"The only problem is this green film in my bellybutton when I take out the emerald at the end of the night."

"Ha. Are you involved with someone?"

I cast around in my brain and came up with Denny D'Amico. What the hell? "It's strictly extramarital."

"With which . . ." Bridget hesitated.

"Him," I said confidently. "He gave me $60,000 in cash."

She smiled. "Wait till everyone hears. You can't even lie well anymore."

"Where's Happy? At the bar?"

"Hap and I called it quits," she said curtly. "He got cut from Salomon because he's basically alcoholic."

"So he's what, a telephone psychic now?"

"I hear he just got a job at Wilde, Coventry. Labor relations."

"Union busting, you mean. I thought as much."

"You do think that much, I'm sure."

"Honey, I feel like something's the matter," I said. I smiled at a couple of people from my graduating class I swore I'd cross the earth to avoid and momentarily thanked myself for not moving to New York. "What's up?"

Bridget glanced over her shoulder, then started speaking in a low voice. "Actually, Fred, I feel like this: I freed up all this emotional shelf space for you last year, and then you seduced my best friend's boyfriend. I'm having a lot of residual anger toward you right now."

"Oh, my God," I said. "You're seeing an analyst, aren't you?"

Bridget was prevented from answering by the approach of a tall, thin, boyish man in a rumpled gray suit. He put his hand around Bridget's waist and she allowed herself to be tilted into his embrace. I stared in mild shock. It was an abomination.

"Fred Layton," Bridget said happily, "this is Dr. Saul Wolfensohn. He's at Yeshiva Hospital."

"Hi, there," I said. We shook hands. "What sort of doctor are you?"

"I'm a cardiologist," Wolfensohn said. "That's a heart doctor."

"Bridget," I said in surprise, "I never thought there was anything wrong with your heart."

"And you?" Wolfensohn said.

"I'm an art dealer. That's a—"

"Fred," Bridget cut in, "can I get you another shot of something?"

"A dealer, are you?" Wolfensohn said. "I was just up on Fifty-seventh Street last Sunday looking for some prints for my office."

I grinned with pleasure. This would be too good. "No kidding."

"I was looking for something after Herring or Stubbs," Wolfensohn said, "but the people up there were so . . . okay, I'll say it—so undereducated."

"Well, we've got a great stock of Stubbs and Herring up at Park and Seventy-fifth, where we are."

"You do?" Wolfensohn showed the first glimmer of interest. "Bridge, we should stop up to Fred's place tomorrow and look at some of his prints. Will you be there?"

I glanced at Bridget, who had half closed her eyes and was mouthing the sentence "No no no no no no no."

"Absolutely!" I said. "Come over at ten and I'll give you an early-bird discount."

"A discount, you hear that?" Wolfensohn said. "All the other places mark their prices up when I walk in."

I tapped my thigh. "It's the pager."

"Fred," Smooch said behind me, "we're about to go to dinner. Are you coming?"

"Of course." I handed the doctor my card. "Would you like to join us? We're going to a wonderful place on Avenue A that lets you pick the roaches out of your salad niçoise."

"We're eating in," Wolfensohn said. "Thanks anyway."

"Hello, Smooch," Bridget said, obviously fed up with me. "What are you doing these days?"

"I'm editing," Smooch said, "and working with the home-less."

"Oh, très chic," Wolfensohn said.

I bowed for my potential clients. "Until tomorrow, then."

Smooch pulled at my hand. "Nice to see you, Bridget."

Bridget was looking at the floor. "Don't depend on us tomorrow, Fred."

"I'll get her up in time," Wolfensohn assured me.

"Bridge always did oversleep," I said. "Ciao."

Bridget looked up, flashed a private, exasperated smile at me, and scratched her nose with her middle finger. "I hope you get a good salad."

## 28. Run for the Roses

Bridget's reservations about a ten o'clock appointment with me the next morning were well founded, because I promptly overslept. The day began when I sat up on Clint's hide-a-bed couch to check my fuck-you money and cut my head on a framed poster of that Tiananmen Square scene of the four oncoming tanks and the defiant man standing before them, above whom someone had taped the word-bubble: "Okay, who had the shrimp roll?" Smooch emerged, fed me coffee, and shared a cab with me to the merrily decorated corner of Fifth and Fifty-seventh. I got out at the corner of Park and Seventy-fourth, cursing everything I'd drunk from midnight on.

"Fred!" Bridget waved at me from under the gallery building's awning and pulled me inside. "You're going to lose your commission if you don't hurry up. Saul found all this stuff he likes."

"Did he bring his checkbook?"

She swatted me. "You owe me the most incredible favor for this."

In the gallery, a thoughtful Saul Wolfensohn was pacing back and forth in front of two folio-size fox-hunting prints. Marjorie Warren, the receptionist, was on the phone. She raised a pantomime lorgnette to her nose, frowned, and reluctantly gestured me closer.

"Our director is not pleased about this."

I rubbed my dehydrated face. "Tell him to gripe to Nelson. This guy didn't know we existed until I met him yesterday."

Wolfensohn strolled over with his hand extended. Were all his suits wrinkled?

"Fred, how are you? I've chosen two images."

"That's great," I said. "You've done all the hard work for me."

"But I can only afford one of them," Wolfensohn said. "If I frame it here, can you do security hangers on it? I don't want my patients running off with genuine art."

"We can do it any way you like." I escorted him back to the fox-hunting prints he'd chosen, which were leaned against two large windows that faced Park Avenue. "Now for a single image, my favorite is *A Few of the Sort Who Have Done the Thing.* Good artist, great engraver, nice original color, plenty of energy in the composition, and a full range of expression in the riders. The other one might do all right as half of a pair, but it doesn't have any strength to stand alone. I mean, great book, but where's the movie?"

"That's true," Wolfensohn mused. "I see what you're saying."

Actually, every fox-hunting print I'd seen in the last four months had blurred into one, but this image was a bit better than most. I said, "Takes you a minute to find the fox in all that action, doesn't it?"

"Oh, yes, there it is." His pale face lit up. "I should tell you, Fred, what I'm really planning to do is buy this for the office and take business depreciation deductions on it for seven years. Then I'll take it home. I plan to build my collection that way, one piece a year."

"I expected something like that," I said. "I mean, that's good long-term planning and everything."

"His secretary will be sick of seeing it after seven years anyway," Bridget said.

"Good point." Wolfensohn nodded. "Bridge, you see any frames you like?"

"One question, Fred." Bridget picked up a two-inch-wide molding corner and aimed it at me threateningly. We had repaired to Nelson's bedroom, where the frame samples were stored. "Are you doing this to get back at me?"

"Doing what?" I asked, all innocence.

"Selling my boyfriend one of your overpriced prints!" she whispered fiercely.

"I told you I'd give him a discount," I said. "We really do have the best stuff, Bridget."

"I'm sure."

"And if I ever need triple bypass surgery, Saul's my man."

She frowned. "In any case, I don't appreciate your judgmental, snobby attitude about my life right now. Can I ask that much, that you cut me some slack?"

"When did I make a judgmental comment?" I whispered.

"I don't have to see any evidence," she shot back. "I know the way your wheels turn. You're just jealous that I've found someone and you haven't."

"You call that a someone? The guy is twice your age."

"Saul is very sweet to me," she argued. "And at least he can get it up."

"Touché," I said blandly, though I cringed inwardly. "Shall we start sending out wedding invitations?"

"No, because he's Republican," Bridget confessed. "He told me last weekend at Tatou. So it's bound to be temporary."

I placed a sympathetic hand on Bridget's shoulder. "Honey, if you really think it's going to be temporary . . . do you mind suggesting a gold-leaf frame?"

"Oh, you are such a *jerk*." She clocked me in the stomach with her molding corner in a way that rendered me supine on Nelson's mattress, then began ripping a row of three-inch frame corners from the Velcro-covered display panel near the bed and throwing those at me. "You men and your fucking egos!"

"I expressed an honest opinion about framing design, what do you want?" I balled myself up tightly until I saw Wolfensohn appear at the bedroom door.

"Anything wrong?" he said.

A Venetian frame corner struck me in the spot where I'd cut my head earlier, but I rolled off the bed and attempted to stand. "Just getting to yes, aren't we, Bridget?"

She frowned. "Sure."


Two hours later I exploded out of a cab to meet Nelson and Ruth in the York Avenue lobby of Sotheby's showrooms. Outside, the sky was threatening snow. Nelson, judging by the look on his face, was contemplating murder. He shook my hand, handed me a hardcover catalog for the sale, and gestured up the staircase.

"Fred, I want you to register for a bidding paddle. Fifty grand limit, just in case. Then I want you to look over any lots numbered 101 to 150 that I've checked off. There's a *grand papier* Redouté *Roses* in that group I'm very interested in. Ruth, you cover lots 51 to 100, please." He wrestled off his coat, a new cashmere chesterfield whose seat Choix had smeared with unseen Play-do, and stuffed it into Ruth's arms. "Thanks, guys. I'll see you in a minute." He marched up the stairs to the second-floor display space, pulling his soiled cords up so that pale blue socks peeked out from underneath the cuffs.

I kissed Ruth, who looked strangely serene and Pre-Raphaelite. The auction house bustle already had me intoxicated.

"Who ate the frosting on his cake?"

"Sotheby's," she said. "They cut his credit limit for this sale to $200,000. This morning he wanted me to go in and apply for $500,000 worth using my parents' house as collateral."

"What about the bidding paddle?"

"Oh, you just have to have a pulse to get one of those."

"How much does he owe Sotheby's?"

She raised one eyebrow and did calculations. "Somewhere in the area of a million."

"Good God," I said. "How does he pay a bill like that?"

She smiled. "Spins a bigger web, I guess, and waits for another Helen Wheeler."

"Enough. So is this an important sale?"

"Fred," she scolded, "it's the Julius Medveckis library. Nelson got an erection going through the catalog."

"Fred!" Nelson boomed above me. "One hour to show time, let's *go!*"

Ruth relieved me of my coat. "If you've got a Visa card, cut it up before he finds it."

Ten minutes before the Medveckis sale began, Oksana Outka wobbled into the viewing rooms in a sable coat and hat that looked as if they had been dragged in from the steppes of Russia, and Swifty Lazar sunglasses large enough to hide half her face. She sat across from me at one of the viewing tables and handed twenty call slips and a fifty-dollar bill to one of the gray-coated Sotheby's attendants. After he hurried off, she replaced the sunglasses with a pair of dowager's half glasses and began to scan a copy of *USA Today*. Her bloodshot eyes met mine momentarily; she produced a shallow, fabulous smile; and I was suddenly dead certain who had directed Jetty Smith's attention to the now infamous newspaper article on the Baltimore Antiques Show.

"Oksana!" a man behind me whispered across the table. "Another all-night brawl at the UN Plaza?"

"Hallo, Jay," she croaked to the man (obviously the person she'd been smiling at), then stopped herself and put a hand to her throat. "I've been soaking in a tub of Porcelana all morning."

"What are you doing at a print event anyway?" the man whispered. "The furniture lots aren't until tonight."

"Oh, I'm merely passing the time," she said evasively. "That chap in the gray gets me heavenly Bloody Marys."

"Just don't get in Nelson Albright's way at an auction," the man warned. "Why do you think I walk like this?"

The two shared a little chortle and the first of Oksana's books arrived with the call slips sticking out. She arranged these so as to block most people's view of her and began to compare the Sotheby's descriptions with the actual lots, making little notations in her catalog with a gold Omas pen.

After another moment my few remaining books arrived. The first title I picked up was Redouté's *Les Roses,* a three-volume set printed on extra large folio paper. The volumes actually constituted a pre-photographic record of the Empress Josephine Bonaparte's rose gardens at her Paris estate, Malmaison. There were 169 images of red, yellow, white, and varicolored roses in the set, each one a super-realistic stipple engraving that was printed in color and finished by hand at the printer's studio. It was one of the most exquisite print collections since the invention of movable type, and easily the best coffee table book of the early nineteenth century. The catalog described it as one of the finest copies extant and estimated its auction value at $90,000 to $110,000. Nelson had scribbled in, "Home run. Check plates 15, 47, 98, 150. Go to $200,000, then break off." Breaking off is the ignoble practice of bidding a lot up to an artificially high price with no intention of buying it after it has risen beyond your limit.

As I was examining the set in a kind of stunned joy, Oksana broke my reverie by tapping the table with her pen. "I'll have a look at that Redouté when you're done," she said. "Try not to get any peanut butter and jelly on the pages. It's quite valuable."

I looked up and smiled at her, my twenty-two-year-old face burning. "A little easier to get off than sixteen half-digested rum and Cokes."

Oksana drew in a breath and gave me her best George Washington profile. "Little sod. Address one more word to me and I shall have you ejected from this building."

Our enmity established, I went back to the Redouté. I was checking the last of Nelson's queried plates for foxing and discoloration when I heard a definite tearing sound behind me. I turned to see my bug-eyed boss pretending to inspect one of three known copies of the eighteenth-century nursery prospectus for plants as seen in Mark Catesby's *Natural History*. Since he'd just accidentally torn the edge of the prospectus loose from the points along the top where it was taped to the mat, he was in fact trying to slip the sheet back in without being noticed. Two Sotheby's attendants sniffed about in their oversized lab coats but kept a respectful distance. They appeared to know Nelson from previous sales.

"Oksana," I heard him say, and realized it was her presence that had caused him to inadvertently tear the print. Then the bell rang to call everyone into the auction room.

At auctions Nelson usually sat in the last row of chairs so he could get up, walk around, or pace at will. He did not deign to use a bidding paddle himself, merely nodding his head when he wished to raise the price. The phlegmatic British auctioneers never seemed to mind; in fact they seemed to enjoy Nelson's erratic antics. That left the rest of the crowd, usually forty to seventy print and map dealers at natural history sales, to sneer upon him. On this particular afternoon I counted more like a hundred.

Oksana took a seat in the front row and reapplied her sunglasses. "She's bidding for someone, she's bidding for that starfucker Danny Finch," Nelson kept saying, though he didn't seem to believe this theory and neither did Ruth or I. Any questions about Oksana's motives at this session of the Medveckis sale were answered when she bought lots 29 to 37, undistinguished books on gardening with ho-hum lithographed plates, at three to four times their high estimate. The atmosphere in the room became electric. Oksana Outka the antiques bed-hopper was moving into a new area—natural history prints.

"Shit buys shit," Nelson muttered, as he scribbled the relentlessly high realized prices into his catalogue with several exclamation points following. I knew that whether or not the rest of the lots bombed—and some of them would—our prices on everything were already going up by fifteen percent. Or at least those prices Nelson marked up before something else distracted him.

Over the course of the next ninety minutes Nelson managed to break off a few high-priced lots in Oksana, but the early excitement of the sale didn't return until the auctioneer arrived at the Redouté roses book, the closing lot and the cover illustration for the sale's catalog. The three women in red riding jackets at the telephones readied their receivers for bids, and the white-haired auctioneer leaned forward in his walnut pulpit and opened the bidding at $80,000, to rise in increments of $2,500.

Nelson, who thus far had spent $50,000 on a rare nine-volume set of orchid prints, took this moment to stand up and bid $82,500. Then he stepped back behind his chair and folded his arms. This gesture meant that anyone silly enough to fight him for the lot was welcome to try. Ruth gave him a thumbs-up.

Oksana entered the bidding at the $105,000 level, when Nelson and a man in a silk lumberjack shirt who'd beaten Oksana on some major Italian fruit books were the only bidders left. The silk lumberjack went up to $110,000, Nelson countered with a full

$115,000, and the man made a sour-milk face and dropped out. I looked back at my boss and he glanced at me just long enough to wink.

"One twenty-five," Oksana called from the front. A low mumble spread across the room. Nelson had gone up $5,000, now she'd skipped up $10,000. The most bloodless of the phone women spoke a few conciliatory sentences to a mystery bidder and replaced her receiver. Ten seconds passed.

"One hundred twenty-five thousand from Ms. Outka in the first row," the auctioneer said clearly. "Is there any advance?"

"One-thirty," Nelson said, practically cutting him off.

"One hundred thirty-five thousand dollars," Oksana said, and now turned fully around to glare at Nelson.

"She just paid for both our college educations," Ruth whispered.

"One hundred forty thousand dollars and fifty cents," Nelson spat back. A few enforced coughs spread through the room, though the man in the silk lumberjack shirt felt free to clap his hands and giggle for the space of several seconds. The auctioneer frowned down a smile.

"Is there any—"

"One hundred forty-five thousand dollars," Oksana exclaimed icily. She was sounding more and more like Margaret Thatcher with PMS.

Another tense silence. Then Nelson called out, like a pro squash player returning a weak serve, "One hundred eleven thousand one hundred and eleven British pounds and ten pence at one pound thirty-five pence to the American dollar."

Several people in the room now began to laugh openly. There

was a mad dash for pens and writing surfaces to calculate the bid. The most bloodless of the phone assistants leaned into her mike and said, "Please, Mr. Albright. We are accepting bids in American dollars only." This only succeeded in sending the laughers into new gales and drawing a dozen curious onlookers into the seating area.

"I beg your pardon," Nelson shouted. He was beaming from ear to ear. "I meant $150,000."

"One-sixty!" Oksana said. The room went dead silent again and Ruth pinched my arm so hard that my head snapped back.

"One seventy-five," Nelson said.

"Oh, no!" Oksana thundered, the color of her face momentarily matching that of her hair. "I beg your pardon, Mr. Hollinghurst, but I believe your records will show that Mr. Albright's line of credit ends at $200,000 for this sale. He already has spent a total of $50,000, which makes his last bid invalid."

Breaths were drawn in sharply. Heads whipped between the front and the back of the room. Nelson, though it took him only a second to recover, was for the first time I'd ever seen him completely taken aback.

"Mr. Hollinghurst," he addressed the auctioneer, with something approaching awe, "am I to understand that Miss Outka here has a special arrangement with your auction house to screen the credit limits of its customers before sales?"

"Foul!"

"Bid the lot over!"

"Bid the sale over!"

"Order!" Hollinghurst banged his gavel angrily. "Order, I say, or I'll clear the room!"

Instead the room filled with more outraged cries. Two chairs turned over as a dealer who'd been beaten out by Oksana on several lots surged up to protest. Oksana's voice rose above everyone else's, however. She waved her hands for silence and said passionately, "I am insulted by that accusation in every way, and I will not forget it. I merely overheard Mr. Albright discussing his credit line with another dealer in the lobby. It was completely unintentional. All I mean to say is there's no sense in having him bid this lot up into the stratosphere if he does not possess the resources to buy it. It is a complete waste of time and moreover immoral."

Without being fully aware of having stood up, I was suddenly on my feet with my bidding paddle in my hand.

"Mr. Albright has just agreed to transfer his first lot to my number," I said, my face going crimson and my voice cracking miserably like a thirteen-year-old's. "His credit line remains at $200,000."

"That's a bald-faced lie!" Oksana shouted. "That person is an employee of Nelson's."

More cries and accusations. I felt Nelson's hand on my shoulder, his voice whispering, "God bless you!" Then he bellowed, "Given that I and Mr. Layton have already agreed on terms, could we please proceed with the sale?"

"Mmm, well . . ." Mr. Hollinghurst shook his wattles and looked down at a list on his pulpit. "One sixty-eight," he said unsurely. "One sixty-eight, yes, Mr. Layton does have a legitimate number. I would advocate to continue the sale."

"In that case," Oksana said petulantly, "I bid one-eighty."

"Oh, well, I . . . I'm afraid," the auctioneer sputtered. "I mean I'm afraid that this rather exceeds *your* total credit line for the sale, Ms. Outka. In which case . . . I believe that one seventy-five will have to stand as the top bid unless there is any advance. Is there, um, any advance?"

Oksana sat down like an anchor hitting water. The foam in her chair hissed, to be replaced in the room by nothing but white noise. I don't think anyone breathed for the next minute.

"Once . . . twice . . . fair warning . . . um, sold to Mr. Albright for $175,000," the auctioneer said quietly. He rapped his little palm gavel on the pulpit. "And I believe that concludes this portion of the sale. You may pay for your purchases at the appropriate windows."

As the crowd applauded and two tourists who'd slipped into the row in front of me exclaimed that the sale had been "better than *Cats,*" Oksana's red hair literally drooped. She stared at Nelson, at me, and at the auctioneer, then regained her ladylike composure and left the room without another word. For all the cunning she'd displayed I felt awful for her. Nelson, blond hair all awry from his yanking on it, crushed me to his chest. I could feel the sweat running down my back.

"Fred!" he hissed in my ear. "You are absolutely incredible! Incredible! I'll see you get Whitney's job for this!"

"That might be a little premature," I said into his wide chest. "How about some more of that fuck-you money?"

Nelson hooted and pushed me back to arm's length. "Broke already, huh? I love that, Fred. I love that!"

## 29. Entering the Humidity Chamber

Besides lugging the Sotheby's orchid books from Nelson's car into the festively lit front hall of Château Delapompe for the holiday party, I was also to oversee delivery of a cracked black portfolio to Denny D'Amico. The portfolio contained a pair of Denny's Catlins which had started to ripple on their backing sheets and had been placed in a humidity chamber to flatten out. I wasn't sure yet, but I hoped this delivery meant Nelson was about to make the D'Amicos my personal clients, which would give me a ten percent commission on all sales to them.

Despite my foreboding about Denny's fury over—or at least suspicion of—the rippling prints I'd sold him, it was just like the guy to be genuinely happy to see me.

"Fred!" Denny called. He had a supernal tan from some tropical atoll and strangled my hand in the vestibule. "You haven't come down to my store to pay me a visit lately. I've been back a week."

I smiled and shook out my hand. "I don't go to the North End, Den. Everyone tries to sell you raffle tickets."

He grinned. "Hey, man. Meet my wife, Jenny."

"Hi, Fred!" Jenny D'Amico, the woman who had indirectly won me my job in the first place, walked up and gave me a big kiss on the mouth. She had disheveled dirty-blond hair and huge gray eyes. She was one of those bright, dynamic people in their mid-thirties you meet at Christmas parties and then never see again.

"Happy holidays," I said, "I—"

"Let's get some champagne going," she cut in. "I'm ready for a good time."

Denny patted my ass in sportsmanlike fashion. "Don't let Nelson make you do any scutwork tonight, because you're a guest too. Let's have a drink later and we'll talk about my Catlins."

"Let's," I said. "Good to see you." I carried the portfolio down the central hall, which smelled of hot cider, cinnamon, and about three hundred potpourris. On my way through I waved not at all sarcastically to Marty Ifft, who was talking to a short, well-dressed older couple I had yet to meet. On the floor of the dining room, Choix was coloring with Kimberly D'Amico, a very pretty and reserved five-year-old with black hair and porcelain skin who could have walked out of a Bronzino portrait. Choix had a glossy magazine open to a full-page ad for a diamond-encrusted Ulysse Nardin watch and was explaining to Kimberly how Santa Claus was bringing her one for Christmas. At a corner nook in the central gallery I passed a twelve-inch orchid plant in a tiny red pot, then another, then two more. The whole house, in fact, was bedecked with orchids. Now that I thought about it, Denny D'Amico had once mentioned a passion for them. It figured.

"Fred!" Nelson called from a corner of the gallery. "Please set up in the living room!"

I had arranged several volumes of the orchid lithographs on a coffee table before I realized that Marty had sat down in one of the chintz-drowned chairs, and that he was talking to me.

". . . look at your contract," he was saying, "you'll see you get no commission on sales made at parties attended by clients until you've been with us for a year."

"Mele Kalikimaka to you too." I wiped my damp forehead

with a cocktail napkin. "By the way, you'll have to explain some of the humidity chamber technology to me, in case Denny asks."

He frowned, his defenses up. "What technology?"

"How many watts the chamber runs on, what the process is, all that stuff."

"Watts?" Marty threw back his head and laughed. "Fred, a humidity chamber is a wooden box with a tray of filtered water in the bottom. You put the print in overnight to soak up moisture and take it out the next morning."

"That's it?"

"A print is ink and watercolor on paper," Marty droned, "it's not like you're gold-plating wire."

"And we're charging Denny D'Amico a thousand dollars to put two prints in a box overnight?"

"Look," Marty said bluntly, "the man is a former coke runner who owns a twenty-room house. This is not a situation where you call an ethical foul. And just in case you were wondering, carrying the portfolio in from the car doesn't get you a cut of the deal."

"Marty, if a tree falls in the woods and no one's there to hear it, would you claim commission on it?"

"I'd keep to the shadows of that tree if I were you," Marty said. "It's embarrassing enough to watch you pining after Denny's butt. I doubt he'd like hearing about that, and I know Nelson wouldn't."

This accusation shocked me into silence for a moment. Anyone with two functioning eyes could see Denny was a stud, and yet I felt found out somehow. Precisely the way Marty wanted me to feel, I realized. I smiled at him and said, "I can't say I've seen it yet, with your face there all the time."

My comeback appeared to strike a nerve, because Marty

surged out of his seat and brought an index finger up to my face. "Watch your step, Fred. Your next one may be your last around here."

"You must be sniffing those potpourris," I said. "You're becoming melodramatic."

"Am I interrupting something?" Denny said, as he stuck his head in at the living-room arch.

Marty replaced his sneer with a friendly smile. "Of course not. Fred was just leaving."

I said as I brushed past him, "That's what you think."

The Christmas party swelled in the gallery, rose to a climax in the dining room, and died in the living room. By 1 A.M. the high point of interest was Nelson chuckling with Denny over a print of a Malaysian orchid you needed a sixteen-inch tongue to pollinate. Their mirth was only momentarily interrupted when Denny asked Nelson what he thought of Oksana Outka's move into antique botanical prints, a move she'd just announced with a full-page ad in the new issue of *The Magazine Antiques*.

"I'll tell you what I think of Oksana," Nelson said. He turned and spat violently into the fire. The room fell silent, and for a moment you could almost see the white smudge of Oksana's face hovering in the flames.

When all the guests but the D'Amicos had gone, and I was pretty much gone on the strength of three vodka tonics, Nelson moved Denny to a remote corner of the room for serious negotiations. Although Marty and I had been parrying for Denny's attentions all night, Nelson made it clear he now wanted to be left alone with him. They began to speak in low tones beside a bay of windows frosted over with frozen rain and snow. A log popped in the fireplace near my chair, and I found myself following its overheated hiss down into unconsciousness. How I could have achieved sleep, drunken or otherwise, with the rumbling thundercloud Nelson Albright and his wife the Texan lightning goddess so close by amazed me even as I drifted away. Although I quickly dismissed the thought, it occurred to me that Marty might have slipped something into my drink.

When I woke again, the living room was deserted. A fiftieth-anniversary bottle of Grand Marnier sat empty on the lamp table beside me, and beyond it I could see the abandoned orchid books. I stirred a little and felt the blanket someone had thrown over my shoulders. The cold air just within hand's reach told me much time had passed, for the fire had obviously burned itself down to ashes. It was so silent in the house now that I could hear snow beating against the panes. In a moment I heard another sound, too, distant and very strange: a tinny guitar and a soft, tone-deaf falsetto following along with it. I sat up and discovered that I wasn't under a blanket at all, but under Nelson's chesterfield coat.

I got up and put on the coat, then walked around the living room eating hors d'oeuvres off of trays. For a second, with my cashmere coattails dragging along the tiled floor, it was as if I owned Château Delapompe. Every Montana landscape painting and Iroquois warrior watercolor, every Persian carpet and shelf of rare books, every sponge-stuccoed wall and polished ceiling beam was mine. And out through the snow-caked windows everything I could see was mine too, every sagging tree and tennis court and outbuilding. And I could get to this. Fred Layton, whose parents fought twenty-nine days a month about the bills to be paid on the thirtieth, whose aunt and uncle had sold all but a sliver of their land to pay their rising property taxes and exploding medical bills: I could get to this world through my own efforts. I could and I would.

As these thoughts blazed through my mind, I approached the set of orchid books and found one of Nelson's business cards on the morocco leather cover of the first volume. "SOLD, $85,000," it read. No wonder I hadn't been awakened.

I was pouring myself a club soda at the bar in the gallery, praying that I wasn't setting off any motion alarms, when the strange singing started again. I walked up into the dining room, then back into the living room and over to the gallery niche near the grand fireplace. Six potted palm trees stood there with red ribbons round their waists, but none had been wired to broadcast music. When I turned from the niche, however, I noticed a crack of light under the door of Nelson's library office. As I walked down the gallery toward it, the sound grew in volume and the single voice resolved into two. One, I realized, was Roy Orbison. The other was Nelson. They were both singing "Only the Lonely."

I crept up to the door and listened. The song played itself out to the end, a few seconds of silence followed, then a tape machine clicked off. Casters squeaked over the floor.

"Come on in, Fred."

I bit my lip and pushed the door open. It was true, he was still working, shirt sleeves rolled up over his muscular forearms, three legal pads in a circle around him. A single log was burning itself out in the fireplace to the left of his desk. Nelson looked completely sated after the five-figure sale, the same way an African python must look after swallowing a large hare.

"Greetings," I said. "I was just getting some more club soda."

"You had more than club soda tonight," he said.

I nodded. Nelson motioned me toward an oversized library chair and I sat down. For a moment he was silent, and I let my eyes trail over his leather-topped desk. It was strewn with auction catalogs, invitations to openings, a nineteenth-century lithograph of a flying squirrel with genitalia added in ballpoint pen, a luminist watercolor of an Indian squaw in a powder-blue Ultrasuede mat, a microcasette dictating machine, his legal pads, the latest issue of *Oui,* on which two halves of an apple wobbled like red breasts, and a vase of fading calla lilies with an attached card that read: "Nelson, thank you so much for coming to the party and for your note of apology. We actually feel sorry for you . . ." and then trailed off beyond my line of sight.

"I needed you to be at Sotheby's today and you were there," he began. "And your first instinct during that sale was to save my ass, which you did. I didn't want to pay two hundred grand for that Redouté, but then again you saw the forces we were up against. I like the way you took that risk. I think you're proving to me in a very short time that you're made for this kind of job."

"I hope so," I said. "I certainly like working for you."

"The feeling's mutual, Fred." He stood up, took the long way around his desk, and approached my chair. "I feel more and more that I made a good decision, regardless of what Kak and Whitney and Marty and Doug say about you behind your back. I feel I can trust you. We're more alike than you think, you know."

I smiled weakly. "How is that?"

For an answer he let one of his fat, powerful hands fall onto my shoulder and squeeze. It felt wonderful and reassuring, the same way it felt when my father used to rub my neck and tousle my hair as I read the Sunday funnies at the dining-room table. Actually, he did it only once, but I'd relived the memory so many times it hardly mattered.

"First thing I'm going to do is make you a codirector with Marty. So your base goes up to $30,000 and a six percent commission applies to every sale you make. I'm also thinking of letting you have Denny and Jenny D'Amico as personal clients. They're going to continue to be very big hitters for us, and Jenny really enjoyed meeting you."

"That's terrific," I said. "But won't Marty have a fit?"

He frowned. "Marty, Marty. Do you shake Marty's dick for him when he's taking a piss, Fred? Marty blows all the money he makes on clothes and the pack of faggots he runs around with. That's half the reason Denny feels uncomfortable with him."

"He doesn't shop at Illusions?"

"I mean the faggot part," Nelson said. "Don't play dumb with me."

"Sorry." I felt both relieved and stung. I'd hoped to tell Nelson at a time like this that I was gay, so that he might stop trying to set me up with clients' daughters and would perhaps delete absurd observations like "All gay men love monkey prints" from the general chatter that went on in my presence. Unfortunately, it looked like I'd be forcing that part of myself underground to stay in someone's good graces. Again.

"So as of now the D'Amicos are yours," he continued, "though I might want you to see me sell to them first. It's too bad you passed out when I was closing. Do you have a drinking problem I should know about, Fred?"

I blanched. "No, of course not. Just celebrating the holiday."

"Because at this point if I put you in solo with six drinks in your belly I feel you might fuck it up."

"I had three drinks," I said defensively.

"Three doubles makes six drinks in my book," he said. "Anyway, think of it like this. You're asleep in your room at the Ritz in Paris. It's about three-thirty in the morning, and Kathleen Turner comes to the door. You let her in and she slips off her fur coat right in front of you. Then she heads for the bed, so you know you're gonna get that big payoff. You get into bed with her and you try your best, give her everything you know, but you can see, you can *just see* as she's slipping back into her fur coat an hour later, that she's a little bit unsatisfied with the experience. And since she's a little bit unsatisfied she probably won't come back."

"I thought I was weaving a web," I said.

"A web, a lay, whatever," he said. "If you're that cocksure, then it's up to you. If you want to develop people on your own and you can make your own sales, fabulous. You can have all the special clients you want. So here's your play: I want you to make sure the D'Amicos get a follow-up letter. 'How nice it was to see you tonight, how I look forward to serving you again.' Shit out three or four paragraphs, really convoluted. Then invite them to the gallery downtown. Invite them in once a week if you have to. But establish the links. I want you to be in Denny's shorts, okay?"

"In his shorts. Super."

"There's a lot coming up for you," he said, as I scribbled down the note "Write to Kathleen Turner," then amended it to "the D'Amicos." "I think you'll know how to take advantage of it, too. I can feel that. Just stay off the booze and keep away from the coke and you'll be all right."

"What about Oksana Outka?" I said.

"Ah yes, Oksana." The chummy laughter returned to his voice. "That British bag of shit has the gall to assume she can *compete* with me now! But we'll bury her." He slapped my shoulder and walked back to his chair. Behind Nelson's head I could see that the sky was growing light. My boss hadn't stayed up late at all; he was already back at work the next day.

"By the way," he said suddenly, "did Denny give you the check for his Catlin restoration?"

"The check?" I held Nelson's stare as the anxiety of displeasing him rushed back with full force. I took my hands out of the chesterfield's pockets and patted them over my trousers. To my amazement, since I could barely remember the exchange, I pulled a check out of my inside blazer pocket. Denny had even included tax. I leaned forward to deposit it faceup on Nelson's leather desktop.

"Here you go."

Nelson nodded as his lips rose in a slow, wily grin. "Good man, Fred. Good man."

Part

2

## 30. Walls Have Needs

Denny and Jenny D'Amico either responded to their mail the day it came or received very few social invitations, because they were standing at the display window of the Newbury Street gallery forty-eight hours after I dropped my convoluted four-paragraph New Year's card into a mailbox and began my career as a codirector. Ruth had just left in a van with some supplementary stock for the annual New York Winter Antiques Show, which in Nelson's hierarchy of pivotal world events fell somewhere between the crucifixion of Christ and the signing of the Magna Carta. Whitney and Marty also had been recruited to work at the show, as had veteran salespeople from the rest of the gallery network.

Denny stepped up to the vestibule to ring the bell, and I buzzed him and Jenny in and offered them coffee.

"We're in a rush," Denny said, "but I wanted to say thanks for the really nice card."

"And congratulations on your promotion!" Jenny added.

"Thanks very much." I grinned. "What can I do for you today?"

"You should tell Fred about the decorator," Denny said to his wife.

"I can barely think about the decorator," Jenny said, suddenly anxious. "I can't think in fur, period. God, but our bathroom. I'm becoming a stress victim. We're doing our master bathroom and we've run into some budget problems."

I frowned with concern, though I was secretly delighted that the D'Amicos were confiding in me. "Tell me all about it."

"Fred," Jenny said, "walk through my bathroom with me. We're walking in and we have a twelve-foot space on the right. Two stairs, and then a thirty-foot space before you hit the tub. And here are our Adam mirrors and our sink."

"But you look at the left side of the room and it's like night and day," Denny said.

"Night and day," Jenny echoed. "And our decorator has been very good to this point. She helped us pick our marble, the fixtures, the fountain, all of that, but she cannot do anything with these walls on the left."

"I see." I rubbed my chin thoughtfully and stared at my new clients. Bathroom walls . . . I was sure the D'Amicos wouldn't want anything like the last bit of decoration I'd seen on a bathroom wall, but I was rather stuck on what else to suggest. I made a sympathetic noise and Jenny D'Amico made one back. Time slowed. The sun set behind us and rose again. Years passed and still we stood, pondering the D'Amicos' naked sinistral bathroom walls.

Finally Denny held up a framed Abraham Lincoln letter he'd taken from the front desk. He handed it to me with a platinum American Express card and said, "History—it's like I'm there!" I glanced at my watch: eighteen seconds had passed.

"Let's solve this wall problem before the autographs," I said. "I don't want to think of you both being upset in your bathroom."

"*Ab*solutely," Jenny said. "Fred, you are so terrific. Let me tell you what we've done. Our decorator Jane Dare, who's based in New York, is somewhat new to prints. If it's okay with you, we'd like to have you meet her. She's already shown us ten or eleven images she picked up at the New York show preview yesterday."

"We saw them last night, on approval." Denny made a mezzo-mezzo sign. "They're . . . ehh."

"They're not really us," Jenny admitted. "In fact it's gotten to the point where I don't know if we should be thinking of prints at all. Maybe a tapestry."

"Maybe autographs!" Denny exclaimed. "Or sculpture!"

"In a bathroom?" I pulled myself together. "What you've sketched out for me says you could benefit a lot from prints. If I've got the dimensions correct, the first part of that wall would need two or three prints, and the bigger section might even need a foursome."

"You *hear* that?" Jenny reached behind me and poked her husband through his leather coat. "I told you Jane should talk to him. Those walls need prints, Denny. Walls have *needs.*"

Denny bit his lip. "It's a whole new world, babe. I'll get the car."

# 31. The Principessa
# of Rame

I welcomed Jane Dare, the D'Amicos' decorator, later that day, even though it was nearly impossible to shake her hand since she held her fingers together as one and pointed them straight down. My first reaction on seeing photographs of the D'Amicos' on-approval prints—three lower-range Weinmann mezzotints, a few skimpy Redouté crocuses, and a tiny pair of *Botanical Magazine* peonies—was that Jane had simply stopped in at our bargain rack at the New York show. When I flipped the pictures over, though, I recanted this judgment: every price was forty to *six hundred percent* higher than what Albright Galleries charged. The fact that anyone could get away with charging a penny more than we did for anything made my head swim.

"Twenty-nine hundred dollars for a Redouté crocus?" I laughed. "We've got bigger images at *half* that price. If half. In much better condition."

"You're not seeing mats or frames in any of those," Jane Dare said gravely, "but I get your point." Jane Dare was an attractive Upper East Side redhead with flawless posture and a host of other value points. She brought a sterling silver tape measure from her purse and approached the print rack at the front desk.

"These I haven't seen anywhere. Tell me about these."

I looked over her shoulder. "Pompeiian fresco prints, engraved in Naples in 1778. I was going to give the D'Amicos a jangle about them. They're just in."

Jane pulled out two vibrant yellow and blue prints of mosaic tiles, then placed four more underneath them on the front desk. "'In-cee-say in Ram-ay, 1778,'" she read from one of the title lines. "What does that mean?"

Good question. Rome was "Roma" in Italian—what the hell was "Rame"?

"Well," I said, hoping this point would end the discussion, "'Incise in Rame' means that these were engraved in a little town called Rame."

"I traveled through Italy quite a bit," Jane said at once. "Years ago. I've never heard of Rame."

I paused before responding. Jane's knowledge of Italy left me standing just within the entry gates of another invented story about art. I could back out now by admitting my ignorance, thereby losing Jane's confidence (and probably the sale), or I could let my imagination take over and try to snow her under. I supposed if I embellished a bit, it couldn't hurt.

"Well, Rame was destroyed during the nineteenth century," I explained. "I'm just trying to think. It was about ten kilometers south of Rome, the way Versailles is so close to Paris. Have you ever been to Versailles?"

"I love Versailles, but tell me more about Rame. I thought you said they were engraved in Naples."

I looked at Jane Dare with new respect. Unlike most decorators I'd dealt with, she seemed to be fully conscious. "The first volume *was* engraved in Naples. . . . Then Casanova, the artist, got into a terrible argument with his biggest patron there, over the principessa of Rame."

Jane edged up some top mats and had another look at the prices. "There was trouble?"

"Yes," I said, and added, before I could stop myself, "a terribly stormy affair. It caused lots of political repercussions in Tuscany, and then the second volume had to be finished with another publisher."

She looked at me skeptically. "Were these cut out of a book?"

"We prefer to say 'liberated from a bound portfolio.'"

"That's pretentious," Jane said. "You should say 'cut out of a book.'"

I smiled. "Aren't those blues in the one on the left handsome?"

"They are gorgeous," she said, "whatever they are. I think I'll return those other images to Oksana. These are much more suitable for a bathroom."

"Great," I said, then did a double take. "You mean Oksana Outka, the 'Unpacking the Past' person?"

"'Unpacking the Past' is so last year," Jane said, though as far as I knew we were only six days into the new one. "Oksana's gone whole hog on botanical prints for '88. Golly, the matting she's got is *just* . . ."

I raised my eyebrows expectantly. "Have you got any samples?"

"Sure." Jane Dare dug in her purse and produced a copy of the 1988 Oksana Outka Collection catalog. It was called, simply, "Wallflowers." Within lay some botanical antics that made our frame shop's fleur-de-lis-matted Brookshaw cherries look like the tightest-assed fare you could buy on Charles Street in Beacon Hill. I saw $185 Weinmann weeds placed in five- and six-layer multicolored French mats, mats whose designs were *copyrighted* according to the footnotes along the bottom of each page, then finished off with 3½-inch faux gold-leaf frames and priced (I caught my breath) at $3,000 a pop. The other two dozen pages of the catalog followed the same theme—the lowest-level botanical prints matted and framed and priced like the masterpieces. There were familiar prints from the Medveckis sale at Sotheby's, too: prints torn free of their bindings and placed in Pollack-spattered mats, sponged pastel mats, and rainbow-colored mats with appliqués made from dried wildflowers and strips of old Renaissance psalters. Obviously, Oksana had just combined her Medveckis sale take with a few hundred pieces of good schlock she bought from some dealer pal and framed it all to the point where the print was merely a necessary evil in the overall design. She didn't even identify the artist or medium, just "Peony, 1764, $4,150." It was blasphemous. It was style over content. And for the targeted market we shared, it was completely brilliant.

Nelson would wig.

"I wanted to get photographs of these in mats," Jane noted over my shoulder, "but everything framed *or* matted in Oksana's booth is sold out. I practically had to kill to get this catalog. *W* is doing a two-page spread on her next week."

"Well," I said, and could say no more.

Jane Dare relieved me of Oksana's glossy catalog. I noticed that a clothing designer had even advertised her perfume, with sampler, on the inside back cover.

"Just write up those mosaics on approval and I'll swing by in my car," she said. "I don't want anything billable being done to me. I'm driving a coppery-red Mercedes. *Rame* is Italian for copper, by the way."

"Oh, of course," I said, smiling in what I hoped resembled a charming admission that I'd known all along. "But just think how much Jenny D'Amico will love that story."

"She will." Jane Dare paused at the door to put on her gloves. "I'll have to tell it to Oksana, too."

"If you do," I said, "tell her I own the copyright."

## 32. Gila Monsters Meet You at the Analyst's

Jane Dare ultimately sold four of the Pompeiian prints to the D'Amicos, which meant about $1,200 in commission for me. As luck would have it, Jane also bumped into a friend she hadn't seen in years on the way to Oksana's booth to return her botanicals. The friend wondered why Jane hadn't come by his booth, and she had to confess she'd found a wonderful new contact in Nelson Albright's Boston shop, a young man just out of Princeton. At this point Jane's friend went quite pale and excused himself to a nearby phone box.

"You back-stabbing little *prick,*" Marty whispered, while the New York show roared on in the background. "If Jane Dare is working with the D'Amicos, then she's *my* client, just as the D'Amicos are *my* clients. The D'Amicos also happen to be referrals from Woody and Jeri Bodega, who were at the Christmas party this year and last year and the year before that, when you were still popping zits in junior high school. Which makes all of them *automatically* my clients."

"I guess it's all the same to you that Nelson made me a codirector and gave me the D'Amicos because you've already got fifty-three special clients and can't give them enough attention," I said.

"Codirector," Marty spat back. "Excuse me while I vomit blood. If you're not out of that gallery when I get back I will make your life sheer, unmitigated hell. As will Whitney. Please consider this a direct threat."

"Please consider pounding sand," I said. "I don't work for you."

"Unmitigated hell," he repeated, and hung up. I handed the phone receiver to Geena, who had at last tired of following the Grateful Dead and returned from her three-month leave of absence to tell us she was quitting the next day because Nelson put too much pressure on her. "Fred," she said, "you're still not getting along with Marty, are you?"

"I refuse to kiss his ass," I said. "Does that make me a bad guy?"

Geena flicked over a page of *Vogue* and watched an ambulance race down Newbury Street. "You've changed since I left."

"You don't say." I began to flip through the print rack at the front desk.

"Kind of uptight, like you're trying to fit in even though it sucks?"

"Must be nice not to have to make any real choices."

Geena leaned forward in her chair. "Excuse me?"

"I said that sounds like a fair description of life to me."

"I'm choosing to leave, Fred. That's a choice."

"I stand corrected."

"Anyway, you'll probably just go to see Alfred to straighten this out."

"Kak's haircutter?"

"That's Kenneth."

"I knew that."

" 'Kak's haircutter'?" she mocked. "I'm like . . ."

"So who's Alfred?"

"Alfred's our analyst."

"We have a company analyst?"

"We all had to go see him last August. He's good. It's much better to talk out your issues instead of walking around with everything bottled up having a bird. Don't you think?"

I smiled, though it felt forced. "I guess that depends on the situation."

Whitney returned from the New York show Monday morning, though Marty stayed on through Wednesday. Whitney didn't mention anything about the D'Amico/Jane Dare incident beyond relaying Nelson's order that we all meet with Alfred on Wednesday night. Ruth and Doug would also be joining us. Apparently they had some issues too.

Dr. Alfred Berg shook my hand at his office door, which was located deep in the bowels of Newton-Wellesley Hospital. He was a tiny, bald man with a white beard and brown eyes whose voice was a purr of calm understanding.

"Hello, Fred," he said. "Hello again, Whitney."

Whitney shook his hand warmly. "Another journey to the vale of tears, what can we tell you?"

I took a spot on the couch next to Ruth, so that I faced Nelson and Kak across a purple plastic coffee table decorated with rainbow stickers. I wondered at the foot-high Daddy doll sitting on this table, minus its head, as well as the Etch-A-Sketch and the well-thumbed copy of *Gila Monsters Meet You at the Airport* beside it. Then I noticed that two walls of Alfred's office were constructed of one-way mirrored panels.

"This is our analyst?" I whispered to Ruth.

"He's Choix's analyst," she said.

Alfred sat down in a Superman rocking chair and thanked us for coming. "I'm going to start with an observation," he said, "if that's all right."

"You're in charge," Nelson said.

"Absolutely," Kak echoed. "We've got to resolve this tonight."

"We certainly do," Nelson went on. "I just spent a fortune on a set of Redouté roses I can't move because Oksana Outka is selling shit at premium prices to all my best clients. I mean, I'm coming down to my last fifty thousand dollars! I'm not even treading water."

"We're barely keeping one *nos*tril above water," Kak said.

"And it certainly doesn't help when people in your own company are trying to push your head under," Marty observed.

Whitney and Nelson looked at me expectantly.

"You know," I said, somewhat stunned at Nelson's financial update, "maybe we should let Alfred share what he was going to say."

Out of the corner of my eye I saw Marty make the international sign for brownnoser to Whitney. Ruth tisked.

"Go on, Marty, speak your thoughts to everyone," Kak said. "It's okay."

Marty crossed his legs. "I've said enough already. I don't have any explaining to do."

"What I was going to say," Alfred purred, "if you'll just let me get things moving here—"

"Let him talk!" Nelson boomed.

"Oh, my God," Ruth moaned in my ear.

"I sure won't be able to concentrate with Ruth telling secrets," Doug grunted.

Nelson's face filled with blood. "All right, I am officially pissed. The next person who talks is fired!"

Alfred paused with his eyelids lowered, looking a bit annoyed. I was sure his fee for the hour had already increased well beyond what Kenneth charged Kak for a wash and trim. "I would continue," he said, "only now I've forgotten what I was going to say."

Whitney examined her flawless cuticles. "I can't imagine why."

"So, let's go around the room now," Alfred said, having glanced gratefully at his watch to see that our time was up. "Marty, what have you learned from communicating with Fred tonight?"

Marty sighed and rubbed his temples. "That I shouldn't jump to conclusions before I've got all the information, and that I should give Fred a chance."

"And, Ruth, what have you learned?"

Ruth pondered. "That I should ask Doug what he has time to do before assuming he'll do something for me."

"Doug, what about you?"

Doug, who was now cradling the headless Daddy doll, said placidly, "That I should never threaten Ruth with an unlicensed gun until we've talked about her needs."

Alfred nodded. "And Fred: has communicating with Marty tonight helped you clarify what you want?"

I hesitated, having tuned out completely once the analysis descended into a glorified sales meeting on how we should market our new Redouté *Roses* set. Besides, I'd won the fight: I was still a codirector and the D'Amicos were my clients to keep. "I only hope that Marty will trust me a little more," I said, "and assume I have the company's best interests in mind."

"Good." Nelson shot out of his seat. "And what I want is everyone to communicate with each other, so we can run this business like a business and I can stop hemorrhaging money. I also want to communicate with all of you on some new selling techniques. We can start right here, in fact. Fred, try selling Marty two canisters of toxic waste."

I blinked. "Um, think of the heirloom value."

Alfred tapped his watch face. "Excuse me, Nelson?"

"Oh, right," Nelson barked. "Time's up. So let's meet at my house at eight o'clock Sunday morning for a focus session."

"Let me communicate with you on that," Whitney said. *"No way."*

As the conversation descended into chaos again, I leaned over on the couch. "By the way, Alfred, have you and your wife ever considered investing in antique prints?"

"Hmm." Alfred scratched his beard contemplatively. "I made a rule with Nelson never to discuss that sort of business around Choix. On the other hand, those Redouté roses everyone talked about sound quite nice. Why not give me a call?"

## 33. The Laura Ashley Memorial Crack Den

In early February Nelson decided to liberate his Redouté roses from their portfolios and offer the whole set to clients in an afternoon. Those interested would purchase a suite of six prints at a lottery drawing where all the images would be pinned to the walls of a display room. I was unsure of the strength of this marketing idea, since each client would end up taking home at least two weedy roses from the lesser regions of the set, but arguing with Nelson on the point was a waste of breath. The "Redouté Public Offering" was his sole strategy to flatten Oksana Outka's extremely popular "Wallflowers" concept.

We sent out several mailings on the Redouté drawing over the next three months, promising preview parties and receptions to rival a Roman wedding with a 2,000-person guest list, and to my amazement people signed on. By the week before the event, we had sold twenty of the twenty-eight available slots for $12,000 each. Even Alfred the analyst had wanted to come in, but the date conflicted with a hypnosis seminar on bed-wetting he attended annually.

Nelson decided to hold the drawing in an unused library at the Weston headquarters, and Kak volunteered her expertise to decorate it. So it was that the afternoon before the event I dropped by to pin up rose prints in the wake of the recently departed Doug Morrow, who'd been found making obscene phone calls to Ruth from within Château Delapompe, and discovered that Nelson's wife had repainted the entire library ostrich-shit olive and hung it to the point of design asphyxiation with navy swags and bows. Since the paint on the walls was tacky when I arrived, I was still pinning up Mylar-wrapped roses four hours later as our preview party began over at Château Delapompe.

Shortly after eight that night, Denny D'Amico knocked on the library door and stepped in to request a quick look at the set. He was impeccably dressed in a deep violet Missoni suit, on his way to meet Jenny for some fund-raising dinner, but when I told him he was the first person to see the entire *Roses* set up on the walls he beamed and dropped his overcoat on a chair.

"Looks like our own little Garden of Eden," he said.

I decided to ignore this vaguely sexual allusion. Besides, to me the long rows of roses looked more like a set of headshots from a botanical Most Wanted list.

"So, kid," Denny said, and slid a black cashmere scarf from around his thick brown neck, "tell me one more time how this'll go?"

"You'll pick a number out of a hat," I said professionally, "and that number tells you when you can choose a print. Then we have six rounds of selections, and in each round you get to pick one rose off the wall. So if you pick number eight, say, you'll get a rose after the people with numbers one through seven have gone. In the second round the order reverses."

Denny frowned. "But by the fourth round all the good stuff will be gone, don't you think? All that's left will be that lame-looking shit on the other wall."

"Those are wild roses, actually," I said, though I completely agreed with him. "They're not really bad when you get up close.

And the first dozen top ones are just salon roses they hybridized to death to get seven or eight layers of petals. They're like roses with breast implants."

Denny thought a moment, nodded, and handed me an envelope from his inside pocket. His thickly veined hand released it, moved up to pat my cheek twice, then continued on to smooth his glossy black hair. Although we were completely alone in the room, he leaned over to whisper in my ear.

"Fred," he said, "help me out tomorrow. I'm in, but I want a couple with the implants."

As if by a sort of extrapecuniary perception, Nelson was waiting for me in the vestibule of Château Delapompe while the big preview party droned on behind him. He tore open Denny's envelope at the door, looked inside, and chuckled.

"Here, Fred," he said, "I just got a message from Denny to come meet him for a minute. You better give this to Marty. He's going to make the deposit tomorrow."

"Sure thing."

When Nelson's Merc pulled away I peered inside the envelope. A check for $12,000 was there, wrapped up in a glossy magazine photograph. In the photograph a naked black man of prodigious endowment was lying on his back in the midst of a tidal, self-produced climax. Denny had written "Twelve Big Ones Coming Right At You" at the top of the page.

I examined the photograph for a moment and shook my head. Whatever.

A caterer with a tray approached, and I handed her the envelope and told her to deliver it to Marty.

Nelson returned without Denny D'Amico in tow. I could tell from the big vein bulging in his neck that we had a problem. He came directly through the crowd of clients and salespeople to the bar, where I just happened to be making a stiff drink to celebrate my $1,200 commission. A moment before, Choix had gotten hold of the "Twelve Big Ones" photograph and was now waving it high above her head as she ran among the guests.

"You saw D'Amico tonight," he said. "He seemed okay to you?"

I thought. "Sure. I got the check, remember?"

"Right." His jaw trembled. I began to fear I'd neglected to do something. Then I noticed that Nelson was mixing a double Scotch. I'd never seen him with a drink in his hand before.

"Hello, chum." Kak flowed up in a long red dress with an enormous black ingot around her neck.

"Hello, honey," Nelson said crisply. "The next time you decide to decorate a room in one of my houses, can you please come talk to me about your plans for a tiny second before you start? Would that be okay?"

Kak's charming veneer evaporated faster than spring dew in Dallas. "What do you mean, 'your houses'?"

"My library looks like the Laura Ashley Memorial Crack Den, that's what I mean. Am I clear now?" He swung around, hand extended, to a trim, white-haired man with thick glasses. "Woody Bodega. Good to see you. Hello, Jeri!"

"Now *that's* service." Mr. Bodega pointed to Nelson's hand. "You've even memorized my drink."

Nelson chuckled. "This one is for me, Woody, but I'd be

delighted to make you another. Fred, please get Woody a drink. Has Marty shown you our new Van Goebels? Best fruit painter of the seventeenth century." He took two long gulps and emptied his glass. "I think it's a total home run."

I handed Mr. Bodega his drink and everyone began to walk through the central gallery toward the Van Goebels, which Nelson and Ruth had hung on one of the walls flanking the living-room entrance. It was a darkly varnished 40 by 20-inch oil that to me resembled a mutant Renaissance watermelon vomiting out of the top of a cornucopia.

"It's rather pretty from back at the bar," Mrs. Bodega said diplomatically.

"I've had it for two weeks now," Nelson explained. "Guy I bought it from said, 'Nelson, that painting is like a three-breasted woman. Everybody's interested in her but nobody wants to take her home.'"

Mr. Bodega chuckled. "I suppose you wrote a check on the spot, Nelson, after hearing that."

Nelson nodded proudly. "I did indeed. I like three-breasted women."

"Hon-ey," Kak said into Nelson's ear. "May I please see you for a moment alone?"

"I wish I could," Nelson said, "but there are some fine people here to take care of."

Woody Bodega cleared his throat and stepped back. "Perhaps Jeri and I will stroll around a bit."

"No, no! Don't move." Nelson took a glass of red wine from a waiter's tray and threw back half of it. "Kak just feels a little subjugated now and then. I remember one time last summer—"

"Honey," Kak warned.

"—it was about seventy-five degrees out, sunny and dry, and she came into the kitchen to ask me if it was a nice day. I told her to check the paper." He nudged Woody Bodega and barked out a laugh. "But for really subjugated, in my opinion, you've got to cross the big pond. Pinckney Outka, father of Oksana. Whew! Never lifted a finger in his life except to slam his bedroom door shut when company came over. Absolutely crackers. The story goes that his wife poisoned him by running his toothbrush around the inside of a toilet bowl. A month after she went to jail, the three kids each inherited two million pounds. Oksana was a coke addict by the end of that *week,* and the two sons instantly became screaming faggots and moved to Europe."

"Cocaine, is that so?" Mrs. Bodega frowned. "What is it about that awful drug?"

Nelson closed his eyes and nodded profoundly. "It's the scourge of our nation, Jeri."

"Come on now," Kak insisted, and relieved her husband of his drink. "I think you're going a little off the deep end tonight, honey. Don't y'all go away, we'll be right back."

You could have emptied a ton of broken glass into the silence Nelson and Kak left behind. I stared after them as they moved down the central gallery and into the dining room, then turned to smile at the Bodegas, who were looking intently at me. Where the hell was Marty, if these people were supposed to be his special clients?

"So," I said, "have you got your hearts set on some roses?"

"We have," Mrs. Bodega said. "I love the ones that show their habit as well as their shape."

"Will you be framing them with us?"

"Jeri does her own framing," Mr. Bodega said, and added, with a slight note of resignation, "She's artistically inclined."

At that moment a loud shriek came from the direction of the kitchen. It sounded like Yolanda, the maid. All conversation stopped.

"What in the world?" Mrs. Bodega said.

"Probably an hors d'oeuvre tray," I said. "Let me go check."

I strolled casually to the end of the gallery and along the entry hall, then scrambled around to the front kitchen entrance once I was out of sight of the guests. Ruth, coming in the opposite direction through the dining-room door, met me near the dishwasher. Nelson and Kak were nowhere in sight.

"Fred, get out there and save him!" Ruth said.

I grabbed a spatula and made several threatening gestures with it. "Who? Out where?"

"This is serious! Nelson's got a chain saw!"

"Nelson's got a chain saw and you want me to go out in the dark after him?"

"All right, all right." She pulled a flashlight from under Kak's butcher-block table. "We'll both go."

Ruth and I ran along the west side of Delapompe, keeping close to the taller trees and parked cars. The cloudy suburban night swallowed Ruth's tiny flashlight beam as it played over the damp ground. Rounding the south side of the château, we heard something like a buzz, or the echo of one. It sounded illogically distant. Ruth stopped and listened intently for a moment.

"He's on the other side, near the dining room!"

"It sounds like he's—"

"Oh, my God."

We ran and stumbled and fell and ran again, skidded over the flagstoned patio, then edged around the back of the house and stopped in our tracks. Warm yellow light was flooding out of the dining-room bay, and each windowpane, like some Austrian Christmas decoration, was filled with a gazing face. There in the footlights of his own makeshift stage, chain saw buzzing, Nelson was making short work of a forty-foot red oak that showered leaves and twigs onto his thinning blond hair and the exposed roll of fat between his blue cotton sweater and his sagging cords. As we advanced out of the darkness I recognized faces in the windows: here was Whitney with the Schochs, there was Marty with the Bodegas, and there was our L.A. gallery director Jim Damon with two clients who'd come all the way from Beverly Hills. The buzzing sound veered off now, the oak began a shuddering, reluctant descent toward the ground, and the crowd inside, whose faces were set in something like envy, reacted as one.

They applauded. Without a word, Nelson held the chain saw aloft in both hands and stepped back to survey the effect. As the oak crashed down into the underbrush, I leaned back against the house and tried to make sense of it all. Nelson's trees were his babies. He'd drive from New York to Boston at 110 mph if his groundskeeper called to say that one of his trees was sick or dying, yet here I'd just witnessed him destroying a prize specimen over an argument with his wife. I don't know that anyone else took note of this fact, but when Nelson began to destroy what was dearest to him we were on the verge of some serious trouble.

As Ruth and I turned back toward the kitchen she put her hand on my arm and caught her breath.

"It pains me to admit this," she said, "but I never liked that tree there myself."

## 34. Albrights in History

ere." I held out a steaming black mug as Nelson's sweaty face loomed in the mudroom light. He licked his lips tentatively and spat several small twigs into the bushes behind him.

"What's this?"

"A hot toddy."

He nodded and drank deeply. "What'd you tell them?"

"That Kak needed more firewood."

Nelson sighed and looked out into the darkness. "I was just thinking about an eighteenth-century ancestor of mine . . . a Tory named Accepted Albright. The story goes that Accepted was drinking one night at a tavern up in New Brunswick, and another man called him a coward. So Accepted walked right out and chopped down the tamarack tree in front of the tavern. First one he ever felled in his life."

I shivered in the late spring chill. "That's excellent."

"Tree fell right on top of him," Nelson said. "Killed him instantly." He glanced into the mudroom and beyond it to the kitchen. "Denny returned his Catlin portfolio tonight."

This news went through me like bad coffee. "I knew it was something," I said. "That's rough."

"The interesting point is why." Nelson's hard stare bore into me. "Do you know *why* he might have returned it?"

I shook my head, terrified that I'd botched part of the sale, and Nelson inhaled dramatically. "Because that British bag of shit offered Denny a Catlin portfolio, two original letters, and a *sketch* for $70,000."

My eyes widened in surprise. "Where did Oksana come up with material like that?"

"From the Christie's sale you covered in my office," Nelson snapped. "Remember, when Choix stole the fax? Were you in an alcoholic haze that day too?"

I ignored this dig and tried to make sense of the news. "Wait; she bought that lot back in October for $70,000 and just sold it at cost to Denny? Why would she do that?"

"I almost murdered him when he told me," Nelson said calmly. "He was jabbering away about expanding his breadth in Catlin, how much Jenny loved the French mat on the sketch at Oksana's shop, all the excuses you hear from a pussy-whipped husband, and I thought, 'My God, if he doesn't shut up in ten seconds I am going to reach over, take his throat in my hands, and squeeze the life out of him. It would be the easiest thing in the world.' Do you know how close I came to *doing* that?"

I glanced out into the (remaining) trees in the yard. "Do I want to know?"

He handed back the mug and stepped past me into Delapompe. "No, Fred, you probably don't."

The mudroom door slammed and I stood alone for a moment. Nelson would put a good face on things for the rest of the evening like the consummate salesman he was, but there was no denying the fact that Denny's decision to return the Catlin for a refund had just eliminated any profit we might make on the Redouté deal.

Months later, I would look back on this moonless evening and see it as a pivotal point, the one at which Nelson's control over the clients and art and possessions he loved began to unravel. Ironically, it was the same evening my fortunes really started to take off. Within an hour of returning to the party, I'd sold another $24,000 worth of Redouté prints.

## 35. Moving Sidewalk Sale

The first annual Albright Galleries Redouté Public Offering went off without a hitch, even after Nelson brought out a stopwatch during round four and offered free French mats to anyone who made their remaining picks from the walls in thirty seconds or less. Jenny D'Amico said that Oksana Outka never made you rush, and I thought I'd have to remove her from the room, but Jeri Bodega came to the rescue by announcing that it always took a long time to choose at her shop because everything was equally vulgar. Nelson kissed the tops of her pumps then, and everyone laughed and received a free 23-karat gold bevel with their framing order, except the D'Amicos, who were to be given a 14-karat gold bevel as a lesson to them for mentioning Oksana's name.

The next day Nelson called from his car as I was leaving the gallery. I expected we would discuss a bonus for my work on the Redouté offering, or at the very least warm congratulations.

"Fred, what's going on?" he barked.

"I just sold three McKenney & Hall Indians for twenty-two hundred," I said. "How about you?"

"Me?" he said dramatically. "Jesus, haven't you heard? The landlord is throwing us out of the New York building on a zoning technicality. He sold the place right out from under me. I just spent a million and a half dollars for a new space at Seventieth and Madison."

I dropped into the chair at the front desk. "Why would he throw you out?"

"Because the landlord got a little call from a certain British friend of ours who said I'm not allowed to run a retail gallery in the building, that's why. She got me when my back was turned. Disguised herself and went snooping around with her lawyer while we were doing the Redouté offering. Fuck!"

"Can you really afford a million and a half?" I asked delicately.

"Would you suggest I relocate to the Lower East Side?" he snapped. "Of course I can't afford it! I'm going insane just thinking about it."

"Hey, we'll be okay," I said. "Boston's sales will be great this month. We don't have to stoop to Oksana's level."


This, at least, was my sentiment until I realized we were going to be moving the New York gallery all those blocks *ourselves*. By ten the next morning I'd lost count of the number of hot lead enemas Oksana had taken in my mental torture chamber. Marty, my moving partner, was running a close second.

"You idiot, look out!"

I snapped back to where I was—the corner of Madison Avenue and Seventy-second Street—and lifted my leg over a small tricycle. The wall-sized map in my hands shuddered in its Plexiglas glazing. Marty glared from the other end of the map, which appeared to be half a block away. For someone who commented so much on his great strength, he didn't appear to do much heavy lifting.

"Aren't you awake yet?" he snapped.

"I'm dandy," I said. "Let's go."

We continued down Madison toward Seventy-first Street, being more or less followed by a youngish, affluent blond couple in aviator sunglasses and a photographer who emerged from behind an antique car parked at a Ralph Lauren store to take shots of us. The photographer, who wore a black cape that billowed to her knees, appeared to be lost on the way to some Fall/Winter fashion showing.

"May I ask you what you're doing?" she said as she caught up.

I called whoa to Marty and paused. "We're relocating."

"Really? I'm from the *Times*."

"In that case we've been evicted," Marty said.

I glanced down the street and saw Nelson and Ruth approaching with some bulging gallery bags. "Quote only that man with the pizza stain on his shirt," I said.

"Fred," Nelson called, his face set in a pugnacious frown, "need you. Ruth, take over his end."

It was during Ruth's replacement of me that I observed the preppy couple in the aviator sunglasses trying to slip across the street unnoticed. Nelson's sudden grin made it clear that he'd recognized them.

"Tim!" he shouted. "Tim Preucel! And Delia! How are you both? What are you doing here?"

"Oh. We live here now," the man said quietly.

"I thought you were up at Dark Harbor," Nelson said happily. "Hey, Marty," he said, "this is Tim Preucel. An old buddy from prep school."

I looked on with amusement as strained introductions were made. Despite his Mayflower heritage, Nelson really was the wealthy snob's worst nightmare. He spoke on equal terms with secretaries and millionaire dowagers. He regularly burst out of The Country Club's locker room naked with soapsuds stinging his eyes to shout, "I spend ten thousand bucks a year for a fucking membership and you can't supply fresh towels?" Worst of all, he pitched fine art with the dogged persistence of a used car salesman. I think people were so bothered by him because he represented life lived at a level they didn't have the guts (or scrambled genes) to attempt. When Nelson arrived at your party, it was even money whether he was going to charm every guest or poop in the punchbowl.

"So, Nelson," Tim Preucel was saying, "you're doing some aggressive promotion these days."

"Or did that map fall off the back of a truck?" Mrs. Preucel added.

"Jesus Christ, Delia, are you kidding?" my boss said in awe. "This is an Arrowsmith!" Nelson repositioned Marty and Ruth in front of a wrought-iron tree planter near the curb and pointed at the map's black and white mountain ranges and undecided state boundaries. "I didn't even know I still *had* one of these! This guy cornered the Hudson Bay Company monopoly on mapping America for the British. Here, Fred, hold it a little higher. The most important American map of its day, my friends *And* it's a first edition, 1796. You want Manifest Destiny on paper, you got it."

"I knew we were missing something when we left the house," Mrs. Preucel said drolly.

"It's also backed with the original linen," I added. I knew this because the description tag had been pressed against my eyeballs on the way through the doors of the old building.

Mr. Preucel stepped forward and lifted his shades. "You said all this about our Melish map too, Nelson."

Nelson extended his hands, palms up. "Hey, is there no room in the world for two cartographical masterpieces?"

"What's the damage?"

"Ninety-five hundred," Nelson said. "But if you take it off my hands now I'll make it seventy-five."

Mr. Preucel's bleached, even teeth flashed in the sun. "Does that include delivery? We're all the way down on Sixty-third."

"Are you kidding? We'd carry it to Long Island City for you, Tim." Nelson beamed. The old school friends never let you down.

"Terrific," the *Times* photographer said. "I'll need everyone's name."

"Come look at our new space," Nelson continued. "My wife Kak is working on it. I'll get you an invitation to the opening."

"Where is it?" Mrs. Preucel said.

"Seventieth and Madison," Nelson said proudly. "Second floor."

"Second floor?" Mr. Preucel feigned shock. "In that case I'll give you six thousand."

"Tim is right," the photographer said. "Second floor is retail Siberia. Is that Preucel with an -eu?"

"Who is this woman?" Nelson barked at Ruth.

Ruth, who had no idea, said, "We will have street-level display windows."

"My Boston codirector, Fred Layton, will put together your invoice," Nelson said to the Preucels. "And Ruth and Marty here will deliver the map to your house instantly. Pleasure to do business with you, guy. We'll have to get together."

"Let's," Mr. Preucel said blandly. "Real soon."

"Hold on," Marty said. I could see he was fuming that Nelson had chosen me to write the invoice. "What's the commission split on this?"

"Two for you, two for Fred," Nelson said quickly. "Are we off?"

"I think I deserve three," I said. "I had the Atlantic Ocean and all that heavy stuff on my side."

"Drop dead," Marty said under his breath.

"I'm not carrying it fifteen blocks if they're both getting two percent," Ruth announced.

"Quiet!" Nelson snapped. "You'll all get two percent. Now go."

"Still hiring the hungry ones," Mr. Preucel said, with a slight nod of admiration. "I wish my employees had that kind of spirit."

Ruth winked at me and she and Marty proceeded at a stately pace downtown.

## 36. The Done Deal

The strains of Nelson's new mortgage began to show hours after the nearly deserted New York gallery reopening party in June (the *Times* photographer was right; second-floor spaces really were retail Siberia). I was fishing for my keys outside the Newbury

Street gallery one morning when Nelson barreled up on the other side and pinned me in the vestibule. He had his car keys in one hand and a blank company check in the other.

"Fred," he shouted, "fill this out and give it to the air conditioner guy. I'm picking up a couple at the airport with a Cassatt sketch to sell."

I sighed with relief now that I knew I wasn't about to be mugged. "So we're dealing in Cassatt now?"

"Once I get this baby reframed we'll send out a letter to the entire mailing list," he said excitedly. "Better yet, we'll offer it directly to the paintings dealers! All those shitheads on Madison Avenue are going to drool."

Nelson thrust the blank check into my hand and ran to his car. At that point I knew better than to ask whether he'd actually seen the sketch.

Nelson returned from the airport an hour later with the Mullers, a middle-aged couple who'd flown in from Berlin with their Cassatt. Judging by the dazed looks on their faces, Nelson had examined the sketch, placed several calls to confirm its provenance, and attempted to negotiate a selling price during the drive from Logan. The group retired to Whitney's office, from which Whitney was promptly ejected.

"Fred," Nelson bellowed, "two beakers of club soda with lime for the Mullers, please." Then he shut the door.

When I returned from the deli with the refreshments a few minutes later, Mr. Muller was sitting on Whitney's couch rubbing his right eye and looking mildly exasperated. His wife clutched a small black portfolio close to her chest. Smart lady.

"My *name* is Nelson Albright," Nelson was saying, as he paced the office with his hands folded. "I'm known around the world for my expertise. I do thirty million dollars of business a year."

"I do not disagree," Mr. Muller said in a halting accent. "That is one reason why first we chose you to look at the Cassatt, *nicht?* But you must understand, a retainer check is merely procedure."

"Forty thousand dollars in a cashier's check," Mrs. Muller said icily. "We cannot leave it here otherwise."

"I can write you that check a hundred times over," Nelson said with annoyance. "What I'm saying is, I can sell the sketch this afternoon and we won't even *need* the middle step. I am unable to see your problem with this. I'm only asking to have it on approval for two or three days."

"If you can sell it this afternoon, why do you need the three days?" Mrs. Muller countered.

I finished arranging the glasses and said, "Anything else, Nelson?"

"No!" he said abruptly. "Hold my calls."

"Fine."

I sat down at my desk in the main gallery and looked through client cards for Cassatt lovers. In the meantime the doorbell rang and I walked out to the front gallery.

It was the large, muscular air conditioner repairman. He looked less than pleased, and was also rubbing his right eye. "The bank wouldn't let me cash this check you gave me," he said. "They said the account is overdrawn. I'm not going to leave until I get my money."

"That's terrific," I said, "but you'll have to talk to Mr. Albright. He'll be available shortly if you'd like to wait."

"I ain't waiting for nobody," the man said, and waved the check in my face. "I'm seeing him right now. I got appointments too."

At that moment Nelson burst through the French doors, car keys in hand.

"Keep the Mullers entertained," he ordered. "I've got to call the bank."

"I've got the number right here," I said.

"I need a little privacy!" he shouted back. "These fucking Krauts want to skin me alive before I can even take a photograph."

"Hey, what about my seventy-five bucks?" the repairman said.

Nelson slammed the front door shut behind him. "You might as well sit," I told the repairman, "unless you want to take it in trade."

Five minutes later Nelson returned, a forced smirk on his face. He sped through the reception area without a word. The air conditioner man followed Nelson, and I followed the air conditioner man. I cut him off at my desk as Nelson rolled back in to the Mullers.

"Look, buddy, just give him a few seconds," I said.

"I give him one more minute," the repairman fumed. "This is complete bullshit."

"It's a done deal!" Nelson was announcing. He pushed Whitney's door half shut. "One of my biggest clients, lives right outside Boston, wants to look at it. We're all set."

"Excellent," Mrs. Muller said. She stood. "We will take the check, then."

A long moment of silence followed. Nelson broke it.

"Um, what check is that?"

"The retainer check," Mr. Muller said. "The check we've been talking about."

"Wait, I *told* you," Nelson said. He ran both hands through his hair and exhaled slowly. "My name is Nelson Albright, my name is as good as cash."

"The check, or no sketch," Mrs. Muller retorted. "You are treating us like inexperienced children."

"All right," Nelson broke in quietly. "That's enough. I'm getting angry."

I stepped closer to the door, saw Nelson's face—the same blank stare he wore when telling me of his desire to strangle Denny D'Amico—and stepped back.

"We respect your position," Mr. Muller said, "but—"

"I said enough," he whispered. "Don't say another word, I'm warning you!"

"We'd better go out to the reception area," I told the air conditioner man. "This may get ugly."

The air conditioner man, who was no fool, followed me through the main gallery.

*"Bitte, Herr Albright,"* Mrs. Muller began. "You must learn to channel your energies."

"I said don't say another word!" Nelson screamed. I got the repairman out to the front gallery and closed the French doors. Given the sound of what followed, one of the Mullers foolishly decided to keep talking. You could practically feel the front display window shaking in its frame. The air conditioner man stared through the doors, then looked back at me.

"Do you shoot that fuckin' guy out of a cannon every morning or what?"

"Let's have a look upstairs," I said, as Nelson's eruption continued. "Maybe there's something in petty cash." I reminded myself as we climbed the stairs to save a few dollars for the Mullers, who would probably be taking a taxi back to the airport.

About an hour after the Mullers and the repairmen were gone, Nelson called me in to see him. No one had yet dared to approach Whitney's office door.

"Sit," he said. His face was pale but his voice was unusually even. "You remember Helen Wheeler?"

I thought of her run-over Audubon hawk and blanched. "Of course. I've been offering her something in the mail every two weeks. It's always in the five to twenty-thousand-dollar range, like you said."

"Twenty grand is pocket change for Helen Wheeler," he shot back. "Oksana Outka just did three rooms for her in Palm Beach: two hundred thousand bucks. We're only picking up the change people like her leave on the table. Plus the address Helen Wheeler gave you is her post office box in Florida. She spends much more time in Charlotte at a private estate. Helen Wheeler *herself* is harder to reach than Bunny Mellon. But I think we may have an in here. I think we have just wedged our foot into her door.

"Have a look at this." He handed me a note written in longhand on white letter paper. It read:

*Dear Mr. Albright—*

*Thank you very much for your invitation to the New York gallery opening. I would have loved to come, but my curator and I are*

*mad about finishing a small chapel on my Charlotte property by
the end of the summer. Give my best to Fred Layton.*

> *Wishing you well,*
> *Helen Wheeler*

"She ought to be writing to me," I said, and handed back the
note.

"That's right, except I threw out your invitation and sent one
myself," Nelson said. "But that's good thinking!"

He dropped the note on Whitney's desk and dug in his left
ear. "You can get tickets from Bish. You're on a three-thirty flight."

"To?"

"To Charlotte!" he said, his eyes bugging out. "For Christ's
sake, haven't you been listening? Just look at that letter—Helen
Wheeler obviously wants to do business with us again. You're going
to bring every religious and botanical print above three thousand
dollars and fill that chapel before Oksana or some other shyster
gets their piggy little fingers in the pie. If I don't get forty grand in
here by the end of the week I'm not going to make payroll this
month. We have begun our descent, *comprende?* Please return to
your seat and ensure your tray table is in its upright and locked
position so you can lean down and kiss your ass goodbye. Unless
you help us, Fred. You're the man. Get out there and pump it up!"

I picked up Helen's letter and left the room without another
word. It didn't occur to me until I arrived at the airport that I
should probably call Helen Wheeler and let her know I was coming.

# 37. Going to the Chapel

enna Spaight, Mrs. Wheeler's short, busty, twenty-eight-year-old curator, drove her red German convertible the same way Nelson broke the spine of a color-plate book—with the assured, controlled savagery of a master. Her blond hair danced along the top of her bucket seat as we wove through traffic on the freeway outside Charlotte. An enormous series of billboards whipped past on my right:

**FAITH?**

**HOPE?**

**CHARITY?**

**First Assembly Free Baptist Has It All**
**And Right Next Door, Freddy Dent's Living Will Texaco**
**With Award-Winning Restrooms!**

"Home at last," I said under my breath.

"We were quite surprised to hear you were coming so suddenly," Jenna said. "I hope you don't mind waiting until tomorrow morning to see Helen."

"Not at all," I assured her. "I needed to get out of Boston anyway."

"Well, you must have sensed how desperate we were getting. We've got to find some suitable religious material for our current project. On a large scale, the way we do things around here."

"You're in luck," I said, "I've brought lots along. Are you considering botanicals, too?"

"Flowers we've got enough of," Jenna said dryly. "Take a walk through Mrs. Wheeler's front yard and you'll be covered in cherry blossoms before you can say boo, beans, or peanuts. What we've got to finish up is that chapel. On the first of August we're looking to dedicate it to the memory of Helen's husband."

"Ah. Was Mr. Wheeler also a collector?"

Jenna drove on for a quarter of a mile, almost speaking at several junctures, then said flatly: "God rest his soul, Mr. Layton, but I'll never know what was going through Billy Wheeler's mind the last years of his life."

"How do you mean?"

She glanced over. "For example. For a while he used to fly us out to art shows in Dallas every month. New cowboy art. We'd walk into this big gallery like an airplane hangar and there'd be fifty paintings on the walls: ropin', bustin', guttin' a wild boar, lots of hills. Lots of *orange* hills. Anyhow, every painting had a box in front of it. You put your name on a little card and put it in the box if you wanted to place a bid. At eleven o'clock the impresario took a stroll around and picked a card out of the first box. If your name was on it, you had sixty seconds to pay your $300,000 or whatever. In full, I kid you not. When it was over we'd all have repechage facials and lunch."

I smiled optimistically. "There was the facial, at least."

As we hit open road Jenna pushed a button near her stick shift that said POWER. The broken center line bled into solidity and I felt a new fontanel opening in my skull.

"It wasn't ever a very good facial," she yelled above the wind. "I just thank the Lord to be working for Helen now. She's always got a quilt in the loom, and we're finally making some important acquisitions for her collection. God knows we'll never sell those orange hills."

I thought of Columbus's powdered bones and the tire-ribbed

Audubon and rubbed my face to hide the pained expression. That *Louisiana Hawk* still pecked out my liver in guilt-ridden daydreams on a regular basis. "That's super," I said. "I'm glad for you."

"And I'm glad you're here." Jenna took off her sunglasses and downshifted, as if fully aware of me for the first time. "We're really in no rush, Mr. Layton: why don't you tell me a little bit about yourself?"

## 38. Town Without Putti

I woke the next morning covered in magnolia petals and stared up into a lightening blue sky. Then I shivered and rose off the damp grass to my haunches before the deep philosophy of sleep could argue me back down again. The guesthouse off the Wheeler chapel, where I'd planned to sleep, lay somewhere behind me. According to my watch, I had eighteen and a half minutes before Helen Wheeler arrived at the chapel to look at large religious prints. As I hugged myself I could smell Jenna Spaight's perfume still on my skin, and now I recalled the party in Charlotte the night before with the five men dressed as nuns, the dartboard propped against the stomach of the cop who'd passed out on a piece of patio furniture, the young white women in their mother's hand-me-down gowns nervously circling a table of catered seafood while Italian disco blasted out of a stereo, and last but not least my tree-scaling midnight rescue of Pimples, the hostess's cat. I also recalled going back to Jenna's rooms on the Wheeler estate and at some point viewing her collection of photos of HRM the Queen Mum caught picking her nose in public, photos that Jenna clipped from Mrs. Wheeler's royalty fanzines on slow days.

Before I got all the way to a stand my head was spinning with numbers. Besides the number of copies of "Raphael's Bible" produced in Rome, which I'd forgotten, there was the number of Absolut gimlets I'd consumed with Jenna Spaight in her bedroom; the number of times Jenna had dive-bombed me out of sheer stir-craziness at living and working on this vast and nearly empty property with only a grounds crew to talk to; even the number of times I'd had to repeat my story of the wrinkle in the airbag that didn't inflate in the car accident, which rendered me unable to have an erection until I was at least thirty.

Five, I knew, was a very important number: the sale wouldn't take more than five minutes, according to Jenna, because in her own homes Helen Wheeler's opinion was instant and unswerving. I stumbled toward the guesthouse in the first rays of morning sunlight and hoped Helen would be unswerving enough for both of us.

Helen surprised me from behind as I stood in the dim vestibule of the chapel. It was some sort of Tudor re-creation with timber-beam ceilings, from which two cast-iron chandeliers hung. The altar and cross looked like they'd been raided from an appropriately important English site, circa 1600.

"Fred!" she exclaimed.

"Helen," I said. Just seeing her kind, lively eyes made my hangover seem inconsequential. She removed a pair of blackened gardening gloves, her face ruddy with exertion.

"A nice cold handshake to you," she said. "I've just been looking in on my tomato plants before I get on the plane to New York. Never enough hours."

"No."

"Have you had a chance to see your old stomping grounds again?"

"This evening," I said. "I've got an aunt and uncle about fifteen miles from here."

"Well, I hope you let one of the groundspeople give you a lift. This is an awfully hard place to try to find, even for a local driver."

"I'm sure Jenna will be happy to oblige," I said. "Anyhow, I think we can make this short and sweet for you. I've got an easel and some samples all ready to go."

"Wonderful. But hang on now, before I forget." Helen turned and tossed her gardening gloves out into the bright morning, then joined me and led the way into the chapel. "If you don't mind, Fred, I've set out a new book for you up at the house. I just bought it this past weekend. It's by Edward Lear, the children's book illustrator. Gorgeous big plates of parrots."

"The *Family of Psittacidae?*" I said. "That's an amazing book."

She patted my shoulder and whispered, "My goodness, it better be. I paid $200,000 for it."

I thought for a second, shrugged. "These days you never know. I wouldn't be shocked at all if a copy in perfect condition brought that much. Did it have the original paper covers for all the subscriber parts bound in or something?"

Helen looked worried for a moment. "No, I shouldn't think so. In fact, I laid it out for you because it needs some restoration work. Your people can remove all those marks and spots and so on, isn't that right?"

"Absolutely," I said. "I'll take it back to Boston and get you an estimate."

"You appear troubled," she said. "Are you sure you can take it back?"

"No, no, it's not that," I said. "It's just . . . I have to say, Helen: I can't imagine who would charge so much for a Lear *Parrots* that wasn't obscenely clean."

"Well, she's right here, actually. She's going to look over the selections you brought."

"You got it through Jenna?" I asked, though I already knew that the woman in the front pew was too tall to be Jenna.

"No, Jenna's not feeling quite up to snuff today. Oksana, I'd like you to meet Fred Layton. Fred came all the way from Boston to show us some images."

Oksana turned in her pew. When she recognized me her half-glasses slipped from her nose into her bosom.

"Oh, I say," she said cheerily. "How super, Helen. Yes, I've met Mr. Layton before. He works with Nelson Albright, doesn't he?"

"He does indeed. Well, that's great," Helen said. "Although I'm never surprised when two art dealers have known each other since Jesus was a child."

Oksana and I forewent a handshake as Helen sat down in the opposite front pew. I could definitely feel my hangover coming back.

"Are you working on the decoration of the chapel?" I said.

Oksana smiled slowly, not meeting my eyes, and said to Helen, "I noticed Mr. Layton has only one case of prints. Not quite bringing the boat out if he's come all the way from Boston."

Helen laughed and settled into her seat. "For heaven's sake, Oksana, let's at least see what he's got."

I smiled at Oksana. "I think I've skimmed off the best ones. This won't take long."

"No. I don't suppose it will," Oksana said breezily. She turned to the easel I'd set up with titanic condescension and added, under her breath, "Little sod."


I stood at the altar beside the first engraving—a blue, red, and black classical pilaster about three feet high, studded with tiny inset views colored in opaque gouache—and deliberately directed my comments at Helen.

"To give you a little background," I began, "these images came about because, in 1519, Raphael was working directly for Pope Leo X, Giovanni de Medici, on his last great commission—"

"Helen," Oksana cut in, "what do you say we skip the frilly bits: do you like this one or not?"

"I'm not sure, but I am intrigued," Helen said. "What were you saying, Fred?"

"About the frescoes," I began again; "these frescoes were to be the major testament of Raphael's life, a marriage of the mythical and the biblical that would literally sit within the walls of the private galleries at the Vatican. Raphael worked for nearly a thousand days sketching and applying color, setting Old Testament tales next to views of Athens, juxtaposing putti from the peristyle walls at Herculaneum with views of Palestine. It was a brilliant synthesis of forms."

Oksana put on her half-glasses and lifted an imperious finger. "Just a moment. Is he saying these are frescoes? I do beg to differ."

"No, that's absolutely not what I'm saying," I said firmly, and watched Oksana's painted-in eyebrows jump with facetious expectation. "This is a print. What we see here is one of the twelve double-page pilaster panels that Giovani Volpasto and Giovanni Ottaviani engraved, printed, and colored by hand with gouache and watercolor, *after* Raphael's work. The print project ran in Rome for six years, between 1772 and 1778. They called it 'Raphael's Bible.' Given these dates of production, you shouldn't be surprised to see fragments worked in from the new archaeological excavations then under way at Pompeii."

"My goodness, I do see," Helen Wheeler said, her voice echoing airily in the chapel. She removed her Cadillac-fin glasses and let them hang around her neck next to her beloved Columbus pendant. "You've done your homework, Fred. I could hardly take all that in."

"He's quite the little scholar," Oksana said. She slipped out of her pew in the cool, mildewy air, picked up one of the oversized, rectangular prints, and stood behind it. She walked it to the chapel's first diamond-shaped window and held it high.

"Helen, can you really envision eight or ten of these on each side, matted and framed up?"

"What, that? I sure can't," Helen said at once.

"Well, you're jolly good there," Oksana said, and made a sound of disparaging agreement that recalled a whale clearing its blowhole.

"Oh." I paused as I bent to remove another pilaster print from my case. "You can't?"

Helen shook her head. "I've got my doubts about those anatomically correct putti running around. My minister and his wife haven't been able to have children, and my husband would never rest in peace thinking I'd put up naked putti in his name, if you see what I mean. Not to mention what that woman in the corner is doing with the swan."

"Yes, well," Oksana said brightly. "Hard cheese for Fred, I suppose. Better luck next trip."

"Hang on a moment, Helen." I dropped to my knees quickly and began rifling through the case. Yes, no, no, no . . . I knew there was a match for the one I held somewhere. If Marty had removed it from the case and stashed it in his Hold drawer I would skin him alive and mount his head on a pike in the middle of the Public Garden. Ah, there it was! I pulled free a pair of the Raphael pilasters based solely on botanical and architectural themes and held them up. "What about these two?"

Helen stood and approached the pair of prints. "Oh, my land," she said. "Oksana, look at these two."

"If you can imagine them with about two and a half inches of oyster silk matting and a two-inch Venetian molding," I said, "you'll really get the effect."

Oksana marched over from the chapel window, her shoes clicking sharply on the stone floor. "How in the world is she supposed to imagine the effect if you haven't brought any samples?"

"As a matter of fact, I have," I said. I laid the two prints on the altar steps, grabbed several mat and molding samples from my case, and framed up three corners. "How do you like this look?"

"I don't like it," Helen said. "I *love* it! Now how did you know that oyster is my favorite shade?"

"I went over all the important points with Jenna," I said. "Naturally."

"Venetian gold-leaf molding with a silk-wrapped mat," Oksana said. She shook her dyed red hair doubtfully. "Cost you the earth, I suppose."

"Quality always costs," I said, "and it's certainly not like the cheap junk mats you see some people cranking out these days. Of course, there would be a twenty percent decorator discount. That's what you're here for, I suppose."

The look on Oksana's face at that moment made me feel grateful that British citizens couldn't legally bear firearms. Helen said slyly, "You know, Oksana, I'm sure I can get a later flight to New York. Let's pick out a few more pairs. Oh my, this is going to be marvelous fun."

Two hours later I was packing my case and Helen's stupendously overpriced Lear *Parrots* volume into the trunk of Jenna's car when a door opened in the main house and Oksana emerged. She walked stiffly up to the bottle-green Jaguar beside me and got in with an overnighter bag. As Helen came down the walk with Jenna at her side, Oksana applied her huge sunglasses, started her car, and revved the engine. I smiled to myself and was about to climb into Jenna's passenger seat when the driver's-side window in the Jaguar descended. The fact that Oksana actually looked in my general direction was enough of a surprise that I met her tinted eyes as well.

"Nelson, you know, never makes good on his promises," she began in a low voice. "He burns out his people in a matter of months. Whatever you think now, you're on the same road."

"Oh, really?" I said, as if this were not a news flash. "I've lasted nearly a year already. I guess that makes me different."

"You are different, a bit," Oksana said, more to herself than to me. "Rather unlike the cast of ninnies he's usually got running about. Ah well." She elevated her window halfway and added, "Ought to be working for me, I suppose. You'd certainly be taking home a few more pennies from this deal than you will be with Nelson."

I glanced up at the walk in surprise. Helen and Jenna were nearly upon us. Was Oksana Outka offering me a job? Against my better judgment, I was thrilled.

"I'm all set for now," I said, "but if I change my mind I'll let you know."

"Before he uses you all up, I hope," she said. "That's Nelson's way, you know."

I was about to respond to this jab, for my own sake if not for Nelson's, but Oksana's window lifted shut and from that point on she acted as if I didn't exist. All the way out to my aunt and uncle's place in Jenna's car, however, I felt wonderfully sure that I did.

## 39. Misspellings

My Aunt Agnes and Uncle Bill lived a few miles outside a town called Pineville near the South Carolina border. A ring of whispering pines stood between their trailer and the highway, while a crumbling brick firing house a farmer once used to blanch peanuts defined the back edge of the property. A cherry tree grew near the tiny attached porch for extra shade.

"Look at you," Agnes exclaimed at the kitchen sink, as I

backed in through the screen door laden with shopping bags. "Who is this strapping young man, Bill? He must be taking them thyroids."

"Steroids," I laughed. "And I don't."

"A little resemblance to my brother Jack, I think." Bill worked himself out of his recliner and strangled my hand with slow pride. He was a big, red-faced German-Scottish man who'd inherited all the sternness of both races. Yet without the formal education and academic airs of my father—that secretive, superior look that made you think he was working on the atomic bomb rather than another seminar paper on Egyptian papyrus production—Bill seemed to walk forth from an early black and white photograph on some farmhouse mantel. Agnes had obviously twisted his arm to get him to put on his tartan tie. She was in her church dress and jacket set with the blue orchids. I grinned at her. She had a farmer's tan from the edge of her neck to the top of her bust, and was still combing her permanent down into a fringe bang above her eyebrows, thereby uncovering a bald spot not unlike the landing pattern produced by a helicopter touching down in loose brush. Like most of my Southern relatives over fifty, she was approximately spherical in shape and so consistently good-natured it boggled my mind. She squeezed my cheeks as she kissed me.

"What's in the box, Fred?"

"It's a wok to cook dinner," I said. "You can plant something in it afterward."

"Did you bring my cigarettes?" Bill said.

Agnes tisked. "I should have handed the phone to this old cuss, he could've placed an order."

"I've got them," I said. "And a case of beer in my trunk."

"You appear to be strangling in that tie," Bill said.

I popped the top button of my shirt. "So do you, old man. Let's have a brew."

I tossed some chicken, peppers, and cashews in the wok and served it over couscous, which Bill picked at suspiciously. Meanwhile I inhaled half a dozen of Agnes's exquisite biscuits, the ones for which she no longer needed a recipe and measured out the ingredients by hand. Neither my aunt nor my uncle was in the least bit bothered that the guest brought the groceries, certainly not when the guest was Fred Layton, the two-year freeloader who'd once borrowed their psychic neighbor Madame Lorraine's red neon hand and set up shop in a bar until he'd raised enough cash for the senior high trip to Disneyland. Our talk came slowly, a combination of thawing familiarity after a long separation and the leisurely speaking pace Agnes and Bill preferred.

"You still selling that paper?" Bill asked, as he cleared his plate.

"I sold eight copperplate engravings today," I said. "From Rome, eighteenth century."

"I know some Italian," Agnes said. She spoke a beautiful sentence of about a dozen words.

"What in the world does that mean?" Bill said. "I never heard that before."

"It means 'Please do not throw solid objects out the windows of the train.' I learned it when I was over in Padua with Father O'Neill, the winter of '81."

"How was the winter down here?" I asked.

"Not bad at all," Agnes said. "You know the schools, though, one flake on the ground and they close down. I said, 'Why don't y'all wait and see if it's gonna *do* something?' Back in October, Jane Geena brought over a Micmac Indian woman who was passing through with some Pentecostalists from Nova Scotia. She said the bee built its nest close to the ground and we were gonna have an open winter."

"As we did," Bill added. "Better than the Farmer's Almanac."

"You still going to Mass, Fred?" Agnes asked.

"You bet," I said, and winked at Bill. "Nine o'clock at St. Mattress of the Bedsprings."

"How many girlfriends you got now?" Bill said. "You lose count?"

"Well, let me see," I said, pretending to add them up as a familiar queasiness rushed through my chest. I looked across the room and noticed that my junior prom picture from Princeton still held a place of honor atop the television. There stood Bridget and I, filled to the gills, two big sets of grinning teeth in formal attire. "Bridget," I said, for lack of anything better. "She's a sweetheart."

"Something in her recalls your mother, everyone says so." Agnes rose to clear the dishes. "Now how long has it been since you've visited?"

I counted, and color rose to my face. "You came up for graduation, so I guess . . . three years."

"Don't you worry about seeing us old birds," Bill said. "We understand you've got to make your way in the world. It's not getting any easier."

"Sometimes it's hard and nothing else," Agnes echoed.

"Still," I said after a moment, "I should be more responsible. You're really all I've got."

Bill lit a cigarette and slipped the package into his breast pocket. "You going back tomorrow?"

"Yes," I said, and realized I regretted this fact. I hadn't felt so welcomed anywhere in a great long while. "Flying out of Charlotte."

"You get yourself a seat in the back of that plane," he said. "That's safest."

"Oh, yeah?" I gestured with my fingers for a cigarette. "How so?"

"Last part to hit the ground." He squinted and coughed out three or four laughs. Agnes came back to the table shaking her head.

"You'd better stop trying to scare Fred and get to work clearing out the junk in that room so he has a place to lay his head." She sponged a few crumbs off the table and planted a kiss on Bill's temple. We both went on laughing together.

"What do you call this stuff, Ass beer?" Bill held the lavender-labeled bottle up in the last rays of daylight.

"Aass," I said. "It's from Norway. The licorice taste goes with spicy foods."

"Not bad." This was about as exultant as Bill waxed toward anything not a part of his life for more than ten years, so I was pleased. At the same time I noticed that he elevated one of his black-haired pinkies a fraction of an inch from the bottle. "Delightful. Isn't that what the fellow on TV says? But I gotta be careful now, talking around this Princeton man. Don't want to make a mistake."

"Damn right," I said. "First split infinitive out of you and I'm gone." I aimed his new Winchester rifle at the last of the empty bottles on the back fence and blew it away. "You want to finish this case inside? It's getting dark."

"Fine by me." Bill lifted and lowered his meat workers union baseball cap, as if in farewell salute to the paprika-red earth in the field beyond the fence and the soft green forest at its edge. "I'll clean that glass up tomorrow, Freddie."

"Thanks, old man. That's a way cool rifle."

"It's the shorter barrel everybody likes," he said. "You only got sixteen inches, so you can swing it around in the brush easy."

We started over the rocky ground toward the trailer's plastic-sheathed porch light. In the process of directing my inebriated steps there I nearly amputated a leg on an enormous wheelbarrow. On closer inspection it turned out to be half wheelbarrow and half produce stand.

"Watch yourself," Bill said.

"Thanks," I said flatly. "What is this, the beginnings of a still?"

"That's our summer project." Bill walked me around to its opposite side and showed me the sign. It said OCRA in wavering, painted letters. "We set this up across the road and sell okra to the tourists and what have you. We split the proceeds with Henry Geena. It's his crop overflow, you might say."

I ran my hand over the weathered gray wood and was rewarded with two splinters whose extraction would occupy me on the flight back to Boston the next morning. "You make money sitting out there in the blazing sun?" I must have sounded incredulous.

"It passes the time on a long day," Bill said, starting to get defensive, "and you talk to the people passing through. Agnes and I will play a little crib."

"How much you make last year?"

"We made about two hundred dollars apiece once we split it up," Bill said. "Why, you gonna report us to the IRS? I'm afraid my share went into half of that rifle."

"You bet I'll report it," I said. "Didn't I show you my Young Republican tattoo?"

Bill smiled, the tension gone. "If you're heading in, let's head in. Agnes will tell you who went down at the charismatics when she gets back."

"Actually, I think I'll hang out for a second," I said. "It's so beautiful here. I forgot a place this beautiful still exists."

"America," Bill said, and spat into the dust. "Look what you get."

I watched the bathroom light go on in the trailer and decided to decant against Agnes's cherry tree. As I did I gulped fragrant night air and leaned my forehead against the trunk. It was just like old times, another one of the hundreds of leaks I'd taken against Agnes's poor tree after my high school friends had pulled away in their cars. I glanced around the yard, the five intervening years erased, until my eyes landed on the crooked letters of the OCRA sign. It hadn't registered with me until now that the sign was misspelled. Here were my aunt and uncle working the whole summer with a misspelled sign for two hundred dollars apiece, and I'd jumped around in a chapel like some Courtauld Institute yuppie gone AWOL for one morning and made 24 times that in commission!

I turned my head away slightly as I zipped up and looked out toward the dark field beyond the fence. Who was I to criticize Agnes or Bill's spelling, come to think of it: the best I'd been able to do was make it to the quarter finals in my middle school's annual spelling championship, only to be tripped up by the easy word "cemetery" in a late round. I remembered that night very clearly, all of a sudden: it was the year they hadn't been able to scrape together enough acts for the school's variety show, so the spelling champs were to be decided as a climax to the event. Seeing my parents' faces in the audience that night had been bad enough: my mother, stitching all her absurd hopes to my tiny achievement, looking crushed as I was called offstage, beside her my father, who'd stayed after his classes with a bottle of something, twirling his mustache and looking down on it all from the infinite height of his condescending sneer. I'd barely crossed the stage with my two-inch-high trophy for fourth place before they were going at each other. It was one of the mumble-hiss fights they had in public places. Mom would hiss in a kind of attention-hungry fury and Dad would mumble for silence in a way that set her off like a Saturn booster rocket. When the meager applause for me died down, I could still hear their voices cutting through the silence of the auditorium. The shame I felt was so familiar I was actually relieved not to have to wait in suspense for it.

"Don't you worry, honey," Mom said, three sheets to the wind herself, as I took my seat beside her, "you're better than any of these kids." And in a loud stage whisper that could be heard ten rows back into the staring audience: "They don't come from quality people."

Then Dad: "The word 'cemetery' is from the Old French, son, so I can understand your keeping the second *i* in there. Perhaps if you go back up and explain they'll give you the gorgeous two-dollar trophy instead of the fifty-cent one."

"Jack, don't you mock the boy like that. He's only twelve, for God's sake."

"Would you shush?"

"Don't you shush me, you jackass! I've got a right to speak as much as anyone else!"

"Shhh!"

At this juncture I told my parents I had to go to the bathroom, though it took them twenty minutes to realize I might not be coming back. They found me a quarter mile from the school outside a Kroger's grocery store, waiting for Bill and Agnes to pick me up in the parking lot. I certainly could have called a friend from my soccer team for help, but I figured if I planted myself in Pineville my parents would have to acknowledge that Bill and Agnes existed. In the reality they'd chosen for us, a suburban settlement where you had to shampoo-vacuum out your personality before passing papers on a house, Bill and Agnes were a sort of misspelling themselves. The irony was that I'd found my mother passed out on the couch when I got home from school that day. In fact, I'd had to pull her upstairs and out of sight before her classy friend Alice dropped by and saw what kind of people had moved into the neighborhood. Days like these cultivated a good, healthy sense of the ironic, not to mention the absurd.

"Come on in the car, Fred," my mother pleaded in the parking lot. "Don't cause a scene like we're some trailer trash family."

"You're the trash!" I screamed at her. "Why don't you both die and leave me the fuck alone!"

Agnes and Bill happened to arrive at that moment, and I was quickly forgotten as my mother whipped up some fantastical custody battle. I remember walking over to sit on the curb in front of the grocery store, then looking up to see hundreds of fireflies and moths dancing around a streetlight, and beyond them a sky encrusted with stars. As I stared at those two overlapping groups, flies who would live less than a week and stars whose light had traveled thousands of years to reach my eyes, I was for the first time in my life able to comprehend the true enormity of time and how insignificant the noise of my parents was in its wake. At that moment I saw my mother and father in the same cold, indifferent light the stars shed on me, and although they would live for another four years after that night, in my own mind I sealed myself off from them as dead things. My mother thought she'd won a victory as I walked over to their car and got in, but nothing would ever be the same between us. Now I was merely biding my time until I could get away.

I pulled back from Agnes's tree and wiped my eyes before my head was permanently indented with a bark pattern. Coming back to Pineville was just like old times, all right: that was precisely the problem. In Boston, at least, I had some space to breathe and reinvent myself.

Eventually Bill's head appeared at a window. "You having a seizure or something?" he called. "You've been out there twenty-five minutes."

"Jesus, Bill," I called back, and jerked my thumb toward the OCRA sign. "Can't you spell a simple four-letter word?"

# 40. Wasps in the Wild

lbright Galleries?"

"Hi, how much."

"Nelson?"

"Fred. How much?"

"I had a nice trip, thanks. Helen says hello."

*"How much money?"*

"Forty-eight grand. It's in the bank."

"God, you're amazing. Whitney's taking you out to celebrate."

"That was fast. Where are we going?"

"I scratched and scraped, didn't buy my daughter the shoes she needed, just so I could land two tickets to the Arboretum Animal Rights Jubilee. People come from all over for this party, Fred; national guest list. So go, with my compliments. I've also given Whitney a photograph of a Visscher map of Italy that you should offer to Denny D'Amico there, okay?"

I sighed. Some celebration. "Fine."

"Is everything all right, Fred?"

"I was hoping to rest up a little after my trip, but—"

"This'll be great for you."

Click.

I had to admit that my boss's efficiency was becoming startling. I'd stepped off a plane in Boston less than an hour ago and already he had me feeling like I'd been back a week.

Since our hundred-dollar tickets only provided admittance at the Monkey level, Whitney and I had to wait at the gates of the Arnold Arboretum for the Gazelles and the Eagles to enter the party before us. Besides getting first crack at the liquor tents and receiving splits of Monopole Red Top in their box dinners, Gazelle patrons were permitted to hold a blue macaw on a stick for up to two minutes. Eagle couples, moreover, stood for *Town & Country* portraits beside a live hippopotamus named William Penn. Yet even if one was deemed a mere Monkey, even if all the animals had been shipped to the grounds just for the party, the early summer night was stirringly beautiful, as were the lush botanical walking trails. Go strolling, I told myself. Imbibe and go forth pollinating with your business card.

"Quite a crush," I said, as we handed over our tickets.

"The MFA's a big sponsor this year," Whitney said automatically. "There's some kind of anniversary tribute to Duncan Phyfe the cabinetmaker tied in with it."

"That'll draw in the fur—" I began, though the words "furniture dealers" caught in my mouth as a tall, pale woman with a gorgeous shock of black hair a few steps ahead of us pulled at a man's hand to dislodge him from a chattering group of people. To my amazement, the hand was connected to none other than Valdemar Abbot.

"Fur?" Whitney said. "On a night like this? I think you need a drink, Fred."

"I do," I said, without looking at her. Valdemar Abbot was not the sort of distraction I needed when I was out for a sale to a guy who disliked gay men, and my hesitation showed when he spotted me.

"Hey, there," I said.

Valdemar's large, handsome face lit up like a Brooks Brothers model at a holiday shoot. "Hello, Fred." He walked over with his hand extended, as if to overcompensate for my discomfort. "What a pleasant surprise."

"It is a surprise," I said. "Meet Whitney Buck."

"Hello, Valdemar," Whitney said, obviously acquainted. "Is that Carolyn Stern you're with?"

"Indeed," he said. "She asked me to advise her on a set of chairs. It's a nice break from Texas at this time of year."

Whitney leaned toward him. "Is she as nuts as everyone says?"

"More so," he whispered back. "Which means I must run. Any possibility you can fit me in for dinner before Friday, Fred?"

The mother of all blushes spread over my face. "Well," I said, "I could possibly do something tomorrow . . ."

"Let's meet here." Valdemar scribbled two lines onto a business card and handed it to me. "Six-thirty, casual dress. You're keeping young, Whitney."

"And you," Whitney said. "Maybe we'll bump into you later."

I pocketed the card once he'd walked away and said, "We sort of struck up a friendship at the Baltimore show."

"Fast friends," Whitney said, adjusting her purse and scanning the crowd. "My mother would say, 'What a waste!' "

"How do you mean?"

"God, Fred, he's queerer than a three-dollar bill, didn't you know?"

"Oh, really?" I stumbled. "I just—"

"Wow," Whitney exclaimed. "There's Jack Klake with Mrs. John Moore!" She made a cash register sound, laughed at her joke, and sent me on into the feline pavilion for two gin and tonics without another word about Valdemar. If she'd meant to imply anything about me with the "fast friends" crack, it didn't sound malicious. After all, she'd been working with Marty for years. As for Valdemar, I tried not to think of him, although I knew I'd be looking out for glimpses for the rest of the night.

Inside the packed pavilion, I had just clenched a lime-bobbing glass in each fist when I was suddenly pressed into a woman at the black panther cage. She wore a World Wildlife Fund scarf and a necklace of miniature teddy bears over her gown. Because of the drinks in my hands, I was forced toward her in a somewhat crucified posture.

"Coming your way," I said. Then I started. "Oh, hey, Jenny!"

"Fred!" She pulled off her tortoise-shell sunglasses and relieved me of Whitney's gin and tonic. "Nice to see you! I haven't seen a soul I know."

"Is Denny at the store?"

"No, he wanted to look around by the reflecting pool." She sighed and indicated the black panther slinking around below us. "Denny says I can have one of those in a full-length if I get down and walk like that."

"He's a pest," I scolded.

"Eh, I've got one anyway. What luck to run into you, though. Denny's looking for a new piece for his study. I'm always imposing my taste on him, so this time I want him to choose something that he'll love himself."

My spirits rose. "I've got just the thing. A seventeenth-century map of Italy by Visscher."

"Terrific." She drained half of Whitney's drink. "Tell me all about it."

"It's a little expensive," I warned, "but the blue tones are gorgeous."

"Nelson's not that expensive," Jenny said. "He has the quality. I'd call him high reasonable."

"God bless you," I said. "The centerpiece of this map is a 1682 inset view of Florence. It'll knock you out."

Jenny merely nodded, looking half at me and half over her shoulder. Then her hand shot up.

"Here, you can tell Denny yourself. Den!"

Denny appeared in the party crush, laughing good-naturedly as he battered bodies out of the way to get to us. "Hey, Fred," he said, "I wish I'd seen you five minutes ago."

I pulled him in among us. "Something jump out of the reflecting pool at you?"

"No, I just saw Whitney. She gave me this great picture of a map Marty wanted me to look at. I decided to do it, babe, on the spot."

Jenny smiled and curled her free hand over Denny's shoulder. "That's okay, we know where they live."

"A map, huh?" I said jovially. "Do you still have the picture?"

"Sure do." Denny handed it over. It was, as I expected, a Polaroid of the Visscher Nelson told me to pitch. The two-line description on the back was in Marty's hand, and featured a price five hundred dollars higher than the one Nelson had given me. The little prick.

"Well," I said, "I should congratulate you. That's a fine piece."

"Whitney said not to worry about your commission," Denny added. "She said Marty would take care of it."

"Oh, I'm sure he will," I said. "That's good to know."

"Are you ready to walk like that cat?" Denny said to his wife.

Jenny raised her eyebrows and passed him her empty gin and tonic. "It'll cost you, babe."

# 41. One-Stop Class Shopping

Marty waltzed his big map sale around like a dancing partner all the next day. He accidentally left Denny's check on my desk and then came by fifteen minutes later, all innocence, wondering if I'd seen it. He pulled me away from lunch to ask my opinion on some framing design for the map, then inquired as to where I'd put all the good cartographical reference books, since he was sure I'd had them last. A few minutes before closing time, I watched him run out the door to catch the mailman at the corner box—just in time to mail the invoice for D'Amico's map, he made sure to tell me. I considered double-locking the door to keep him outside in the heat for a while, then noticed some activity back in the main gallery, which Marty was supposed to be covering. I pulled open the French doors and found a willowy man with a mustache and blond hair to his shoulders browsing in our Thornton drawer. Just what I needed when I was trying to leave early and be on time for dinner with Valdemar.

"Hi there," I said. "Is someone helping you?"

"No one's been able to yet," the man said. He leaned against the print case. "Have you got Thornton's *Night-blooming Cereus?*"

"Let me check in back," I said, though I knew we hadn't had one in months. "If I don't have a copy here, I can get one sent in from another gallery."

"Do that." The man reached for a wallet in an inside pocket of his black leather motorcycle jacket. His hands trembled and jerked as if covered with little magnets that were repelling each other. He pulled out a business card and let it drop to the carpet.

"Tom Ashe," he said. "I'm building a collection."

"You obviously know your stuff," I said, "if you're starting with Thornton." Although Mr. Ashe wasn't aware of it, this is what we were obliged to say to customers if they were starting with Redouté, Weinmann, Audubon, Ortelius, or any nineteenth-century British journeyman shmuck who engraved dead birds in London for more than six months.

"Art's new to me," Ashe said, "but I inherited a little money recently and thought I'd buy some class."

"You've picked the right place," I said. "I get mine right here, as part of the benefits package."

"Make sure you have good insurance coverage in that package," Mr. Ashe said coolly. "If you get anything worse than the flu, these insurance companies tend to lose your policy in their computers." He started toward the door. "That cereus is my personal symbol. I want it in perfect condition."

"Good," I said. "I'll call you."

When Mr. Ashe reached out to open our front door, he was nearly knocked back off his feet by Marty, who was letting himself in with his key. Troy, a young Italian carpenter who occasionally met Marty after work, walked in behind him. Troy was far more handsome than beanpole Marty, with a full head of black hair and a great build, but he was crushingly shy. You could tell Marty had intimidated him into bed, probably to compensate for the fact that the narrow window of his attractiveness was rapidly closing. I could tell, anyway.

Mr. Ashe stepped back and grimaced while pressing at his chest. "Just because I'm sick," he said sharply, "doesn't mean I'm invisible."

"I beg your pardon," Marty said, with his jackal-like indifference. I stared after Mr. Ashe as he stepped into the vestibule and then made his way out onto the street. Oh, for a nice poison-tipped Chinese Star when you needed one.

"Nice going," I said.

"I didn't see the guy!" Marty snapped. "It's after six, in case you haven't noticed."

"You sure have."

"By the way, if you made a sale to him I get the commission," he added. "I'm covering first floor today."

That was it. "Marty, go fuck yourself," I said.

Marty feigned shock. "What's the matter, Fred, don't you have something to go home to?"

"At least I don't drag it in to work with me."

His dark eyes narrowed. "Care to repeat that?"

"Marty," Troy said, "leave him alone."

I smiled without responding and stepped back into the main gallery to fetch my jacket. The lonely space in my chest felt so big I feared caving into it. For the first time in months I thought of the Xeroxed Audubon Marty had delivered to me on my first day, with the words "Poised to take advantage" written in along the bottom. I'd show him how poised I was, if that's what he wanted.

At my desk I made several quick phone calls. Our New York, Greenwich, Chicago, and Los Angeles galleries were all out of Thornton *Night-blooming Cereus* prints, New York laughing outright when I requested such a high-demand image. I sat glowering over this state of affairs for several minutes while Marty and Troy made their own calls in the reception area. Another line rang and I picked it up.

"Albright Galleries."

"Hi, how much?"

I closed my eyes. "Oh, lots and lots."

"Don't fuck with me, Fred," Nelson said. "How much did you take in today?"

"I have a sale for a Thornton *Night-blooming Cereus,*" I said. "Have you got one out in Weston?"

"Damn." He sighed. "Try the other galleries."

"No dice."

"Shit."

"I doubt the guy will be back anyway," I said. "Not after Marty and his lover nearly knocked him down at the door."

"What?" Nelson thundered. "Are you telling me he's bringing that guy into my store again? Let me talk to Marty!"

"He's busy on the phone at the moment," I said. "Shall I leave him a message?"

For several seconds there was only hard breathing on the other end of the line.

"Have him call me first thing in the morning," he said ominously. "First thing. And let me thank you, Fred, for being my eyes and ears down there. Don't worry about Marty. He's gone. He's out of there."

"And I need a *Night-blooming Cereus,*" I said miserably.

"You'll have one. I'll get you a pristine one. Don't let this guy drop, Fred. You will have no more impediments to making sales there. I promise."

"Thank you, Nelson," I said. "Have a good night."

I hung up and noticed that Troy was staring through the French doors at me. He hadn't heard the conversation, but I could tell he knew. Marty was history. Marty was history and my hands were shaking and I needed a drink.

# 42. More Nelson
# than Nelson

ey, handsome," a Dallas twang called, "take a load off!"

I stepped into the brightly lit Dixie-style restaurant Valdemar had chosen in a kind of daze. I'd already downed a double vodka on the way to Massachusetts Avenue, which was not the ideal way to start a weekday evening. On the other hand, I'd just vaporized Marty's ass back at the gallery, and I had to commemorate this new personal low somehow.

"You look like you just saw a ghost, or maybe Nelson," Valdemar said. He lifted his thick, compact body halfway out of his seat and kissed me on the mouth. My eyes darted around the room to discover that nearly all the couples were same-sex. I could relax.

"There," he added. "I wanted to do that last night."

"I'm surprised not to have seen you with Mr. President," I said. A waitress stopped by and I ordered a sunrise. "Don't you travel together anymore?"

Valdemar smiled. "He arrives Friday."

"Oh. Sorry to hear that," I said, though this was an understatement. "You'll have to excuse me if I'm snappish, by the way. I'm always a bit tightly wound after leaving work."

"Who isn't."

"Tell me how the chair consulting is going."

"Fine, thank you. Lots of excitement around the top stuff these days." Valdemar reached over and began to massage one of my hands. "But enough about my dull life. How've you been?"

"Same old same old," I said. "Can't complain."

"Sure you can," he said. "You looked ready to snap last night at the Arboretum." He began to tickle the insides of my fingers with his fat index finger, doing it lazily, and I felt my socially constructed self start to slide off.

"Things are a little more whacked than usual, if you must know," I began. "It's hard to stay optimistic when your boss operates under the bizarre illusion that the more money he spends the less serious his debt problem is. It sort of adds to the challenge of maintaining a healthy business, if you see what I mean."

I received my drink and guzzled half of it like ice water.

"Then we come to the delightful people I work with," I continued, "who'd stab you in the back for a $2,000 sale. And of course there's Nelson's lovely wife, who uses the company employees like personal appliances and takes the best stock we buy to decorate her own home. It's like, just name a real-world preconception about this job, Valdemar, and I'll tell you how it's exploding in my face."

He stared at me for a long moment and nodded sagely. Finally he said, "Can I ask one thing here?"

"Go right ahead."

"Don't you find it unusual that you haven't said a single thing about how Fred Layton is doing?"

I spat an ice cube back into my drink. "Nelson's driving me nuts, how do you think I'm doing!"

"And what drives me nuts is that every person I've met who ever worked for Nelson Albright can't talk about anything *but* Nelson," Valdemar said. "Five years later they're still telling little stories about how this or how that he is. You don't have to become his mental slave to work for him, Fred. Define yourself from the inside and let his bullshit wash over you."

"Now there's a pleasant image."

"And if he is driving you crazy, you've got every right to call in sick and knock around a little. Take some long weekends. Go to some clubs and let your libido leak out. Stop and smell the brioche, as Mr. President likes to say."

"I've tried smelling it," I said. "I've probably gone to every gay club in this town at least once, and I'll tell you what: all the men are tanned year round, go to the gym one to two hours every day, seek material gain over all other goals, and are, to the person, one hundred percent *bland-o.* If one of them had an original thought his friends would probably drag him into the street and kick him to death."

"Perhaps so," Valdemar said, "but just because everyone in the world didn't double-major in philosophy and art history at Princeton doesn't give you the right to fault them for it."

"Well, just because a guy's got a nice crack in his ass doesn't make him the Liberty Bell, either," I shot back.

Val looked at me as if the oxygen flow to my brain had been interrupted. "This may sound rude, now, coming from someone who doesn't know you that well, but I might advise a little more humility so you don't have to disappear into your head to have someone to talk to."

"That sounds familiar." I polished off my sunrise and held up the glass for another. "Actually, I'm becoming so numbed by it all that I sit down at my desk in the morning, my $38,000 desk, feeling like the scaffolding around a person rather than the person underneath. I'm becoming this sort of two-dimensional shirt-tie-belt zone who works six days a week and can't make honest decisions about anything. I'm either waiting for Nelson to contact me or recovering from his latest contact. Maybe this is the ideal time to apply to law school."

Valdemar finished his massage of one hand and moved to the other. "Hey, now, it's always hard to start over in a new place. Just remember who you are and never be ashamed of it. . . . Unlike your boss."

"He's really a woman underneath those cords?"

Valdemar leaned forward over the table. "Not too many people know this, but Nelson's actually from the whitest-trash stock this side of Jackson, Mississippi."

"He's what?" I said in amazement.

"Those candy-ass parents of his, John and Hattie Albright, adopted him from an orphanage in Kentucky after Hattie lost her baby. It was all very hush-hush. I don't think he knows who his real mother is. And definitely not his father."

"No shit!" I said. "He tells everyone he's Mayflower stock."

Valdemar chuckled. "Sure, his adopted family is. Not a branch out of place there. But his own blood is pure mutt. That's why he loves selling prints and maps to the society crowd, playing squash at the right club, that kind of quiet status stuff."

"How about that," I said. Now it was beginning to make sense, the way Nelson referred to purebred Wasps as "those people," or the comment he'd made in his office after the Christmas party: "We're more alike than you think, Fred." He was probably ready to tell me right there. "So why hasn't anyone exposed him?" I said. "Couldn't Oksana spread this rumor and kill his business?"

"Oh, I'd say only a handful of people know," Valdemar said. "I had to drive Kak home from a party one night in Dallas back when Nelson was in his lush period and she spilled it all. She was ready to drop him when she found out—which says a lot about her."

"Did I mention he's drinking again?"

Valdemar raised an eyebrow. "He is? Well, that sort of puts your comments in a whole new light."

After dinner, Valdemar and I had an iced coffee and started walking toward the Fenway. Then we closed down a jazz bar on Boylston and strolled back along Commonwealth Avenue to Valdemar's hotel in the muggy summer breeze. While we walked, Valdemar talked about his childhood in Danville, North Carolina; about going to UVA and dropping out of medical school; about sleeping on wooden planks in Korea for eight months thereafter; and about being fitted for eleven suits by his father's tailor, who flew to Korea from Danville to prep him for the Abbot men's biennial cruise to Marseille. He talked about his two-year marriage, too, but mostly he talked shop, antiquing, or what he called "the business." When I got too tired to listen to Valdemar I drifted along on his golden voice. He could have tethered me to that voice like a helium balloon and I would gladly have bumped my head on all the eaves and windowsills in our path and not cared.

"I love this cruise thing you used to take with your brothers," I said at one point. "It obviously meant a lot to your dad, but I'm still not sure why. I mean, what was the guy like?"

"My daddy?" Valdemar considered. "He was a neurologist, a tremendous man. A little too attached to ceremony, maybe, but he's the major reason I tried medical school in the first place. Very open, very affectionate with his boys. How about yours?"

I frowned. "Oh, squandered his career with drink, distant and unavailable. The usual."

"It sounds from all you've been saying like you could never quite win his approval."

"Well, Dad's the one navigating the ship, everything you know as real. Of course you try to win his approval. When he's sober."

Valdemar cast a glance in my direction. "Still looking for him?"

"What do you mean, through Nelson?" I smiled at the thought. "He certainly makes everyone else in my life seem inconsequential, but I think that's a question of sheer volume. It's funny, though . . ."

"What is?"

We paused at a stoplight for two cars to rumble past. "I have thought of my father when he's around," I said. "It's not a very flattering comparison either way. Besides, I gave up on the guy a long time before he died."

"Still, you'd do anything to keep on earning Nelson's approval."

"Are you crazy? Nothing I do for that guy would be enough."

"And you love that about him."

"Not true," I said. "What I love about Nelson is that he takes risks, he breaks the tight-assed rules of social propriety and gets away with it. He doesn't forget the fact that he's alive, for Christ's sake."

Valdemar nodded. "If I remember right, that's just how you see yourself. Or at least that's how you did when you sweet-talked us into that jazz show for nothing."

"Hey, we could have been out-of-town reviewers. Plus the set was half over."

"And some of us become what we despise."

"So I look like Child of Nelson to you, is that it? Hell, why not?" I said. "I've spent my whole life taking on the shape of anything I admired. For that matter, I just used homophobia as a lever to get someone canned. That's more Nelson than Nelson."

I could feel Valdemar staring and realized my run-in with Marty was what had been bothering me all night.

"Do I want to hear about this?" he said.

"No, you don't. I'm oversimplifying it anyway. The guy got in my way one too many times." I shook my head at this admission. "God, did I really just say that?"

"So you want to be rich and Waspy and conservative and straight, is that it?"

"No!" I said sharply. "And here's the funny thing, Valdemar: they hate being it themselves! I can see it in their eyes at these parties and receptions. They're all bored stiff with what they are!"

"Think so?"

"Believe me, they're bored," I said. "I counted four women at the Baltimore Antiques Show who only came into the booth to let me know that their lives bored them silly. . . . And no, to answer your question, I don't want to become rich and Waspy and conservative. I just want to become the best art dealer I can, and find the same kind of joy in my job that an eighty-year-old woman feels when she goes down in a charismatics meeting. If sponged ceilings and outbuildings go along with all that, great. If not, I won't die unhappy."

He looked at me askance. "Uh-huh. And what about the straight part?"

I reached over and pinched his butt. "I'd think our last encounter would have answered that question for you."

"Fine, then," Valdemar said. "If you're as much this rip-roaring break-the-rules guy as Nelson, tell him to go fuck himself when he pushes you over the line. Jump off the bridge again and find a new role for yourself."

"Easier said than done when the guy calls sixty times a day to check up on you," I countered. "You're right, though, I've got Nelson up to my eyeballs."

"But you obviously love the guy on one level, so you're loyal."

"I do love Nelson," I said. "I do. He's just such a fucking prick!"

"Yes, well," Valdemar said, "that appears to sum up the whole dilemma, doesn't it?"

I stopped my fly-by-night friend at a street corner and hugged him, despite the policeman who was walking past. "Thanks for hearing me out," I said. "All this shit is in my head, I just can't get to it on my own. This ought to qualify as charity work for you."

He tousled my hair. "I'd argue for another hour on that point."

"The very thought exhausts me. What time is it, anyway?"

Valdemar checked his watch. "Half past one. We're only a block from my hotel, if you're interested in coming up for a night-cap."

"Oh, right," I said slowly. "To tell you the truth, Valdemar, I think I've probably had enough to drink already."

"I see," he said, not forcing the issue as he gently forced the issue.

I hesitated. "It's just that I keep thinking of Nelson screwing around with this woman he pays, practically in his wife's face, and how unfair it is to do that to Mr. President."

He nodded slowly. "I understand, Fred. You don't feel the same spark you did the first time, is that it?"

I smiled and looked away. "Jesus, guy, that couldn't be less true. You're perfect. I mean, I couldn't believe it when you asked me to dinner down in Baltimore."

"Come on, Fred," he laughed, and took a step closer. "You're making me blush."

"I have to be honest, Valdemar. I've been finding myself doing all these more-Nelson-than-Nelson things. Getting back at a friend by selling her boyfriend a print. Getting this guy Marty fired. Selling Helen Wheeler an Audubon that a truck ran over. Selling prints by making up art history on the spot. I mean, maybe it's time I started improving on that record before it's too late to turn back."

Valdemar sighed heavily, but when I met his eyes he smiled at me. "All right," he said. "But that bed's gonna feel real big without you in it."

"If Mr. President should give you the boot, you've got my number," I said.

Valdemar crushed me in a hug. Then we simply shook hands and walked our separate ways into the night.

## 43. Gum Doctor

So what happened?" Whitney said in my ear as she leaned over to buckle her seat belt.

"It was a personality conflict, all right? I have one and Marty doesn't."

Whitney sighed impatiently as I swung her Jaguar down through Wellesley Hills. We had just ducked out of a Museum of Fine Arts benefit luncheon and were heading for the airport so

Whitney could fly to Miami and close another sale with Bobby Hammerstein, Florida's most famous periodontist. Nelson had called Marty out to Weston that morning and fired him, though Whitney, I knew, was betting he'd be back on the payroll by the time she returned from her trip. Marty might be a pain in the ass, but he brought in a lot of money. I was shuttling between jouissance and mild shock over the turn of events, not to mention my private grief at watching Valdemar Abbot walk out of my life again, leaving me with only a hangover and some fading bits of advice that sounded simplistic in the reality of full daylight. Example: how could I jump off the bridge into freedom with $60.45 in my checking account? With so much on my mind I found myself cruising along in the parking lane until a passing Town Car with an air horn brought me back to sense. I turned to Whitney and smiled.

"Pardon me while I kill us both."

"One other thing," she said. "Don't be surprised if you get a call from Nelson about the Barbash collection. There's a rumor going around that Dodo Barbash is about to start taking bids on her natural history library."

"Is it good?"

"God, is it!" Whitney exclaimed. "Dodo's a few sandwiches short of a picnic these days, but for a while she bought only the best of the best. Like a hundred original Barraband watercolors and all these unbelievable Nicolas Robert vellum paintings from 1660. I saw them on a collector's field trip to New York in college. Today the whole lot could bring fifteen million dollars easily."

"Since when does Nelson have fifteen million to spare?"

She dug around in her purse for a lipstick. "Nelson doesn't, but he can get some pretty impressive money when he needs it. I've seen him come up with $500,000 in half an hour."

"I've seen him spend that much in ten minutes."

"This is also true. On the other hand, if he plays this one right he could make a small fortune. Which we could use right about now. I've already lost two clients to Oksana Outka this month." Whitney tapped me as I screeched up to a red light. "Hang on, Fred; roll down my window, please. *Gosh,* that gets my goat."

I lowered Whitney's window from the control panel on my door as she cupped her hands around her mouth. On top of a grassy knoll near Wellesley's town center, a fat homeless man with cornrowed hair was pulling bunches of day-old sub rolls from a clear plastic garbage bag and flinging them high into the air like juggler's pins. His eyes were wide open in a barely contained ec-stasy of total madness, though at the sound of Whitney's clarion voice he immediately squeezed a roll in each fist and started run-ning toward the car. As I watched him approach I couldn't help thinking that a homeless man seen in Wellesley would probably make the local papers.

"Stop wasting that food!" Whitney shouted, and gestured at the man with her lipstick. "Those are meant for a lot of people!"

"Shh," I hissed. The light had the decency to change then, and I released the clutch just as the cornrowed man raised his arms over the car.

"*Fred,*" Whitney whined.

"Sorry," I said. "I don't want you to miss your flight."

She leaned back in her seat. "I'll bet. You'll have no one in your way to make some big sales now."

"Not at all," I said humbly, in our usual inane role-play. "I imagine *you'll* be making all the sales to Dr. Hammerstein."

Whitney sighed. "Don't sap my energy before I get started. Every trip to this guy it's the same way: the prices are fine, the framing is fine, and then as soon as it gets down to paying he and his wife start arguing over all the quotes. If there's one thing that burns me up, it's having to close a sale with a stingy, penny-pinching you-know-what."

"Gum doctor?"

Whitney smiled. "Exactly. . . ."

"I've been meaning to ask you," I said. "Did you ever make three million dollars a year?"

She threw back her head and laughed. "You mean that memo? Who gave you a copy of that?"

"Nelson did, my first day."

She stared at me in disbelief. "God. That's a satire of a Nelson memo that Marty wrote. I guess we've reached the point where he can't even tell the difference anymore."

"Hmm."

"And no, just to ease your mind, I never made three million a year, and I have not become a millionaire in ten years. He made me the same promises when I started, too."

"Are you angry that they haven't come true?" I said.

"Angry? It's a bit late for anger now, don't you think?"

"I guess so. By the way, would you like me to do daily activity reports while you're gone?"

"Fred, don't be ridiculous. You're one of us now."

"You mean it?" I exclaimed.

"Well," she added, rolling her eyes, "practically."

# 44. Five Rings

oward four the next morning the phone began to ring in the total silence of my bedroom with all the charm of a knife in the face. I opened my eyes and rapidly closed them again, praying it was a dream, then reached from my futon down to the bare wooden floor.

"Hello?"

There was silence on the line, silence and then the distant sound of sitar music. I was leaning back over the futon to hang up when Nelson's voice shot out of the receiver like a cloud of poisonous gas in a spy movie.

"Fred!"

"Nelson," I said, unable to conceal the irritation in my voice. "What's up?"

"What's up?" he shouted. "You and me and eight of the biggest venture capitalists in Boston are having breakfast with Dodo Barbash in New York. She's going to give us the pick of her collection. What the hell are you doing in bed? You're at the airport in forty minutes, kiddo! We leave at five, I told you I chartered a jet!"

"Are you sure I'm the one you wanted to call?" I said.

"Ruth's on her way out there to pick you up. You be on that jet or you can forget your co-directorship!"

"Nelson, I've got to be back in Boston tonight. I'm showing some maps to a client in Dover."

He sighed. "Fine. Just give me a little advance notice next time, okay?"

Slam.

Besides being the first mention of the jet, this was also the first mention that my codirectorship was endangered. Dawn wouldn't break for another hour, and it was already a typical day.

How I ended up on the right Logan Airport taxiway at the precise second to spot Nelson scrambling up the five-step walkway of the Falcon 50 he had chartered to fly to New York must remain a minor miracle. Ruth, my driver, played the latest Rosemary Clooney tape all the way out to the airport to put me in good spirits and waved expressively from the window of the white Ford van as I ran for the plane.

"Steal me a few Barrabands!" she called.

"Hey, Fred." Nelson shook my hand and pulled me past the jet's tiny cockpit to the seats, all ten of them executed in buttery white leather and as wide as bathtubs. My boss's hair was dripping wet, so as I stepped into the herd of CEO types in the cabin I grabbed a hand towel on a low table and passed it to him.

"Morning, everyone," I said. My vocal cords, still addled by pot smoke from the night before, produced a tone half an octave lower than normal.

"Here's my Boston codirector, Fred Layton!" Nelson announced to his fellow travelers. "Fred's our resident expert on botanical art. Thornton, Redouté, De Bry, Merian, you ask him! Fred, this is . . ."

And here the particular names and titles escape me, owing to the overall similarity of the men. They were all between forty and fifty-eight, outstandingly tan and healthy save a large stomach or two, and oversaw turbine companies, nursing home chains, small $300 million public utilities, grocery store empires, and the like. I guessed that they beat people up to stay in shape. Or golf, I thought, moving toward the unoccupied seat beside the largest man, who looked like he'd sired hundreds of children: golf golf golf.

Everyone was fully awake at five-ten on a Friday morning. The common workers were still abed, dreaming of debt, their wide-eyed, power-charged faces seemed to say. As I dropped my briefcase into the free seat I noted that Denny D'Amico had just raised his head in the row behind me, and that he was not with his wife but with his young Japanese receptionist from Illusions. She looked up at me and winked. I assumed that Nelson invited D'Amico on a cancellation. Compared to these guys, he was a poor immigrant cousin. I fell into place somewhere between lower crustacean and bug dust.

"Hey, Denny," I said. "How'd you get roped into this?"

"You tell me, Fred!" he shouted, over the igniting engine. "You tell me!"

Now that the first joke of the morning had been told, entirely devoid of humor and uproarious to the executives, my stock was set up and I could take my seat.

"Lou Smith," the tanned mogul beside me said. "Shame we couldn't take your friend in the van."

"Oh?" I said, blanking. "Who do you mean?"

"Nelson," Lou said across the aisle, "how could I tell this guy works for you?"

Nelson leaned over and replied, with juicy laughter in his voice, "I set him loose at parties at my house and ten minutes later I look out the window and he's got three or four women following him across the lawn!"

"Whatever happened to that Marty guy you had?" Lou asked. "Tall fellow with the sharp eyes and—"

"Marty's gone," Nelson cut in. "I don't need any trouble in my organization."

"I have to say I never felt quite comfortable around him," Lou observed, folding his massive hands on his laptop. "Not even when he sold me that Ortelius map."

"You never want to turn your back on him, that's for sure," I said. This comment produced another mysterious round of laughter.

"Yup; don't drop the soap around Marty Ifft," Nelson shouted, as we nosed skyward. "He'd have you knocked up before your pants hit the ground."

"Ever tried it, Nelson?" Denny called. "You sound pretty familiar."

Nelson sighed, closed his eyes. "It's the scourge of our nation, Denny."

"I thought that was cocaine," I said.

Nelson shot me a murderous look, then Lou shook his head slowly and said, "I thank God I got normal kids. My son Jamie, you should see this guy. Mr. Muscle, I call him. He's probably got muscles in his shit. Twenty-one years old and he still kisses me before he goes to bed every night."

"I'll tell you the secret for healthy kids," Nelson said. "Two things—you gotta love 'em and you gotta listen to 'em."

"Amen," Lou said.

I thought of Choix's latest tantrum, the one involving the windshield of Nelson's Mercedes, and lifted my eyes to heaven as the stewardess approached with an espresso she was holding at a forty-five-degree angle to keep it from spilling. I wondered if she would consider serving it to me with a syringe.

———

Six in the morning Eastern Standard Time, circling La Guardia, and the tap of laptop keys was louder than the engines on either side of us. I drifted in and out of sleep to the sales strategies Nelson pitched to Lou Smith—how he could divide Dodo Barbash's collection into suites as he did the Redouté roses; or better yet, how he could sell the whole lot to the Diet Library in Tokyo. The sales ideas spun out into other schemes; e.g., how Nelson was going to buy a house in Wayland where all his unmarried employees would live and sell around the clock until they were wealthy. He could get the print and map stock, could get the house. He could get twenty million dollars of credit exposure in a day, it would be cake. The more my boss described, the more I kept imagining myself in falls or auto accidents that would keep me out of sight until the last scheme blew over and the Albright Selling House was back on the market again, or I was back on the job market again, or I could get the stewardess to read my mind and bring me another espresso. When it occurred to me that Nelson's impossible scheme making would *never* blow over, I opened my eyes.

That just wouldn't do.

"Selling, I'll tell you about selling," Lou Smith said. "I just finished up a bunch of sales spots for TV. We got some people in from the wheat fields: a secretary, a meter reader, and a guy who strings lines for us, a black guy. They talk about keeping your kids in school, putting in insulation, pretty vanilla stuff. Then I come in and do the pitch: keep on plugging in to us, yadda yadda yadda. Everybody at HQ thought these things were hokey as hell, but they've hit it big. Suddenly I'm known all over western Mass. I was at a store trying out a putter the other day, this guy comes up and says, 'Lou Smith, how are you, how are the kids?' I said, 'Fine, thanks.' Never seen the guy in my life. Then he comes back with, 'Hey, why aren't you at work, Lou? Why aren't you in your office? No wonder my rates are so goddamned high!' Jesus Christ, did that ever blow up in my face."

"Nelson, I called your New York gallery the other day," Denny said, leaning out in the aisle. He had his arm around his receptionist, who was drawing a Total Quality Management diagram on an abandoned piece of origami. "Took them five rings to get to the phone."

"Uh-oh!" everyone on the jet said as one. Nelson laughed and held up his hands.

"It's been busy, all right! Am I supposed to take the blame for that?"

"Five rings," Denny said solemnly. "Think about it."

## 45. Breakfast at Dodo's

Nelson's superstretch limo found a spot at the northeast corner of Eightieth and Third, so we walked up the block to Dodo's house as a group. As we approached the address, my eye was drawn to a frail-looking woman several doors down from the corner. She was bent all the way forward to the sidewalk, madly searching for something in the slanting morning sunlight. She had a puff of snowy hair and white eyebrows over a handsome, square face that had seen more than one go-round of cosmetic surgery. I followed the woman's eyes out to a bright glint of metal in the gutter and stepped up to rescue a penny that had rolled there.

"Here you go," I said.

"Thank you," the woman said. She seemed to move her mouth and then let the sound come out. "I suppose I should have left it there, and been stylish."

"Nonsense," I said. She moved to return to the brownstone behind her and I added, "I don't suppose you could help us. We're trying to find the home of Dodo Barbash."

The woman stood up very straight. She was wearing chamois riding pants and a white linen shirt with a silk scarf at her throat. "I'm Dodo Barbash," she said precisely. "Who sent you to this place?"

Nelson charged up behind me and extended his hand. "Nelson Albright, Mrs. Barbash. We've come along to look at your art collection. You invited us to breakfast, remember?"

"I do," Dodo said unconvincingly. I wondered yet again if Nelson had bothered to call ahead.

"We're interested in buying the art from you," Nelson said, more carefully. "Paying you money for it."

"Well, I'm not interested in selling anything," she said. She dug into her pocket and produced a key, then walked down to the brownstone's below-street entrance. Denny D'Amico muttered something obscene, and I turned back and shushed him. The clump of expectant executives and Denny's receptionist behind them looked like some Daumier cartoon of the business world.

"We're interested for our own sake," Lou Smith said, "even if you don't have anything to sell."

"How can you possibly be interested in a collector with nothing to sell?" she called back. Then she took us in as a group. "My goodness, aren't there a lot of you. I've only got a dozen eggs."

"We'll just bother you a moment," Nelson promised. "Just to have a look around."

Dodo considered this request. Then she exclaimed, "Well, why don't you all come in for a moment, so you can have a look around? Actually, I'd feel better if you did. I've been trying all week to get the asparagus to come and fix up the locks."

"That's always a bother," I said politely.

She stepped into her house and Denny nudged Nelson. "Check it out: I love that little dimple in her chin."

Nelson smiled. "Actually, that's her belly button. It moves up over the chin after the fifteenth face lift."


"There's one canvas here I did in 1941, when I was twenty-two," Dodo explained, as she dug around behind a large breakfront. "Most of you weren't even ideas in the mind of God back then. These days when people ask I just say I'm plenty-two."

I shot a confused look at Nelson and he put a finger to his lips. I and Nelson and the clump of executives were standing in Dodo's cavernous, cat-filled dining room before a nine-foot-high canvas screen painted with acrylic pastels. The screen's three sections showed a balcony scene of patrician seaside bliss, à la Matisse, in the foreground, and a huge blue rose rising out of a blood-red ocean at the center section's horizon. A large jay was also painted about halfway up the sky, and after the jay three plastic budgie replicas of decreasing size hung on lengths of fishing line attached to a thin metal arm that jutted out from behind the screen. Denny D'Amico took a peek behind the contraption while we were waiting and flicked a switch. When he did the metal arm began to jerk back and forth, and the birds on their fishing lines followed suit.

"Hey," Denny said. "I feel more like I do than when I came in."

Dodo put a hand to the small of her back and straightened up. "I'm afraid you're out of luck, gentlemen. The only remaining piece of my collection I'd sell is the screen."

The man who owned the nursing home chain cleared his throat, and Nelson said, "Dodo, perhaps I wasn't clear. I'm sure the rest of your paintings are wonderful, but what we'd *really* like to see is your natural history art collection. You know, the pieces you used to show students who visited here?"

She smiled brightly, thought a moment. "Oh, my. You can't possibly do that."

"We can't," Nelson said. "All right. Did I misunderstand you when you said we could come and look around?"

"Not a bit," Dodo said. "But that was yesterday. The men from Sotheby's came and took it all away last night."

"Sotheby's!" Nelson exploded. The big vein in his neck began to bulge. "You just said you weren't interested in selling any art!"

"Oh, I'm not, really," Dodo said, as she fingered the scarf at her throat. "They only took away those books I used to collect for my library. Fruit books, flower books, little paintings of birds on goatskin. Fantastically uninspired stuff. I can use the extra shelf space."

"But I said we were coming for breakfast!" Nelson said, his face caught between panic and rage. "These are all very important men. We came here to make you a wealthy woman."

"I'd very much like to talk about that," Dodo said. "Why don't you all sit down, and I'll make you an omelette?"

———————

Dodo stopped me at the front door as I brought up the rear of the group.

"I hope I haven't offended Mr. Allbetter," she said. "I didn't want to cancel out for breakfast. It always disappoints people so."

"Albright," I corrected. "No, he'll be fine. He just gets a little ahead of himself sometimes."

"I hope you can come to the auction," she said. "Sotheby's seemed in such a rush to get it going. It's to be on New Year's Eve, my birthday, but I'll be unable to attend."

"Let me guess," I said. "You'll be plenty-two."

She grinned. "I like you, young man. Can I give you an old drawing or something to take with you? I've got piles of them in the basement. My sister used to say they were by Tiepolo, but between you and me she was half out of her mind."

"Fred!" Nelson bellowed from the street.

"No, thanks, but you're very kind," I said. I made a quick mental note to give Dodo's address to an art history professor back at Princeton. "The omelette was quite memorable enough."

# 46. The Man Who Painted Moonlight

I woke up staring at a strange hotel ceiling, though I did know, somehow, that I was in Charlotte. There was a knock at the door, obviously not the first one, since the first one had awakened me at the absurdly early hour of—my head fell over toward the end table—twelve-thirty.

!

I flung myself out of bed, saw that I was still in my clothing of the night before, and croaked, "Yes?"

"Hello there, Fred, it's Helen. Are we ready for lunch?"

"Half of us are!" I stumbled to the coffee table in the center of the room, rewrapped Helen Wheeler's now very clean volume of Lear's *Parrots*, placed it on the bed, and ran around straightening up. I defeated a wave of dizziness, lurched to the door, and launched into High Chipper.

"Howdy!"

Helen Wheeler entered in a splendid red tartan suit, instantly distinguishing the room with her presence. "My land, Fred; your hair looks like the business end of the broom. I'm sorry I couldn't put you up at the house, but we're booked solid for the chapel dedication."

"How's it been going?"

"Oh, wonderfully. I feel like I'm at my wedding again. I keep asking myself, 'How can I possibly be related to all these people?' "

"Sorry to drag you away."

"On the contrary," she said. "This is just the break I needed. I've got a terrific new place picked out for lunch."

"I thought the Raphaels looked super."

She shook her head with admiration. "I was the tour guide yesterday, showing everybody around, telling them the story you told Oksana and me. My nephew said I should become a docent at the Charlotte museum."

"You'd do the place proud," I said.

She smiled wistfully. "Yes, well, if one only had more time. Have you brought down my Lear *Parrots?*"

"I have. The restoration went beautifully."

"*Won*derful. It's certainly taken long enough." Helen sat beside me on the bed and I unwrapped the volume. The renovation of the parrot lithographs, in spite of Nelson's outrageous price, really had been a stunning success.

"Look at those yellows, and that purple." Helen breathed deeply with pleasure. "Simply amazing."

"That's a print and a half, all right," I said. We proceeded to the next image, then looked at half a dozen more. At this point Helen spoke up, almost to herself.

"Strange thing," she said. "I've already had one of these."

I laughed. "You mean you're planning to become the Folger Library of Lear parrot books?"

"I mean we had a lovely library in the house where I grew up, but that's all gone now."

"Sold off?" I asked.

"Lost entirely." Helen flipped another page. A Grand Lori parrot in the most intense shades of red and blue seemed ready to explode off the page, or at the very least turn its hydraulic head around to dig into the feathers on its back. "My mother collected these books in London, but they were all lost in a fire."

I straightened up. "No; how awful."

"Every Friday after tea when I was a little girl, down at the old house in Charleston, Mama would take down a book from the shelves and bring me up to her room. We'd go through the book page by page and make up stories about the images. We had those lovely Eliot pheasants, and those Bloch fish with the gold painted over the top, mm-mmm. It was a terrible thing, I suppose, squirreling away those sorts of books. I don't know that the family was so interested in charity in those days. Official charity, I mean. Hospitality is another matter entirely."

"Yes," I said. The soft lilt of Helen's voice made my skin tingle with pleasure. "What sort of fire was it?"

She looked off. "My brother Hazzard started it. Smoking in bed, foolish with drink. We lost nearly everything and almost lost Hazzard. He was a handsome man before that accident. I'll tell you, Fred, alcohol is the devil's gift. It's criminal what it does to people."

I blushed in agreement. At that point I probably could have lit my breath.

"I haven't taken up collecting with any seriousness since then," she continued. "I've maybe ten or fifteen nice color-plate books. But I can't for the life of me remember what my favorite one was called. It had the most lovely images in it. Huge flowers with stunning backgrounds. Kalmia, and a big cereus with a church or something behind it and the clock at five past midnight, and passionflowers, and an exquisite water lily."

"Romantic, sort of melodramatic backgrounds?" I said, though I was thinking, *Thornton?* She might want a complete *Thornton?*

"That's right. And I still remember one of the prints said, 'Moonlight by someone or other' down at the bottom. I always thought that was wonderful, to bring in an artist who just painted the moonlight."

"Yes." We sat for a moment reflecting on this odd, commissionable skill. At length I said, " 'Moonlight by Pether.' " Helen turned and looked at me with such grateful warmth that I laughed. "I think the book you mean is *The Temple of Flora,* by Robert

Thornton. It's the ultimate flower book. Have you put Jenna on the trail for one?"

She shook her head and turned over another big page of the Lear book. "No, I haven't. Strange, Fred, how I'm thinking of that book all of a sudden. Thornton, yes. Perhaps I put it out of my mind deliberately. . . . I don't know that I'd be prepared to buy another big book until the end of this year or early next. And I've got to be more careful. I think you were right. I paid quite a bit too much for this Lear from Oksana."

"Well, the last one did go above its high estimate at auction," I said gently. "But I'll do everything I can to get you a terrific price on the next Thornton that comes up. That way you'll come out ahead based on what you paid for the last piece you bought." And the piece before that, I thought, and the piece before that, right back to that bloody Audubon hawk.

"That would be marvelous," Helen said. "Why don't you send me whatever information you've got on Thornton, auction prices and so on, and I'll have those handy for when a copy does appear."

"I'll do that," I said. "That would be a good start."

Helen removed her glasses and stared down at her Lear volume. "I'm sorry, Fred; I realize now I'm giving you assignments that really should be Jenna's."

"That's perfectly all right," I said. "She must be swamped."

"She is and she isn't," Helen said ambiguously. "Jenna's changed, I'm afraid. About a month back she inherited a sum of money, $750,000 or something, and she just hasn't been the same. I found her yesterday drawing maps of the refrigerator for the maid: butter here, two percent milk here, cheese there. Now what in the world would bring that on?"

I thought for a moment about what my state of mind would

be after inheriting even $750. "Now that you mention it," I said, "I think Jenna told me she's highly lactate intolerant."

Helen smiled. "I see I won't get a straight answer from you on Jenna. But I will think about everything you've said. I surely will."

# 47. Thunder and Flashlights

Back at the Albright home everything was in confusion. Kak had discovered that Nelson was still carrying on trysts with his best-of-breed call girl, Tang Li, and in retaliation she announced plans to go ahead with a major renovation of her kitchen. Nelson, deep in a funk over the Barbash collection slipping into Sotheby's hands, responded by having his bookkeeper cut up Kak's credit cards and void her account at the florist's. Now Kak refused to leave her nook in the "unrenovated" kitchen of Château Delapompe and launched an intensive round of telephone and fax negotiations with an English cabinetmaker. Choix, meanwhile, ran wild all over the house. According to Ruth, this state of affairs had worsened over the course of the two days I was away in Charlotte.

Though it was only four in the afternoon, I found Nelson asleep on the leather sofa in his library office. Once inside the door I drew back at the smell—a mixture of old Stilton, soured wine, and burnt papers. I walked quietly to the big mahogany desk to lay Helen's check there, but stepped right down on something that split and broke. Nelson stirred but didn't wake. I followed the trail of debris from my feet to the fireplace left of the desk: it looked as if an entire set of Chinese Export porcelain had been flung between the andirons and the half-moon of tiles that met the edge of the Persian carpet. The shards of two champagne bottles lay among this costly wreckage.

"Hey, Fred. What time is it?"

I turned to see Nelson rubbing his eyes and stretching on the sofa. I guess this fact was the most shocking of any—Nelson, the workaholic's workaholic, asleep in the middle of the day. I raised a hand to him.

"About four, I guess."

Now Kak stormed into the room, eyes red-rimmed, her bright blond hair awry. She stamped her foot and Nelson sat up with a jerk.

"*What?*"

"Your friend Denny D'Amico keeps calling," Kak said sharply. "He's bidding on the au pair for the weekend."

Nelson yawned noisily. "Tell him two-fifty. What did he bid?"

"Ask him yourself," Kak said. "It might be refreshing for you to take a little parental responsibility for a change. I'll give you one more minute—that ringing's driving me spare in the head. And get on the phone to The Country Club. If it rains before the guests arrive we've got to find out how to dry the grass." She stomped out without acknowledging me.

Nelson smiled, leaned back on the couch, and closed his eyes. "So," he said. "What've you got from Helen Wheeler?"

"A nice big check," I said, "just for you." I waved the pale blue rectangle over my boss's broad, supine form. He laughed and snatched it away.

"Fucking upstart. What's she need next?"

"A complete Thornton for Christmas. But she would want it first edition, first issue. We don't have one, in any case. I checked."

"Like hell we don't have one," Nelson said. He grabbed at his crotch and rearranged himself. "Dodo Barbash has one. Haven't you seen the catalog Sotheby's did? The big stuff is New Year's Eve, but it's going to take three sessions to get rid of it all."

"I thought Sotheby's cut off your credit for nonpayment," I said.

"Sotheby's," Nelson said, and made a sour face. He strode up to his desk, swept away a pile of papers, and laid down Helen Wheeler's check. Then he grabbed a white plastic spoon and scooped out a large chunk from a round of Stilton that was sitting in a crumpled brown bag.

"Sotheby's is like a 20,000-ton Japanese trawler," he said. "You'd think they'd take some pity on a little fly fisherman like me after I've been giving them a blow job for the past ten years." I crossed my eyes at this mixed metaphor and he snapped, "I mean the people I've brought in! The clients I've turned on to them! I *made* Sotheby's what it is today in natural history, and all they want to do is bitch about a little back payment."

"How much?" I asked.

"Two-point-three million," he said. "That's a substantial sum of money to someone like me. For Sotheby's it's barely a fart in a football stadium. The upshot is they'll let me bid again if I get them half. All I need is a couple of fucking employees who can actually sell!"

I felt momentarily dizzy. Nelson had a brand-new $1.5 million mortgage and owed Sotheby's over $2 million? Was he in some sort of denial?

"Look, Nelson," I said, "I've been thinking about something

related to this down in Charlotte. Let's say Oksana had to pay $175,000 for that Lear *Parrots* at auction and added another $40,000 for herself before it got to Helen Wheeler. With our restoration fees, that's a quarter of a million dollars. That's nuts for a book like that. Things have gotten out of control. People are paying retail prices at auction."

He sighed noisily. "Out of control? You obviously haven't seen the estimates in the Barbash catalog. And I can't even bid on anything—Jesus help me! I feel like I'm about to get laid but there's an electrified cage on the woman's vagina."

"What I mean is, we ought to beat Sotheby's at their own game."

"How so?" he pressed. "What's your idea?"

"Well, we could gather our best clients together at the Barbash auction and do the bidding for them," I said. "I mean, we could advise them lot by lot on how high to go before the sale starts. So we'd be selling our expertise on what the lots are really worth, you know? Instead of fifty unknowledgeable people going crazy and pushing prices out of sight, we'll control prices and please our clients at the same time. We'll also eliminate carrying a lot of overhead because the clients will take all the stock home."

Nelson covered his mouth with his hands. "We could," he said through his fingers. "We could do that. We could preview the whole sale for them and charge them by the lot to bid in their place. They could sit around Sotheby's eating hors d'oeuvres and never even have to worry about lifting a paddle."

"And we could donate some of the bidding fees to a charity," I said. "Ten percent of the fee or something. That would really draw them in."

"Yes!" Nelson ran a small, erratic lap around his desk. "We're out there doing what's best for every client! We're not some impersonal art warehouse like Sotheby's or Christie's. I'll get every salesperson to bring in their top ten clients. God, that's 120 people . . . that's $300,000 easy! I'll get it in advance from them and sell my ass off this fall and bid myself, too! And think of all the stock we could sell them at the gallery afterward if everything goes high!"

"Another thing, too," I said. "I can suggest a charity that would probably interest Helen Wheeler very much."

Nelson's face resolved into a maniacal grin. "Aha! You see, this is what I tell my people! You keep client cards with all the information about their kids and family diseases and prep schools, and eventually it pays off! What's Helen got, breast cancer?"

"It's not her—"

The phone rang and Nelson snatched it up. "Denny," he said, squeezing the receiver, "I'll go to three hundred. Don't be such a cocksucker. You had her Fourth of July and when we were in Australia. What? Sure we'll pick her up, you got it." He hung up and fell back into his desk chair, then took another swipe at his Stilton and grabbed his key fob. "Hold your dick for a minute, okay, Fred? We'll discuss Helen Wheeler in the car."

"Doesn't your au pair drive?"

"The au pair's afraid of 'thunder and flashlight' storms. She prefers to stick to the house. What she's stuck to is Denny, if you get my drift. But if Brigitte wants a little rooster, we'll get her a little rooster."

Presently we heard a low rumble across the early autumn sky. This rumble was followed by the delicate tapping of rain on the windows. Nelson started and turned around. Then he pulled a roll of money from his back pocket and stuffed it in my hand. "Here.

That's about four grand you can put toward the party. I'll get you another ten or twenty thousand tomorrow. This is going to be great!" On scanning his desk one final time he saw Helen Wheeler's check.

"Wooh!" He kissed the check. "Fred, when you come around dropping this kind of money I seriously think I should be working for you."

"Working for me?" I thought a moment and shook my head. "Nah, I'd make your life hell."

## 48. Down's Syndrome Is a Total, Total Sellout

ood morning, Manhattan Philanthropy Consulting."
"Hello, this is Fred Layton of Albright Galleries. I want to find out whether anyone in New York is doing a substance abuse benefit party over the Christmas holidays. Alcohol in particular."

"Substance abuse? Sure, I can check that in our database. . . . Let's see: MS is taken, arthritis is taken, Lyme disease, cancer, Down's syndrome—wow."

"No one interested in Down's this year?"

"On the contrary, sir, Down's syndrome is a total, total sellout. We've still got six or seven sponsors in line for Down's syndrome. Now, you were interested in . . . ?"

"Alcohol abuse. But we don't want to do a tie-in with AA. This would be a sort of preview party for a Sotheby's auction with nonalcoholic drinks and so on."

"Got it. . . . Hmm. You said you were interested in late December?"

"Actually, for New Year's Eve. There's a sale at Sotheby's that night and we'd like to get some people together for it."

"New Year's Eve, very good, sir. In the city you're competing with the Hand Institute Ball and the Eye Institute Ball, though they've both downsized this year."

"Great. I think we could easily coordinate with Hand and Eye."

"I'll pencil you in on my screen, then . . . Albright Galleries. Now, I'd be happy to put you in touch with Sotheby's and that charity, though I can also talk to the representatives directly on your behalf. This is a new service we're offering that's extremely popular."

"Yes, that would be helpful. Why don't you take care of the whole ball of wax—invitations, catering, valet parking, blumpety blump. I'll fax you an invitation list and you can call me with any questions."

"Will this be a local guest list, sir?"

"National. Oh, and we are targeting a donor from Charlotte, North Carolina, in particular. We want to send her a special invitation with a small gift. Dance around her a little, if you see what I mean."

"I do, and there's no need to worry, Mr. Layton. We dance around a lot of significant donors. She'll be danced around."

"Excellent."

"And we'll be back in touch tomorrow with a full estimate. Can I do anything else for you today?"

"No, thank you. . . . Oh, wait; there is another thing. Do you know how to dry grass?"

# 49. Related to Money

A nd so it was that the Sotheby's/Albright Galleries Alcohol Abuse Benefit Ball became Nelson's Holy Grail. If we hit it big on the party and auction, we'd never look back. If it failed, we'd all go down together. That is, if you considered the boss going down in his $5 million mansion and yourself disappearing into a $5.00-an-hour temp job a fair definition of "together."

The invitations for the event were liver-shaped and printed with the words "Optional Dry Bar" in red at the bottom. Kak insisted they be sent out via airmail to arrive faster. We didn't have to wait long for a response.

For the Boston gallery's younger customers, whose fêtes regularly consisted of one safe, deadly band, two dozen bottles of hard liquor, and several bowls of taco chips, the benefit ball promised an intriguing climax to a social season whose local highlight thus far had been an MFA event called the Polaroid Party, where a hundred and fifty of the area's best and brightest had driven around town in limousines taking Instamatic shots of homeless people on steam grates. For the region's elders, brought up on golden rules such as "Never eat bread," often eliminating entirely the need for comestibles among the tall stands of Scotch and gin, an alcohol-free party was as daring an idea as an Hispanic or homosexual on the board of one's investment management firm. Some of the more parsimonious society folk had thrown what were sarcastically referred to as dry parties, but declaring one's party dry in advance was to put quite a new spin on things.

Within a week, all Boston's spots for the ball and auction were fully subscribed, and note-laden pages from the Sotheby's Barbash Collection catalog began to arrive in Federal Express envelopes and on long, flowing curls of fax paper. The only dark spot in this picture was Helen Wheeler's decision to escape to a health spa in Arizona until further notice, leaving the question of her Thornton volume open until after she returned.

As each day passed that fall, I decided that New Year's Eve couldn't come soon enough to suit me. The promises and early cash flow from the auction party subscribers distracted Nelson for a week or so, but in retrospect I see that losing the opportunity to buy the Barbash collection whole had dealt him a deeper psychological blow than any of us realized. It also hatched some revenue-generating antics to reduce the immediate debt to Sotheby's that were, shall we say, less than fully thought out. Nelson's main sport was to pick an item at random from Oksana's "Wallflowers" catalog, find the same item in our stock, and have it framed in a day as brilliantly as our shop could muster (thereby wreaking havoc with the regular framing orders). Then he would try to sell the garish piece to some salesperson's client for twenty percent less than Oksana's list price—or twenty percent more, depending on his mood. As for Nelson's own clients, sending them invoices for items they hadn't purchased and hoping they wouldn't notice became a favorite pursuit. One of his biggest hitters went over to Oksana when he realized he'd been charged $48,000 for nine Seba snakes to hang in his billiard room. The only problem was, the man in question didn't have a billiard room.

By November, Nelson began to display an alarming lack of scruple at calling anyone's clients at any hour to offer them items they couldn't possibly afford, items he often described one or two hundred years out of context. He sold the same John Speed 1611 map of Bermuda to three of my customers and sent me racing around the world by phone to find anything in substitution that might keep two of them from initiating lawsuits or, worse, asking for a refund. I would be on the phone with him to confirm a price and he would suddenly throw down the receiver in Greenwich or New York and start a firing spree ("You're out in two hours! And *you!* And *you!*"), though by the end of the day everyone would be hired back. For Thanksgiving he broke up another Redouté book—this one *The Lilies*—and sold the prints in lots of ten. After two rounds of this event he told all the clients in attendance to run to the remaining print they most wanted and let him work out any conflicting requests based on their place in the draw. This was an easy task for Nelson, who had a threshold for chaos Alexander the Great would have admired, but not so for me, since I was choosing prints for four clients who couldn't even attend. At times I swore that if I had to listen to him bootlick his top Dallas client in a fake Texan accent one more time or hear him crow for five more minutes about the importance of family values while having Ruth disconnect his daughter's pediatrician on the other line, I'd go insane.

Then, on December 1, came the penultimate straw. At five minutes to closing time Nelson stormed into the gallery with my pale, sickly client Tom Ashe in tow and sold him a third-edition copy of Thornton's *Night-blooming Cereus* for the price of a first strike.

"This is absurd," I told him, after Ashe had left the shop (albeit happily). "You just ripped him off for $7,000. Nelson, this is not an oversight I can live with."

My boss waved off this protest as he sat at the front desk and returned the usual pile of phone messages. The pouches under his eyes were nearly black. "They must have forgotten to fax you the new price list from New York," he said, between chomps from a mustard-slathered pretzel. "Our lottery edition *Cereus* now goes for $7,000. The Barbash results have made all the old prices moot."

"Nelson," I said with disbelief, "the Barbash sale isn't for another month!"

He swallowed and belched loudly. "Not to worry, Fred: we'll cross that bridge when we come to it. Provided Teddy Kennedy isn't driving."

"Jeez, Oksana was right. This is inflation in action."

"Don't you mention that British bag of shit to me!" he shouted. "And get with it, okay? That guy Ashe is going to be dead in six weeks. Has the word AIDS not entered your vocabulary yet?"

"Don't worry, it's in my vocabulary," I said.

"Oh, really?" he said, his interest piqued. "And why is that?"

I waved off this lame attempt at outing. "Look," I said, "just answer one question. Why are you in this business? I mean right now, today, not the day you started it."

"Why am I in this business?" he said, with furrowed brow. "Jesus, Fred, to keep the wolf from the door. To clothe my wife and feed my child, even if the little bitch just throws her food back at the walls. To grow my wealth, to crush my competitors."

I nodded, my suspicions confirmed. "Don't forget supporting Tang Li."

"That's right," he said. "That's a big line item."

"So instead of cutting back on Tang Li's apartment on Berkeley Street you force Ruth to babysit Choix and save ten bucks an hour?"

"Choix is a delightful child, Fred."

"You don't think she's the slightest bit traumatized after you sold every stick of furniture in her bedroom for $40,000?"

"It's that or you don't get paid tomorrow."

I handed him Tom Ashe's check, uninterested in arguing the point further.

"Hey, what am I supposed to do?" he went on in an injured, whiny tone. "Oksana Outka is eating my shorts! She's stolen eight of our top fifteen clients this year! She wants to see me living in a Maytag box under a highway overpass!"

"Nelson," Whitney hissed, and stuck her head through the opening between the French doors. "I have customers back here and you have exceeded your fifteen-minute weekly limit on visits to this gallery. Would you please scream out on the sidewalk with the other lunatics?"

"All right, all right!" He stood up and sent the front desk chair banging into the wall behind it. "Doesn't anyone realize the amount of pressure I'm under?" He raged out the door, his new cardboard-box attaché streaming copies of invoices behind him.

I turned to Whitney. "You know what I'm realizing? He not only enjoys this chaos, he prefers it! He courts it!"

Whitney shook her head as she watched him go. "I'll tell you one thing: that is not the Nelson who hired me when he started this company. At least he cared about the art then."

"What does he care about now?" I said.

"Oh, I don't know," she said, and laughed sarcastically. "Do you think it could be related to money?"

It could, indeed. The next day our paychecks bounced.

# 50. A Lesson in Newtonian Physics

can't stay there, I can't!"

I held Ruth's sobbing body tight against me, then moved her slightly to the left so the crowd of Christmas shoppers who'd congregated at the Sotheby's display window wouldn't stare. I'd been waiting half an hour or so for the doors to open and anticipating Ruth's smiling face to accompany me for the first day of the Barbash preview. Instead, she pulled up in a taxi, saw me, and broke down. Three minutes later I still couldn't get out of her what was the matter.

"Honey," I said, and patted her frizzy brown hair. "All I can understand is the part about Kak monogramming her dishwasher in gold leaf. That's odious, but it's nothing to get so upset over."

She pushed away from me, her tears replaced by impatience. "Fred, please. I haven't lost that much perspective."

"So what is it?" I said. "Come on, have a sip of this." I handed her the cup of mulled cider I'd bought on the walk over from Nelson's Madison Avenue shop.

"The plaster dust was bad enough," she said. "Every time I turned around this week Kak was knocking out a new wall in the kitchen. Not that I've been doing anything but bookkeeping since half the Weston staff quit when their checks bounced again. Then yesterday afternoon I had to cut off a phone call with Michael Kornbluth, who wants me to bid on fifteen lots for him in the Barbash sale, just so I could take Choix to the eye doctor."

"Ah," I said. "And Kak was too busy overseeing the mono-gramming."

"No, too busy talking to the bank," Ruth said raggedly. "I think she's bounced checks on four continents already this month."

I smiled. "Tell me something I don't already know."

"So I took Choix to the eye doctor, and he said she had an infection that was probably related to an animal. I told him to call Kak and explain it to her while I drove to the pharmacy to get her this cream. You know how Kak loves to kill the messenger who bears the bad news. Anyway, I walked in the door and immediately had to babysit again, which screwed up my plans to get here last night and surprise you for dinner—"

"Sweetie," I said. "Just for that I'll take you to lunch."

"—so I had to get up really early to take a van full of stuff to the New York people," she continued. "And when I left Château Delapompe at about five this morning, I looked over into the space behind the garage where Choix plays with her rabbits, and Nelson was there . . ." Ruth's eyes filled up again.

"What, honey?" I said. "What's so awful?"

"He was carrying a red jug of gasoline over to the hutch," she went on, her voice halting, "over to the rabbits where they were sleeping, and then he got out this box of fireplace matches and . . ."

"No way," I said quietly. "He didn't."

"I mean, maybe the rabbits had passed along an infection, but there's the cat, too, and what the hell are vets for, right?" She began to sob with renewed vigor. "And I didn't know what to do, Fred. I couldn't just stand there while he lit those rabbits on fire. So I ran over and sort of . . . stopped him."

"You . . . stopped him."

"I sort of tackled him around the ankles," she said hesitantly, "and before he could get up I unlocked the hutch and got the rabbits out. He must have hit his head on a rock, because he didn't get up right away. But I did. I got the hell out of there."

I stared at her. "You knocked out our boss at five o'clock this morning and left him on the ground unconscious. Is that what you're saying, Ruth?"

"Stop it, he wasn't unconscious!" she cried. "He's probably going to sue me for assault and then fire me."

"And what happened to the rabbits?"

"They're over at the gallery," she said. "Do you want one?"

"Look, honey," I said, ducking her question, "as long as you got the infected rabbits off the property I'm sure Nelson won't give it a second thought. Sotheby's is letting him bid again, the party's all lined up, everything's cool. Just put the whole thing out of your mind."

"I can't," she said, and teared up again. "I keep thinking what would have happened if I wasn't there. I close my eyes and see flames shooting out through the hutch while the rabbits thrash around inside . . . then I see that fucking asshole walking back inside his house! Is that what the rich do with the things they don't need anymore? Is that it?"

Ruth buried her head in my chest as a host of thoughts rushed through me. First his trees, then his prized Chinese Export porcelain, now his daughter's pets? This time I couldn't duck the conclusion: it was all getting a little too weird. Maybe Oksana Outka was right, maybe Nelson did eventually use up anyone who came too close to him. Which meant, based on my extremely limited knowledge of Newtonian physics, that there was only one safe direction left in which to travel.

Away.

## 51. The Lascaux Effect

As badly as our day had started out, Ruth and I ended up like two kids in a candy store. Since we were first in line with our request slips, we were able to survey the Barbash collection like guests at Dodo's house—minus Dodo Barbash, who would have called it all down as junk or quite possibly pressed several volumes of it into our hands to take home. Not every item was a star—every collector, after all, has his or her own idiosyncrasies and slip-ups—but so many copies of so many books were first rate that the oddities seemed to round things out rather than bring down the overall effect.

Within minutes of entering one of the three examination rooms set aside for the collection's viewing, we were surrounded by piles of mellow brown morocco leather volumes embellished with gold and marbleized endpapers in every color of the rainbow. There were unique copies, signed copies, author-annotated copies, first books on subjects, best books on subjects, and worst but most entertaining treatments of everything in between.

Barbash had a Crispin van de Passe *Hortus floridus,* probably the best book on flowers of the early seventeenth century, that was bound into four separate volumes—by season of the flower's bloom, just as Van de Passe had envisioned it. She had a dozen Nicolas Robert pen and ink drawings of carnations, roses, and clematis that made Ruth squeal with pleasure, her tears momentarily forgotten. She had all the great women of natural history—Elizabeth Blackwell, Maria Merian, Mrs. Edward Bury, Margaret Stones—and some of the men, such as Pancrace Bessa, whose great insight and delicacy were almost completely overshadowed by the celebrity artists of their day. She had a complete collection of John Gould's forty-odd volumes of birds, all with original paper wrappers bound in at the end of each book—the nineteenth-century equivalent of saving and preserving every style and iteration of McDonald's french fry container from the chain's first design. She had a set of George Brookshaw fruit books so mint that the prints made my stomach growl. This growling signaled to me it was time for a break, so after making some notes on how high I might bid on the set for a client, we stepped out to a deli to get coffee and croissants.

"I feel like a pig," Ruth said in the deli line. "I haven't seen stuff this good in so long."

"You haven't seen stuff this good in so long because Nelson's been buying junk to out-schlock Oksana Outka," I said.

Ruth nudged me and whispered, "Speaking of the witch."

I glanced demurely over my shoulder and saw a familiar George Washington profile with a head of windblown red hair in a full-length mink coat.

"Oksana," I said, as she came forward.

"Oh, it's you again. Good morning," she said, not unpleasantly. "A quick cup before you sniff out the kill?"

"A break, actually," I said. "We've been here since nine. There's a lot to sniff."

"I'd hurry back," she said, and stepped directly in front of us to the cash register. "Don't want to lose track."

Ruth narrowed her eyes at Oksana's tall mink-covered back. "We marked our places, thanks."

Oksana turned, a placing smile on her pursed lips. "Make sure your friend remembers the order," she said to me. "Tea first, then the milk."

Ruth grabbed my arm and pulled us out of line. "Come on," she said. "I don't need any caffeine now."

Ruth and I worked right through the day and into the four forty-five dusk. My head was spinning with factoids about books: a twelve-year run with 360 subscribers, 450 plates, 456 with the supplement, 240 in color, 114 tinted, 475 total copies, on and on. The gloves I wore to examine Dodo's books had gone black at the fingertips, and I'd nearly filled a legal pad with notes for my clients. I had yet to examine a few special items, such as the complete Audubon and the boxed set of *The Beauties of Flora,* one of the rarest botanical books ever produced. Unfortunately, when I inquired about these titles from a troubled-looking young page in the rare books department, he told me that they and ten or so other lots were off limits until the day before the sale and required an appointment for viewing. Appointments could not be made until the week before the sale, and official applications for appointments were only available during the mornings. I could clearly see Dodo's hand in that rule.

"So is the Thornton *Temple of Flora* a special item?" I asked the page.

The man's eyes rolled to the ceiling and he sighed shortly. "No, but it's limited to ten-minute examinations. That's enough time to flip through it once. Very slowly."

"Darn," Ruth said. "I like to tear through it ten pages at a time so all the flowers run together."

"We'll have a look at it right now, if that's possible," I told the page. "We're only in town for the day."

The man glanced down at my legal pad full of notes and well-thumbed Barbash sale catalog; he softened somewhat. "I'll bring it now," he said, "if you don't mind viewing it quickly."

"Fine," I said.

"Were you interested in the first-edition or the lottery copy?" he said.

"Oh," I said, "I didn't realize there were two. Hang on." I flipped to entry 200 in the catalogue and browsed through the three-page entry. The provenance alone on Dodo's Thornton volume could have won it a knighthood in most European countries. At the end of the entry there were a few lines of white space, then an asterisk and another entry which I'd mistaken for a bit of marginalia about the first-edition copy. "Lot 200a," I read. "A second *Temple of Flora*, late second edition, struck from the lottery-edition plates after 1812. Good condition with heavy foxing to some plates. Spine cracked and in need of repair."

"Sounds charming," Ruth said.

"Could we see both?" I said. "Since we're here."

"Certainly," the man said. "But I'll be timing you."


Ruth was still deep in note-taking on a volume of Seba snakes when the page returned with the Thorntons on a little wheeled book cart. Even from the outside, the lottery edition was a sorry sight. Where the first edition had been bound in a turtle-green Russian leather and gold-tooled at the borders with infinite refinement, the second copy's covers were peeling brown cloth, completely off the spine and held to the body of the book with pink librarian's cord. This second book also bore a telltale odor that escaped me until Ruth raised her head.

"Feh!" she said. "I smell cat piss."

The page smiled to himself and slid the book about an inch toward Ruth's side of the table. "There may indeed have been a few storage problems in the Barbash residence, but I'm afraid Mrs. Barbash stipulated the books were to go untouched until they reached their next owners."

"Fred, get that away from me!" Ruth waved the air in front of her face. "I'm going to pass out."

"Ten minutes," I said. "You'll survive."

She pushed back from the table and closed her notebook. "I don't think so. I'm done for today. I'll see you outside at the Fabergé egg display."

Ruth and the page went out together, leaving me alone in the small room to flip through the first-edition *Temple of Flora*. It made me proud of Thornton to do so, even if the guy's grandmother thought he was nuts and his parents probably suspected until the day they died that he was yanking their chains about a career in medicine. I personally loved the idea of someone throwing a whole inheritance on a project that lasted decades and ended in ostensible failure—in Thornton's case, going bankrupt and having to sell off an edition of blurry, late-struck copies of his masterpiece in a raffle. Yet what remained bettered any other outcome; even if, like his contemporary Wordsworth, Thornton only got a few feet off the launching pad toward fully realizing his plans. What remained was still art: aquatint, stipple, and line engravings that brought to studied life scenes like three lilies glistening in a quiet pool with the Giza pyramids in the background; cyclamen blooming for a few short days in an alpine meadow; roses gathered into a bunch by a country wind at a turn in the road. These roses were also Thornton's own plate, the only one of twenty-eight in the book he worked on, with his wonderfully turgid poetry to accompany it. The final plate I scanned was Tom Ashe's favorite and probably Helen Wheeler's too: the night-blooming cereus. This copy was so sharply struck and beautifully preserved that I blushed to think Nelson had taken Ashe for $7,000 to give him what was really a pale imitation of it. Nelson was right about one thing, though: most of Dodo Barbash's copies were going to push prices to levels no one would have dreamed possible a few years before.

Two minutes shy of my ten-minute limit the Sotheby's page popped his head in to say viewing hours had ended, and I quickly pulled off the pink cord from the lottery-edition copy and began to examine the contents. In a word, this copy was a mess. The foxing and staining were awful on nearly every print, and what images had escaped the worst effects of aging bore testament to the tired state of the copper plates by that point in the book's convoluted history. In the *Night-blooming Cereus* plate, the blue-green river running below the blooming flower looked more like the toxic sludge you see when you enter New Jersey in a train from Manhattan, and the castle tower with the clock at four minutes past midnight could have been reading nine-fifteen for all you could make out. The cereus blossom itself appeared to be another flower entirely: outer spikes yellow, central petals orange, inner bloom white. In every other copy I'd seen the order was orange, white, yellow. It would genuinely surprise me if the book reached its upper estimate of $60,000. I wrapped it up and set it aside.

I got halfway into packing up my things before I paused and reconsidered. This was an artist, Dodo Barbash, we were talking about. What would possess her to own a ratty, late-edition copy like this when she already had one of the finest in the world? According to the acquisition code she had penciled in the frontispiece of every book, Dodo had bought the lottery copy eleven years after the first edition. I put down my coat, reapplied my protective gloves, and picked up the volume again. Something drew me back to the cereus, so I bent over that page with a loupe and perused it more carefully.

"Hello, what's this," I said. In the left-hand credit line, which always read "The Flower by Reinagle. Moonlight by Pether," it read "The Flower by Reinagle. Moonlight by Thornton." That was a fun touch, but something anyone with an engraving needle could pull off. Only why wasn't there anything on record about such an oddity in some of the lottery-edition copies?

"Mr. Layton, this is last call," the page said through the door. "The final readers are leaving."

"Sorry," I said. "I'll be right along."

"All right, Fred," I thought. "Enough conspiracy theories. Maybe Dodo just loved Thornton. You've been here seven hours. You need a cold beer and a warm baguette and some hot onion soup." I handed the page the first-edition Thornton, but when he stepped out and loaded it onto a larger cart of books I suddenly thought of Ruth's comment about preferring to flip through all the Thornton plates at once. This struck me as a mildly naughty idea for some reason, and I knew it wouldn't hurt to see the effect on the lottery-edition Thornton in my hands. I clutched the book's weak spine and bent the page-ends up into a slight buckle against my thumb, almost like the pages of a simulated animation book I was about to flip through to see a flower opening or a chick hatching. What happened then amazed me.

As I fanned the pages back and held them, the gold paint covering their edges disappeared to reveal an exquisitely colored English street scene, painted right there on the edges of the pages. The signature I saw along the bottom of this little painting caused my heart rate to double, then triple when the Sotheby's page reappeared behind me. What I felt was probably a variation on the young French girl's experience when she stumbled upon the fifteen-thousand-year-old paintings in the Lascaux caves—a breathless awe and a sort of warming delight. Now I knew what had hooked Nelson on this career in the first place, even if he'd recently lost track of it: the joy of discovery.

I knew another thing, too. If this fore-edge painting really was by Thornton, I would win the copy for Helen Wheeler if I had to lose my job in the process.

"Everything all right?" the page said.

"Sure," I said blandly, to cover my excitement. "I couldn't get the pink cord all the way around," I told the page. "I forgot it's threaded through that little metal ring so you can pull it tight."

The man looked at me suspiciously. "Your hands are shaking," he said. "You're sure everything is all right?"

"Exhaustion, that's all," I said. "I think we got here about two hours before your shift started. Have a good evening."

"You too," he said, looking only slightly appeased. "It's snowing out there, you know."

"I didn't know," I said. "I think I'll find my friend and celebrate."

Ruth would soon know that there was a lot more than the first snow of the year to celebrate.

## 52. Quilt in the Loom

I squeezed the phone and prayed. Six rings. Seven. Then:

"Wheeler residence, can I help you?"

"Hello. Is this Jenna?"

"Yes, who is this?"

"This is Fred Layton, from Albright Galleries."

"Oh, hello, Fred. You're in luck. Helen is right here with me. Was it her you wanted to speak to?"

I grinned. "Helen is there? Fantastic! Yes, I'll speak to her."

"Hang on, then."

The phone was put down, then picked up.

"Hello?"

"Helen, how are you! How was the Southwest?"

"Dry and hot, Fred, as usual. I'm afraid I'm in the middle of something serious here, so you'll have to be quick."

"I will. Helen, I found something very exciting in the Barbash sale."

She sighed. "My goodness, is that all you called to say? I've been reading that the whole sale is full of exciting things. Nelson calls me every hour to tell me how many exciting things are in it."

"It's the Thornton, Helen. The *Temple of Flora.*"

Her tone warmed. "Oh, now, you know that's what I have my heart set on, don't you? I just can't spend more than $200,000 on it, and Oksana assures me it may double that."

"That's not the one I mean, Helen. There's a second Thornton in the sale, right after the first one. I can get it for you for sixty thousand, tops."

"Doesn't sound like a very good one, if you don't mind an amateur's opinion."

"It doesn't," I said, "but I've done a lot of research on this copy. I talked to Dodo Barbash, went over some records, and visited a lot of libraries. I'm sure of what I found. Sotheby's overlooked something about this copy that makes it much more valuable."

"Sotheby's did?" Helen said in a perplexed voice. "Oksana tells me they never make mistakes. They've got teams of experts looking at whatever comes in through the door, don't they?"

I tried to make my voice calm. "Helen, I know you've worked with Oksana for years, and I'd say this more gently if we both had time, but in some matters Oksana doesn't have the slightest idea what she's talking about. I'm afraid this is one of them."

"Well, what can I say then? I'll see you the evening of the sale, that's my best hope. In fact I'm trying to get out to the airport to go to New York right now, if you can see my predicament."

"Just let me bid on it for you," I said. "I promise you won't be sorry. . . . Helen? Are you still there?"

"I am. Why don't we talk before the sale starts, all right? I'll just let you be in touch with me."

"Great. Great! Have a terrific flight."

"My land, Fred. My little nephew at Duke would say you're 'stoked.'"

I laughed. "I've got a quilt in my loom, Helen, and you're going to love it."

## 53. Appearing to Need Air

Ruth, my partner in crime, reached behind my shirt collar and tugged out a hair. I stifled a shout and whirled on her.

"What are you *doing?*"

She smiled. Like the rest of the packed reception hall, my friend was dressed to befit a New Year's Eve benefit party and auction. The buzz of Nelson's clients gossiping about him was deafening, and quite drowned out the sound of the other hundred and fifty people who'd come to the sale of their own volition. "Just calm down," she said. "I think Helen Wheeler is arriving downstairs."

"Oh, my God. Where?"

Ruth pulled another hair from my neck and I took a very deep breath and let it out. "Okay, I'm fine," I said. "Maybe I need another glass of that faux champagne."

"Be my guest. We have enough left over to flood Times Square."

"The night is young," I said, "and that champagne is a hell of a lot better than anyone gave it a chance to be." I didn't add that, if I had anything to do with it, nonalcoholic beverages would be the only ones passing my lips for the next six months.

Going on the wagon was not my only New Year's resolution, however.

"I hope plants thrive on the stuff," Ruth said. "That's the only
place I'm seeing it land."

I looked down into the reception area and tensed up again.
"You're right, it is Helen. Let's see if we can show her the Thornton."

"Remember; a true buyer wears a poker face at auctions,"
Ruth said. "And don't run up to her until she's been here at least
five minutes. Let Hirschl & Adler and Arader and the rest of the
jackals have at her."

At the word "jackals," Oksana rushed past us to greet Helen
and Nelson pounced on me. A small bandage was taped over his
right eyebrow, and he was bearing on his arm Tang Li rather than
Kak, who'd slipped in her new kitchen two days before trying to
find the first-aid kit for Nelson and sprained her coccyx. He'd been
explaining to clients all evening long that Tang Li was his spon-
sored guest from a local AA halfway house. Who just happened to
be in a Versace dress. It no longer surprised me that people believed
him.

"Fred," he rasped, knocking me back half a step with his ever
enlarging belly, "did the Smiths and the Slaters give you their
checks?"

"I've got them right here," I said, and patted my lapel.

"Good," he said, his eyes bulging. "Now here's our plan. I'm
going to get that first-edition Thornton for Helen Wheeler, so
don't you go near it, okay?"

"She won't pay more than two hundred," I said.

"If I can get it for under three I'll take it home, rebind it, and offer it to her next week for $475,000. What you're going to do is work on her; work on her until the moment she leaves tonight, and convince her half a million is a good price for a first-edition copy."

"I'm telling you, Nelson, she'll never go that high," I warned.

"Not for you she won't," he said. "She hasn't had me sell to her yet."

"But she's my special client," I said evenly. "It's in my contract that I'm the only person who sells to her."

My boss shook his head in annoyance. "Fred, get a life," he said. "You'd be asking people if they wanted fries with their Happy Meals if it wasn't for me."

"You've practically brought the business to that point by your-self," I said.

His eyes narrowed. "A warning: don't fuck with me tonight. I'd prefer not to embarrass you in front of all these people."

"I know the whole catalog inside out," I said. "I don't see any way you can embarrass me."

"Oh, I've heard a few things from Marty about what you do after hours," he said, taking great pleasure in this knowledge. "Can't stay in the closet forever, you know."

I was at that moment rehearsed and ready to spill Nelson's secret: allude ever so cuttingly as to what I knew about his shabby family lineage. Yet now that the moment was here, I couldn't do it. Incredibly, I remembered something my father told me instead. I couldn't pinpoint where or when he'd said it, only the ironic tone of his voice: "Two reasons you should never wrestle with a pig, Fred. You get muddy and the pig enjoys it." My father was right, too. There was nothing to be gained from fighting on Nelson's terms and making him into an enemy. It was up to me to maintain control and not give it over to him. If I lost my temper, everything would be lost. An uneasy truce would have to do.

"Here's Helen Wheeler now," I said. "Why not say hello and see how pleased she is to see you?"

"My advice," he said, ignoring me, "is to go after game your own size. We net a million tonight with these big hitters or we're going into Chapter 11, got it?" He strode off, pulling poor Tang Li by the hand, apparently having seen a piece of game worth tracking. I closed my eyes and thanked myself for keeping mum. I also thanked my father, wherever he was.

"Ladies and gentleman," a woman announced over the intercom, "the Barbash sale will begin in approximately fifteen minutes. Viewing ends in five minutes."

"Cretin," Ruth said. "Notice how he ignored me since I gave my notice?"

"He ignored you because you gave him a mild concussion and you're going to work for your father, both of which remind him of his mortality," I said. I tensed and then relaxed as Denny D'Amico passed behind me and slapped my ass. I couldn't say that I'd miss him. "Now look. How am I going get Helen away from Oksana?"

Ruth kissed my cheek. "Leave it to me."

She ran off and I tried to make my way closer to Helen, who was smiling for a photographer. The room was packed with people in party dress attempting to hold canapés and alcohol-free champagne and catalogs at the same time, so getting around was extremely tricky. I found a safe spot fifteen feet away and tried to catch Helen's eye.

"Would Miss Oksana Outka please come to the cashier's window for an urgent message?" the woman's voice announced again. "Miss Oksana Outka."

"God bless you, Ruth," I said to myself, as Oksana reacted with annoyance and gave up her post. I stepped right down on a woman's foot to reach Helen, but slipped behind two tall men to escape a time-consuming apology and from there made a beeline.

"Helen," I said naturally, as I passed in front of her. "Nice to see you."

Her face lit up. She was in a simple silver gown that beautifully matched her white hair. "Fred, don't you look well in a tuxedo. I'm ashamed of myself for not getting to your party on time. My plane just circled the airport for it seemed like two hours."

"Not to worry," I said. "I wonder, though, since we're about to start, whether it would be okay for me to bid on that second Thornton in your place?"

"Second Thornton," Helen said slowly. She looked off into the crowd with her brow slightly furrowed. Out of the corner of my eye I could see Oksana circling back, looked peeved. I didn't think she'd seen me yet.

"The one we discussed, right after lot 200," I said, and leaned forward slightly. "It's estimated at forty to sixty thousand, but I discovered a fore-edge painting of a London street in it, a painting *signed* by Thornton, and a change in the *Night-blooming Cereus* image that implies Thornton colored it. In fact, he could have colored the whole copy himself, but it's too early to say. Conservatively speaking, it's probably worth five times the official estimate."

"Fore-what?" Helen said. "Wait, here's Oksana coming. You can tell her."

"Fore-edge painting," I half whispered. "You bend the page edges back, put them in a press to hold them as a flat surface, then paint on them. When you fan the pages back out to normal, the painting disappears and you can burnish the edges with gold. Trust me on this one, Helen. I'll go to sixty thousand on your behalf and then I'll drop out. But it has to be our secret, okay? I've put together all the evidence for you. You can read it during the sale. Just give me a nod when the lot is called and I'll bid for you, all right?"

Our eyes locked. Helen considered a moment, then smiled ambiguously. "All right, then. I'll get you my paddle as soon as I have one word with Oksana. We'll see how you do."

"Wonderful. I'll see you in a bit." I slipped away behind the two tall men just as Oksana began her final approach. To my immense relief, I watched Helen fold the two pages I'd given her, then tuck them into her catalog and out of sight. We were set.

Whatever I had seen in the past of Nelson and Oksana together or apart, nothing prepared me for their performance during the Barbash auction. As I'd predicted, Nelson couldn't resist the spotlight, so he'd taken all the bids his salespeople had brought in from their own clients and began making them himself, using their various paddle numbers. Oksana, too, gave every impression of bidding for friends and clients as well as herself. Whenever one of them opened the bidding on a lot, the other practically leaped up to do battle. Nelson was particularly shameless. He shouted out his bids so loudly the auctioneer had to threaten him with ejection. Once he even accused the auctioneer of pulling bids out of the air to jack up the prices, but something Whitney hissed in his ear about taking a testosterone antagonist made him apologize at once.

The effect of Nelson and Oksana's back-and-forth banter was

to push some prices so high that the crowd exploded in laughter when the gavel hit the desk. It was like watching an Olympic event where five participants break the world record but still don't win against the sixth. Of course, this rivalry had exactly the opposite effect on prices we'd promised our clients when they signed up to have us bid for them. I wondered, was Nelson aware of the damage he was causing, or did he even care anymore?

I was a wreck, sweating openly and terrified to check my notes on the Thornton for fear another dealer would spy them and outbid me when the lot came up. Helen, who I ensured was sitting directly in my line of sight ten rows up, had her catalog open all the time, so it was impossible to know whether or not she was reading my explanation of the painting Thornton had tucked into the fore edges of the pages. Whatever her final decision, the prices for even the mediocre lots gave me a sinking feeling. For that matter, it was audacious of me to assume I was alone in discovering the painting. If Dodo Barbash had admitted to me flat out that there was a fore-edge painting by Thornton in the collection, she had probably told quite a few others.

By the time the first Thornton volume was on the block, Nelson had abandoned his seat and was standing at the back of the room. Barbash's complete Audubon, which would open at $1.1 million, was the last lot in the evening's sale, and Nelson wanted it to be known in no uncertain terms that he was taking it home for his client, the nursing home chain guy who'd flown to New York with us that summer. Between the first Thornton lot and the Audubon was the ratty, surely useless Thornton copy that wouldn't even attract anyone's attention. Or so I prayed.

"Lot 200," the youngish auctioneer said, after sipping from a glass of water, "a superbly preserved first-edition copy of Dr. Robert John Thornton's *Temple of Flora*. Do I have an opening bid for $150,000?"

"One-fifty," Nelson boomed from the back of the room.

"Two hundred!" Oksana rang out, already at the high estimate.

"Oh, Christ," the dealer in front of me sighed. "All for the cause of art."

When it was over, Nelson had bought the Thornton, using Lou Smith's paddle, for an incredible $390,000, which came out to $429,000 with Sotheby's ten percent commission thrown in. I kept thinking of a facsimile of a 1936 auction catalog I'd seen, where a first-edition Thornton had fetched the tidy sum of thirty-two pounds sterling, six and six. Wherever in the universe Thornton was, he was either proud as Pimm's punch or horrified beyond belief.

"Now, before the Audubon," the morning-coated auctioneer continued, "we have another lot, lot 200a, also a *Temple of Flora* by Robert John Thornton. This copy is a lottery edition with some foxing and spotting, but otherwise in good condition."

Two people in the room chuckled at this inflated claim, which sent several others into private whisperings. The auctioneer polished his glasses for a moment and added, "Would you believe fair to good condition?"

I had been waiting unsuccessfully for Helen's white head to turn to me for the last ten lots, but when I glanced up at her this time our eyes met.

She nodded.

"Bidding is open," the auctioneer said.

At first I was so elated by Helen's vote of approval I hardly noticed that the bidding had already been opened by a stocky man with almost elephantine limbs and a head like a flat Dutch cheese.

"Thirty thousand dollars," he said in a thick Austrian accent.

"Thirty-five thousand!" I said confidently, though my bidding paddle knocked a woman's hat off in the next row as I raised my hand. The auctioneer looked at me with mild bemusement as the hat rolled up the aisle and was still.

"Young man, you may take down your paddle now," he said. "I have noted the bid."

Oksana smothered a laugh with her hand, while Nelson surged up behind me.

"What the *fuck* are you doing?" he whispered.

I ignored him, cleared my throat, and recovered, by which time the Austrian man had bid $40,000 and the auctioneer had gone to second call.

"Third call, do I hear—"

"Forty-five thousand," I said clearly. All my timidity was gone. Compared with my first appearance in these rooms a year before, I was now filled with a certainty that I would win the day, a sense that I could hold my own in these rooms regardless of the competition.

"Fifty!" the Austrian man called.

He turned once with a studied motion and I met his eyes. I wasn't budging an inch. He broke the stare first.

"Sixty thousand," I said. As if I'd predicted it, the man raised his eyebrows at me and dropped out.

"Just a moment!" Nelson roared. He waited until everyone's eyes turned to him in the silent room. "This is an employee of mine, Mr. Davies. At least for the next thirty seconds he is. I have not authorized him to bid. In fact I forbid it."

I stood up, took a deep breath and, looking past Nelson in the aisle beside me, announced, "I am bidding on behalf of a private collector. Paddle number 316."

Davies, the auctioneer, quickly scanned his list while Nelson poked my arm with his index finger. "You sit down right now or you are *fired*, bucko."

"That paddle is assigned to Mrs. Helen Wheeler. According to this schedule, she has signed over authorization to Mr. Fred Layton. Is that you, young man?"

"It is," I said. "Would you mind having Mr. Albright take his seat?"

"Mr. Albright?" Davies said. "Mr. Layton appears to need some air. Could you please return to your seat . . . or your spot along the wall there?"

"I'll have the want ads delivered to your tract house tomorrow," Nelson hissed at me.

He sat, and several people in the crowd cried out for joy. I'd just had Nelson disciplined—Nelson Albright, the spoiled brat of the auction circuit, the man you didn't lock horns with under any circumstances. I wiped the sweat from my upper lip and said, over the applause, "I bid $60,000."

"We have recorded the bid, Mr. Layton. Sixty thousand. Do I hear any advance on sixty thousand?" the auctioneer said. His eyes swept the room slowly while two dozen other pairs locked on me. "Once . . . twice . . . three times . . . fair warning. . . . Then we are sold at $60,000 to Mr. Layton."

Dead silence. A few chuckles. Nelson's bewildered rage be-hind me. Then, from a seat about halfway up the room, came the sound of two gloved hands softly applauding.

## 54. A Lot Going Around

Helen Wheeler handed me her check before the ink on it was dry. I handed her a glass of alcohol-free champagne and we toasted.

"Fred, you were *master*ful," she said, her eyes sparkling, as socialites and dealers spilled out of the auction room around us and their symphonies of small talk filled the air. "I'd surely have cracked under the pressure. All the energy you must have used to keep that secret!"

I beamed. My face was so hot you could have cooked flan on it. "I'm just delighted something like this will be in your collection. There are two people you can take the book to Monday morning who will authenticate Thornton's hand on the fore-edge and the edit he made to the *Night-blooming Cereus* plate. And then I've got photocopies of all Dodo Barbash's notes on the copy. I even know someone at *The Magazine Antiques* who's here and can write up the story."

"Actually," Helen said cagily, "I was hoping you might do all that work for me. You see, Jenna quit her position just before you called yesterday, so I'm without a personal curator."

"Oh," I said. "I . . . guess I could."

"Fred." Helen saw my unsure face and patted her right hand

over mine. "Lord knows I'm not one of those headhunter people, but I do want to say this in any case. I've been so impressed every time I've seen you work. You know so much for a man so young. I admire your spirit and your tenacity. I'm sure you're delighted to be working with someone of Nelson Albright's caliber . . . but I guess what I'm about to ask is whether you'd consider coming to work for me permanently, as my curator."

"For you?" I was speechless for five seconds, a personal record. "Helen, I don't know what to say."

"You don't have to say anything," she said. "We can talk about salary tomorrow or next week."

"No," I said. "I mean that is my dream request, to work for someone like you. God, I'd be honored. Are you serious about this?"

Her face, a moment before concerned, expanded into a wide smile. "I surely am. Oh, this is simply wonderful. What a lovely New Year's present."

"Except . . . wait a minute." I had just accepted Helen's job offer and I was already back-pedaling. "Helen, there are a couple of things I've got to tell you. First, I just can't live in Charlotte. Not that I wouldn't love it, but my parents' memory there is too strong. It's too painful to go back. Besides which, I've been to enough pig pickin's to last a lifetime, if you see what I mean."

She laughed and touched my arm reassuringly. "Fred, I wouldn't dream of forcing you to live in Charlotte if you didn't want to. I'm only there a few months a year myself. I've got an apartment right here in New York you can stay in, with a little car. Closer to those auctions, too. Now what's the second thing?"

"The second thing." I looked off for a moment to see if anyone was walking around with triangular heads or blowing smoke out of their eye sockets, because I was certain I had to be dreaming. I would know for sure in a minute.

"The second thing is that Audubon hawk I sold you. It's a phony. I mean, it's a genuine Audubon, but those tire tracks on it were unintentional. We had a little mishap with our stock on the way down to Baltimore. That's how it got that way. In any case, I'd have to pay you back before I could work for you. Or I could pay it off in installments, $250 a month, or pay to have it cleaned, I mean, but what's the point of going on, you're probably going to withdraw your offer now anyway, right?"

Helen's eyes were wide, not so much at what I'd said, but at the fact that I could say so much in one breath.

"Oh, Fred, aren't you sweet," she said, brushing off my protests. "Of couse I knew that Audubon was damaged. I could see it in your eyes when it fell over that first time in the booth. And Oksana called me the day after I bought it to tell me. I just fell in love with it, even with the tire mark. I consider it one of those lucky accidents of art, don't you?"

"You're saying you knew?" I said numbly.

"I just found you so charming, that's all. I never bought from your Nelson before because I find him so pushy, I guess. Now, did you have anything else to say?"

"Um, anything else." I sensed Helen's fatigue from the evening and the plane ride in and knew that my window of opportunity would close unless I struck now, in this thick crowd of rich, Waspy, conservative, straight art buyers on New Year's Eve.

"Okay," I began. "The third thing you should know is that I'm gay. Homosexual. I don't think it'll ever be relevant to what I do, but I never got that clear with Nelson and I'd like to have it clear with you."

Now it was Helen's turn to pause and look off. She reached down and touched her pocketbook with her free hand, perhaps for balance. "Well, I suppose there's a lot of that going around."

I smiled despite myself, perhaps because I felt like I'd just said, "I do," and married my heart back to my head again. "Helen," I said, "it's not a virus. It's just the way I am."

She closed her eyes, opened them, then said, "Now I'm getting myself all crossed up. What I meant to say was, my brother Hazzard, the alcoholic one, he was"—she looked down—"probably homosexual too. Though we called them 'confirmed bachelors' in those days. Of course it makes no difference to me. I do wish you'd told Jenna, though. My land, how she loved to talk about you."

I cringed. "Well, that's one reason I had to tell you now. No misunderstandings."

She nodded, regained her perky energy. "I agree entirely. Now, I suppose you'll have to find your Nelson and catch him up on the news. You may give him as much advance notice as you like, by the way."

"Fifteen minutes is usually fine with Nelson, but I'll let you know."

At the very mention of his name, my boss came rushing up to us bearing the first-edition Thornton volume.

"Mrs. Wheeler," he gasped, "I want to apologize on behalf of Fred for bidding on a lot for you without the foggiest idea what he was doing. I can make you a fair-market offer of $450,000 on this Thornton, absolutely without markup from the auction price."

It didn't take a Niels Bohr to figure out that Nelson had

already added in a profit margin to the Thornton he'd won for Lou Smith, and it didn't take Helen long, either.

"Nelson, thank you so much," she said, "but Fred already has me sold on the second copy. He did a little investigative work and discovered it was originally colored by Thornton. Didn't you, Fred?"

Nelson's eyes drilled into mine with a ferocity that would have led the average Albright Galleries employee to grovel and plead for his sweet mercy. No longer. I was the one in control here.

"It's not proven that Thornton colored all of it," I said, "and you did say I should do what's best for my customers and do whatever possible to get Helen a Thornton for under two hundred thousand, so I did."

"*Fred,*" Nelson began.

"The other thing I have to tell you is that I'm taking you up on your offer to be fired," I said. "I'll give you the standard two weeks notice, but I'll also leave whenever you like."

The next few seconds would be a blur in my mind, had my friend from *The Magazine Antiques* not stepped forward for some feature shots of the noted natural history dealer, Nelson Albright, and the noted industrial heiress and collector, Helen Wheeler. Among the images he captured was Nelson rearing back with his Thornton, me reacting to the terrifying grin of rage and betrayal on his face and shielding my drink, and Helen attempting to duck out of sight. When my vision cleared, Nelson had lowered the volume and was laughing before a small audience of shocked faces.

"Just seeing how heavy half a million dollars is," he told the crowd, which smiled and chuckled (though Helen did neither). "Call me at eight sharp tomorrow morning," he said to me. "We have more to discuss."

"We do," I said in his ear. "Helen is going to drop Oksana. I'll make certain she does. And if you don't sell that Thornton to someone else by daybreak all the paychecks you reissued are going to bounce again."

Nelson's face was suddenly avid with interest, having completely forgotten about my decision to leave. It was like tossing a Labrador retriever a tennis ball and then tossing him another ball while he was bringing the first one back.

"Shit," he said. "You're right. Who should I hit up?"

"I just saw Denny D'Amico go by," I said. "Now's your chance. Oksana's going to be out looking for fresh blood soon."

Nelson gritted his teeth. "You're right, I'll nab him. Thanks, Fred, you're incredible."

I patted Nelson's back and brushed the champagne from my lapel as he departed on his eternal quest for the next client. "No, Nelson," I said, "you're the incredible one. Trust me."

## 55. I Should Know

In the days that followed I sold off or discarded most of my Albright Galleries life, but not all. Each time I climb behind the wheel of Helen's "little" XJ-6 I see pinned to the overhead sun visor a certain photograph of Nelson about to knock me and my glass of champagne straight out of Sotheby's and down onto York Avenue below with the most expensive Thornton *Temple of Flora* in auction history. For all its journalistic value, my photograph remains unframed and gathers scratches as I move the visor up and down while driving.

And why haven't I thrown this photograph away, burned or buried it? Probably because, for all the bitterness and animosity Nelson could have felt over my leaving on New Year's Eve, he was in fact the first person to call and congratulate me the morning I started working for Helen. He was also the first to call the day the issue of *The Magazine Antiques* came out with Helen's Thornton on the cover. Of course, he called the day after that and the day after that and the day after that, pitching me an astounding array of material for Helen's collection, but each time he did I sensed his pride in my accomplishment—becoming a personal curator on the strength of what a mildly abashed *Sotheby's Preview* later called "the find of the 1988 auction season." I was flattered by the blinding glare of his attention for a time, then I had to have the number in Helen's apartment changed.

I rarely cross paths with Nelson anymore, but in my mind's eye I can see him eternally charging around his desk like an overweight Groucho Marx in unwashed wide-wale cords; forever picking up and dropping auction catalogs on his bed as he wiggles his way to the right one; constantly running numbers through his famous calculator, which rounds totals up to the nearest hundred; and, unto his last breath, screaming orders at his poor secretary, Bish, while the strange, wonderful gears of his brain spin at top speed. Once in a while, after Helen has asked me to expand her collection in a particular artist, or I wake from a particularly claustrophobic dream of my former boss trying to run me off the Mass. Turnpike, I wonder if I shouldn't give Nelson a call and see what he's dug up recently that I can buy. In truth, I never seem to get around to it. For one thing, his new prices are probably outrageous.

I should know.

## Acknowledgments

For their fine editorial insight and general guidance, thanks to Tom Augst, Fred Crane, Phil Cronin, Billie Fitzpatrick, John Gerlach, Lois Geena, Lisa Beth Kovetz, Tamar Lehrich, Dan Melnick, Laura Nelson, and especially Sheila Schwartz.

Special thanks to my agent, Fred Hill, and his assistant, Irene Moore; and a very special thanks to my editors, Nan Talese and Jesse Cohen, for their patience and good counsel.

Thanks also to the Cleveland State University College of Graduate Studies for their financial support during the early drafts of this book.

ABOUT THE AUTHOR

*Hugh Kennedy* attended Yale, where he won the Gordon Barber Prize for undergraduate poetry, and received an M.A. in English (with creative writing concentration) from Cleveland State University. His first novel, *Everything Looks Impressive*, was published in 1993. He currently lives in Waban, Massachusetts, and works as Creative Director for the strategic marketing firm Philip Johnson Associates.